A BLACKGUARDS ANTHOLOGY

SCOUNDRELS

SCOUNDRELS: A Blackguards Anthology
Outland Entertainment | www.outlandentertainment.com
Founder/Creative Director: Jeremy D. Mohler
Editor-in-Chief: Alana Joli Abbott
Publisher: Melanie R. Meadors
Senior Editor: Gwendolyn Nix

Stories originally published in *Blackguards*, edited by J.M. Martin, Ragnarok Publications, 2015.
New edition curated and edited by Melanie R. Meadors.

Published by Outland Entertainment
5601 NW 25th Street
Topeka KS, 66618

Paperback: 978-0-9963997-4-6
EPUB: 978-1-947659-43-8
MOBI: 978-1-947659-49-0
PDF-Merchant: 978-1-947659-48-3
Worldwide Rights
Created in the United States of America

Editor: Melanie R. Meadors
Cover Illustration: Daniel Rempel
Interior Illustrations: Oksana Dmitrienko, Orion Zangara, & David Alvarez
Cover Design & Interior Layout: STK•Kreations

CONTENTS

HONEST TRADE

Elaine Cunningham

MY NAME IS Selena Dove, and I'm a whore. If you're the sort of person who's offended by that, you're welcome to double my fee and call me a courtesan. By any name, whoring is honest work, money earned for services rendered. Sure, it's a little south of respectable and not strictly legal, but at least it's not punishable by death. That's more than I can say for my true vocation.

I was plying both my trades the night the vizier's guard raided the White Raven. Sunset colors still painted the sky and the first star had yet to appear, but I was already hard at work, entertaining a new client and stealing secrets with every touch. I'm a sorceress, and that's my one and only magical ability: I can read a man's secrets with my fingertips.

As impressive as that might sound, I've found most people's secrets really aren't worth knowing. For example, the elite soldier in my bed had never actually used the sword he'd dropped on my bedchamber floor. Apparently Sano—which was not the name he'd given me—owed his position to a former patron, a wealthy older widow who'd talked up his "swordsmanship" with great conviction and a straight face. Now he was stuck with a fighter's reputation and living in dread of the day when he might actually have to earn his pay.

An elegant revenge, in my opinion, on a bed-swerving young fool whose list of playmates included one of the pasha's wives. And as if *that* wasn't stupid enough, he chose Nifridia, of all people. She used to work at the White Raven—an excellent qualification for a spare wife to have, in my opinion, but that particular whore is meaner than a stepped-on viper. I would have been mildly insulted a man so lacking in discernment would seek me out, had I not known a few things about the path that had brought him to my bed.

It was one of those nights when the sand in my bedside hourglass seemed to trickle down one grain at a time, so I wasn't sorry when our resident ravens sounded the alarm.

Every brothel in Ankorish keeps birds for this very purpose. Most of our clients think these feathered sentries are here for decoration, or as a coy reference to the human "birds" for hire in such establishments. Fortunately, our ravens are smarter than most of our patrons, and when they break into raucous song, you know it's time to roll your gentleman friend out of the bed and throw him his trousers.

Sano responded with the alacrity of a man well accustomed to such interruptions. He got one leg into his trousers and hopped about as he struggled with the second, which had been turned inside out in his haste to disrobe just moments before. "What is it?" he demanded between hops. "What's wrong?"

I held up one finger to warn him to silence as I slipped over to my balcony window.

Several men crept down the alley toward the "secret stairs" to the balcony, oblivious to the raven cawing from the railing. They did not, as I had expected, wear the gaudy crimson and bronze of the pasha's soldiers, but rather the plain gray tunic of the vizier's guard.

That was interesting, and by "interesting" I mean the evening had just become a lot more complicated. For one thing, my client was a member of the vizier's guard, but he had no knowledge of the coming raid. Or if he did, he was better at keeping secrets than any man I'd ever met.

"Huh. We haven't been raided in over a year," I said. "I wonder what they want."

Sano's handsome face registered fear, not surprise. Apparently he wasn't expecting a raid of any kind.

"The pasha's men?"

"Looks like. And there's a woman with them. That couldn't possibly be… Nifridia? Why would she return to the Raven?"

My client's fear changed to panic, which proved he wasn't as foolish as he appeared.

"Dung heap!" he swore. "She can't find me here!"

"And she won't," I assured him as pulled aside a tapestry to reveal an alcove that hid a tall pile of books and a door to a narrow stair. "This leads to a cellar we share with the perfumery next door."

"Good. That's good," he babbled as he fumbled with the fastenings of his sword belt. "What shall I do then?"

"Buy me a bottle of scent. Something with patchouli."

I gave him a kiss, a candle, and a little shove. After he'd stumbled out of sight, I nudged one of the books with my foot so that it would peep out from under the tapestry. That accomplished, I pulled a thick silk rope that looked like a bell pull, but which actually lowered a hidden panel and a ladder to the brothel's roof.

There's a practical purpose to the skylight window in my ceiling. Actually, more than one, if you count the coins earned from the occasional rooftop spectator. Tonight I joined their ranks; crouched by the window, I watched as the vizier's men burst into my place of business.

It didn't take them long to discover the hidden stairs. They clattered down the steps and several moments later they charged out of the perfumer's shop and down the street. Sano was with them. Most likely he'd played stupid, a role for which he'd been born. "A pale woman? Young, with white hair? She went that way..."

Since I wasn't sure what to make of this, I took off in the opposite direction, running across the rooftops of the school of magic and toward the home of Fazzimir, also known as the Ears of Ankorish. Or just Ears, if you're feeling informal.

Fazzimir is a big man in Ankorish, in every sense of the word. He's an information broker grown fat and wealthy on the secrets he extorts from me. Since magic of any kind is forbidden to women—and by "forbidden" I mean that any woman with even a hint of magical aptitude is considered an abomination that must be destroyed for the good of society—I didn't have much choice.

I found the blackmailing rat bastard seated at a table in his counting room, shifting coins from one pile to another. He looked surprised to see me, which was useful information.

He quickly adjusted his expression from slack-jawed shock to mild disapproval. "You're early, cousin."

We really are cousins—we have a grandmother in common—but you wouldn't know it to look at us. Fazzimir is the picture of a wealthy Ankorish merchant, with bronzed skin and a bigger belly than most men can afford to sustain. I'm built like a willow branch. I'm also a bloodwraith, which is a rude term for someone born with white hair, pale skin, and silver eyes. A living ghost, in other words. You might be surprised to learn how many people find that notion intriguing. So, while I'm not a beauty in the ripe rounded fashion preferred hereabouts, I know how to make novelty work for me.

I took the seat across from him without waiting for an invitation and slapped down the prepaid appointment card Fazzimir had conveniently lost in a game of cards.

"Sano came to the White Raven, as you arranged."

"Yes? And?"

"He knows nothing about a runaway elf princess," I said, giving Fazzimir the information he'd charged me with discovering. "Assuming she even exists, you can be sure the vizier isn't harboring her."

"Perhaps she is kept hidden away, somewhere beyond reach of the guards?"

"Trust me, if there was a woman in the vizier's palace, Sano would have sniffed her out. That man is as randy as a dog with two cocks."

Fazzimir nodded absently, his dark eyes unfocused and his brow furrowed with the effort of figuring out how his plan had gone wrong.

Since he was distracted, I reached for one of the gold coins on the pile he'd just counted. His immediate inclination was to slap it out of my hand, but he managed to pull up just short of touching me.

A sour expression twisted his plump face. "You're not as clever as you think, cousin."

"The same could be said of you. A runaway elf princess? Seriously? We heard that legend as children."

Fazzimir shrugged. "Legend or not, any information that supports such rumors could be valuable. The vizier is an elf. There are many who resent his very existence, much less his influence with the sultan."

"Including the local pasha."

The flicker in Fazzimir's dark eyes was telling. He knew that Sano was dipping his quill in the pasha's inkpots, and no doubt he'd made sure the pasha knew it, too. That old rumor about the runaway elven princess was nothing but an excuse to get me into bed with Sano and swept up in an arranged raid.

"The pasha is a faithful servant of our lord the sultan," he recited piously, "and a friend to everyone, man or elf, who supports our lord."

"Then who's your client?"

He sneered. "How long would *you* stay in business, if you dropped names like a seabird befouling a dock?"

I ceded the point with a nod. Fazzimir and I had more in common than either of us liked to admit. We knew far too much about each other, and I assumed at some point he would decide the risk of using me outweighed my usefulness. Tonight's arrest would have solved his problem. When whores run afoul of the law, our memories are magically wiped clean to protect the secrets of former clients, not to mention the occasional rat bastard cousin.

What Fazzimer doesn't realize is that I can get nearly as much information from an object he's recently handled as I would from touching him directly. He also doesn't know about Nifridia, who came to the pasha's attention by getting swept up in a similar raid. Since I can out-whore that woman without breaking a sweat, I wasn't worried about being dragged to the pasha's palace. Any man who weds fifteen women places a high value on novelty, and I offer more than the usual portion of that. The secrets I could glean from bedding the pasha could set me up for life.

But now that I'd avoided arrest, Fazzimir would find another way to be rid of me. I needed to find out what that was.

I baited my hook with the juiciest worm I could imagine. "Assuming I could discover a damning secret about the vizier—a real one, not some moldy tavern tale—what would that information be worth?"

His eyes lit up, as well they should. The vizier was the most powerful mage in the kingdom. Meddling in his affairs was not just insane, but suicidal, which would solve Fazzimir's problem rather neatly.

"That information would be worth your freedom," he said bluntly.

"On the day you bring it to me, you may consider our arrangement ended."

"My freedom and your silence," I countered. "In perpetuity."

"That was implied."

"Not good enough. I want your solemn word you will never reveal my secret by words spoken, sung, or written, nor through magic, nor by gesture. Furthermore, you will swear to never again use my secret to force me into servitude."

Fazzimir rolled his eyes. "My lawyers should be so thorough. Done."

Though I didn't believe him for a moment, I fashioned the delighted smile he would surely expect.

"Done and done. Here's my hand on it."

He scoffed. Ignoring my outstretched hand, he pushed three small bronze coins across the table.

"Nice try. Take these, and leave the gold piece."

As I gathered up my pittance, I gleaned from the coins the reason for Fazzimir's long-expected betrayal: He'd been offered marriage to one of his clients' daughters, a girl who'd fallen pregnant by another man. A fine opportunity to move up in the world, but one that required closing less respectable doors behind him. Firmly.

Oh, and I also learned the names of several clients willing to pay a small fortune for any information that might topple the vizier. I should have realized Fazzimir had ambitions along those lines when he dredged up the runaway princess story. His ideas are not so plentiful that he can afford to use any one of them for a single purpose.

What I did not learn, unfortunately, was his plan for me, as he had yet to contrive one. And that meant that my life would continue along the path it had taken for nearly three years.

At that realization, something broke open inside me, a crack in the sepulcher I'd build for a dream long dead. When Fazzimir reached for a bronze bell on his desk, its ghost poured out and filled me with a scream of silent, impotent fury.

The nearby magic school provided Fazzimir with a ready supply of cheap labor—magic wielding guards, mostly. A young man clad in a student's lapis blue robes strode into the room before the last jangling peal faded away.

His assessing gaze slid over me. I answered with a stony stare.

Three years ago, my response to a handsome young mage would have been very different. When I first came to Ankorish, I bedded every mage and magic student who crossed my path, and at bargain rates, in hope of learning what they knew. But I can only steal secrets, not knowledge. The only magic I'll ever possess is my one sorcerous trick. I have accepted that; Fazzimir is still unconvinced.

"Challenge her to the Handstorm," Fazzimer ordered.

The youth looked startled, as well he might. "But she is a woman."

"She is a mage," he snapped. "More powerful than any woman has a right to be. See to it you don't lose the challenge."

The young mage seized my hand. Power surged through me—sharp, painful jolts followed by wracking waves. It felt as if I were drowning in a vat of lightning eels, all of them sharp-toothed and hungry.

The worse thing about this ordeal was it should have been easy to stop. The spell was a common schoolboy challenge, the magical equivalent of arm-wrestling. When force was met with force, the combined spells created harmless flashes of light and sound, but this magic was never intended to go unanswered.

Pain distorts time, so I couldn't begin to say how long the torment lasted. Either this mage was more powerful than most, or Fazzimir had decided upon a direct solution to the problem I presented. I was on the floor, still twitching, before I realized the mage had released me.

"I didn't tell you to stop," Fazzimir snarled.

"You wanted to see how well she could perform the Handstorm. Clearly, she has never learned the spell," the mage said, each clipped word ringing with controlled fury. "Anyone who could respond would have done so."

"She is stubborn."

"That may be true, but it's irrelevant. Once learned, the spell becomes an involuntary response." He turned to me. "A thousand pardons, little dove. Is there anyone I can summon? Or perhaps I can escort you home?"

I waved him away. The effects faded quickly, as usual. In the time it took for Fazzimir to terminate the mage's employment and the mage to observe that Fazzimir was a scrofulous camel prick, I'd regained the use of my limbs and my wits. By the time the door slammed behind the young mage, I had a plan. Desperate and perhaps suicidal, but I'd run out of other options.

Brushing aside the curtains that fluttered over me, I reached for the windowsill and pulled myself to my feet. On the street below, a dozen of the pasha's soldiers marched past on their way to the White Raven.

I glanced at the rising moon. The pasha's men were right on schedule. They would not be pleased to find their quarry missing, but that was Fazzimir's problem.

"The streets are crowded tonight, and I'm not quite up to rooftops. I should probably leave by the wine cellar tunnel."

He grunted and flapped one hand dismissively.

I walked down two flights of stairs and into the kitchens, making no effort to avoid the servants. Most of them nodded politely as I passed. The pastry chef, a favorite client of mine, winked and tossed me a cardamom-scented roll, richly studded with dates and still warm from the oven. I caught it and blew him a kiss.

Munching, I brushed past the grim-faced sommelier who stood like a sentry at the stairs to the wine cellar.

"Slouch a bit," I advised him. "You'll look less like a soldier."

The startled flash in his eyes was gratifying. The vizier's man had been in Fazzimir's household for nearly a year. After tonight, I saw no reason to pretend I didn't know this.

I hurried down the steps into the vast, brick-walled cellar and past long racks filled with dusty blue bottles. The cellar ended in a mural composed of tiny tiles. With the ease of long practice, my fingers found the seven tiles that unlocked the door and pressed them in rapid sequence. A panel swung open, and in the darkness beyond, faint blue flames flickered to life, revealing the two rows of wall torches that marked a narrow, curving passage. Magic of all sorts was easy to come by in Ankorish, as long as you possessed coins and a cock. Someone like me couldn't hope to buy a potion, much less cast a spell.

My jaw set in renewed determination, and I all but ran through the tunnel. It ended with another mural and a hidden panel that led into a greengrocer's root cellar. I emerged from the cellar into a moonlit alley littered with broken crates and rotting fruit.

The shadows stirred, and three gray-clad men stepped into the light. I scooped up a handful of muck and hurled it at the vizier's men.

My aim was good—I got the nearest man full in the face. While he gagged and clawed at disgusting sludge, I shoved him into the man behind him. Luck was mine; they both slipped and went down. The third man lunged at me. I dodged his grasping hands and took off running.

When necessary, I can run like a rabbit. I would have gotten away if I hadn't run face first into a sandstorm.

That's not the sort of thing one expects to encounter on Silk Street.

It's on the edge of the market district and busy by day, but after sunset it's nothing but empty tents lining a cobbled street. Behind those tents, however, is a warren of alleys. I could duck into any one of them and leave the guards pondering which option to explore.

I hadn't gone more than three steps into the street before a whirlwind of golden motes leaped from the paving stone. My first startled gasp drew the glowing, spinning magic deep into my lungs.

If the gods are good, I will never again hear anything half as loud as that whirlwind. I now know what a dragon's roar must sound like—assuming you were inside the dragon's mouth at the time. The deep thrumming shriek filled me to the marrow of my bones with vibrating agony, a crescendo that grew until I was certain I would explode into pieces no bigger than the swirling motes. Darkness, when it came, was a welcome escape.

I AWAKENED TO the sensation of a cool breeze on my face and a silken couch beneath me. Opening my eyes just a crack, I peered out through the veil of my long white lashes.

The vizier sat across from me, and his unfocused gaze indicated his thoughts were occupied with something far more interesting than a captured whore. His age was impossible to tell, but he looked far too young to have risen so high in the world.

Elves are seldom seen in Ankorish, so I had no fair standard to judge this one's beauty. A human with his long limbs and narrow frame would look emaciated, but it suited him, as did the sharp angles of his face and features. His face was nearly as pale as mine, and unfashionably beardless, but then, that was to be expected from an elf. Beautifully dressed in layers of dove-gray silks, he fit in almost every particular my image of what an elf ought to look like. The only unexpected note were the full, almost sensual lips, currently curved in a faintly sardonic smile.

"Now that you're awake," he said in a voice that shamed any music I'd ever heard, "I have a few questions. As you might well imagine."

I abandoned pretense and sat up. When the room stopped spinning, the elf reached for a decanter on the low table between us and poured a small portion of sapphire-colored liquid into a cup.

"Drink that," he said. "It will help dispel the effects of the sandstorm capture."

Since I felt as hung-over as a sailor on the second day of shore leave, I picked up the cup and tossed back the contents. The potion tasted faintly of berries, herbs, and something decidedly less pleasant. Fermented squid, maybe.

The vizier's brows rose. "It is not to your liking?"

I touched the fingertips of one hand to my forehead to indicate that my grimace had more to do with headache than hospitality.

"Where am I?"

His gesture encompassed the elegant room. "These are my private quarters at the palace. I assume you know who I am?"

"Okshiri the Wise, Grand Vizier of Ankorish, First Counselor to Sultan Barzareem," I recited.

"And you are Selina Dove, a woman of many secrets."

I didn't like the sound of that. "Men like to talk. Keeping their secrets is part of my job."

"And yet you have been seen entering the home of Fazzimir, the information broker, on more than one occasion. I wonder why."

"So do I, most of the time," I said honestly. "I loathe the man, but he's family. We're cousins of the first degree."

The elf's eyebrows rose. "That, I had not heard."

"It's not something either of us likes to talk about. If you're asking whether I'm selling pillow talk to Fazzimir, the answer is no. I have never repeated anything spoken by my clients. If I did and word got around, I wouldn't stay in business very long."

"No, I suppose not." Okshiri shifted to lean one elbow on the arm of his chair. "It might interest you to know some of your clients were warded against speaking of certain things, and yet somehow, these secrets came to light. Nothing of consequence, but distinctive enough to trace back to their source."

My throat clenched so hard I could barely draw breath. The vizier knew my secret! Maybe not all the particulars, but more than enough to have me beheaded at dawn.

He took in my stunned expression and confirmed my fears with a nod. "Your response to the potion was conclusive. A person devoid of magic would perceive only fruit and herbs. What, may I ask, did you taste?"

"Fermented squid."

His expression was half grimace, half wry amusement. "My apologies. It's a very individual response."

"Does what I taste tell you what I can do?"

Okshiri tapped his chin thoughtfully. "That would be an excellent refinement, but no, it does not."

We sat in silence for long moments while he mentally tinkered with his potion recipe and I contemplated my own mortality.

Finally I could take no more. "So what now?"

His attention returned to me. "You interest me, Selina Dove."

Finally, a tune I could dance to!

"Take for example the books in your chamber," he said, oblivious to my knowing smile and receptive posture. "You are curious about a great many things, yet you possess not a single book on magic."

"The study of magic is forbidden to women."

"True, but you don't strike me as someone who's particularly concerned with social conventions."

"When flouting social conventions could get me beheaded, I make an exception," I said dryly. "Is this why you sent your guard after me? To ask about my reading habits?"

"Actually, I am more curious about why *you* contrived to meet *me*."

This, I had not expected.

"Your guards had to stun me to get me here," I reminded him. "I would have gotten away, otherwise."

"Yes, it was a fine performance," he agreed. "Very convincing. Now, tell me why you wanted to meet. What secret did you expect to get from me that was worth the risk of revealing yours?"

I considered several possible responses and decided upon honesty. "Elven magic is seldom shared with humans."

"Ah," he said, drawing out the sound. "So unlike the magic taught in Ankorish, elven magic is a secret."

He was quick, I'll give him that.

"So you hoped to steal elven magic, and not for your cousin, I think."

"No. He's done with me."

I hadn't meant to say that, but once truth starts flowing, it's harder to staunch than a knife wound. Everything poured out, and Okshiri simply sat and listened until I was empty of words.

"What must that be like," he mused. "I imagine it would be a great relief, to speak so freely."

It was, actually. "What do I have to lose?"

"Less than you think," he said briskly. "I propose a trade."

I knew this one. "If I steal secrets for you, I get to keep breathing?"

He looked surprised, then insulted. "You are not dealing with the likes of Fazzimir. What I propose is an honest trade: your secrets for mine."

This was more than I'd dared to dream! "You would teach me magic?"

"What else? Is that not the secret you came to uncover?"

His gaze was a bit too penetrating for so simple a question, but I was pretty sure I knew the reason why.

"I'm a sorceress born. All I ever wanted in life was to be who I am. But no one, I think, gets to be just one thing. A whore, a thief—it doesn't matter what else. As long as I could learn magic, I'd happily be a camel, assuming I could figure out how."

"Yes," Okshiri said quietly. "I do believe we understand each other."

The vizier extended one hand. I raised an eyebrow, silently reminding him what he was offering. He nodded in confirmation.

Our fingers entwined, and the storm began.

Knowledge, more than I could possibly absorb in a moment, a day, a lifetime... Magic, most of it veiled by rune and ritual, but still as blindingly bright as the corona surrounding a sun in eclipse... Impossible dreams, and the lengths people like me and Okshiri were willing to go to achieve them... Secrets and lies, and the deep loneliness of living in the shadow they cast...

Sooner than I would have liked, my mind felt like a jar filled to the brim and overflowing. There is only so much anyone can absorb at one time. The faint smile on Okshiri's face assured me that there would be other times, other storms, other ways of communing.

We sat together in silence, hand in hand. A bloodwraith whore and an elven vizier, with nothing in common but the secrets we shared.

"You know, I never did believe you were actually a princess."

TO THE END

Rob J. Hayes

THE BLACK THORN? Oh, I could tell you a tale or two about that fellow and no mistake. Why I was there the time he murdered the Governor of Chade, I witnessed him single-handedly burn Heross to the ground with nothing but an angry glare and, let me assure you, his glares were very, very scary. I could tell you tales of any number of his glories, travesties, and tragedies but really, wouldn't you gentlemen, and ladies, rather hear something else? Something new. How about I tell one my own fabulous escapades, hmm? No? Well fortunately for you miserable cretins I'm one drink away from not giving a damn what any of you prefer and… there goes that last drink.

I have just the story to tell as well. It's called… "To the End…"

Now as many of you fine people may be aware, I have quite a considerable tolerance for the consumption of intoxicating beverages. Fortunately, along with that dreadful burden comes the never ending desire to test the very limits of that tolerance. I consider it a labor of self-growth. So, a good number of years ago I found myself in Acanthia, home of the most powerful merchants in the world, and the richest thieves in the world, and they are not always the same people. I was sitting in a tavern very much like this one, only considerably cleaner, when I first saw her.

Elize A'bth was her name, though I didn't know that at the time, and she was like the first rays of golden sun on the morning. She was like an oasis in a desert and I, a man dying of thirst, though in truth I was more pickled than parched, and that likely prompted my actions. Never let it be said I am not a man to take responsibility for my actions but sometimes there's no one to blame but the booze. She was working as a waitress at the tavern, I forget its name, and it was clear from the off that she took as much interest in me as I her. I know what you're thinking. *Hard to blame her when setting eyes on a man as handsome as I.* And you are completely correct in that thinking, and don't feel bad for voicing such an opinion as everybody here would no doubt agree with you.

We hit it off instantly. She approached my table all smiles, hips, and lips and asked if I would like another drink. I, smitten as babe with its first glance of a tit, stood and put a knife to her neck, demanding the tavern owner pass me all of the day's earnings.

Perhaps this was not the most chivalrous of actions, but you have to take into account that, at that time, calling me broke would have counted as a compliment. I had somewhere in the region of half a million bits of debt and less in my pockets than most beggars would consider nothing. I could not pay for my bar tab, and neither could I pay for the pressing need to eat so, instead of paying, I decided to rob the place.

The transaction went fairly smoothly considering the bar owner was larger than your average mountain with scars on his arms that suggested he was no stranger to knives. He simply handed over the bar's earnings with a smile. "I'm all paid up for the month," he said. "I'd hate to be you when the Guild catches up."

Now I already know what you're thinking. *What sort of a fool does he have to be to commit a crime in Acanthia?* As it turns out, I am quite the fool.

"Pah," I shouted in a tone that left the man under no false impressions that he had just been mocked and ridiculed. "I fear them even less than I fear the notoriety that actions such as this will bring." It was fair to say my witticism left the man a little confused.

"You tell them that Ches N'tt," that was the name by which I was going at the time, "dares, nay, *begs* them to do their worst."

Then, after foolishly and drunkenly throwing down the gauntlet, I gave my toothpick-of-a-knife a dramatic flourish and disappeared out of the tavern doorway still dragging poor Elize with me.

I had intended to dump the unfortunate wench right outside the tavern and make good my escape and, to my credit, I did try but every time I waved my knife at her and told her to be on her merry way I found her following me not fifty paces later. I even started taking random turns into unknown alleyways, a dangerous business for anyone in Acanthia not registered with the Guild, and even passed through the fish market, blending into the crowd as a leaf on a tree. Alas, when I reached the hovel I was calling home I found Elize just a few steps behind me.

"You've been an excellent hostage, really just sublime," I said with a tip of my hat. "Honestly, anyone would think it wasn't your first time. However, our time here is at an end—"

"I want to join you," she interrupted and I saw it then, the spark in her eyes. To this day I will never be certain whether it was truly me she loved or the danger and excitement I provided.

I should have sent her away, I've no doubt in that, but… well she was beautiful and her body… I'm sure I don't need to remind any of the men here how a woman's body can bend a man's will and crush his faculties.

I neither wanted a partner in crime nor needed the burden of a person to tie me to Acanthia, but I was drunk, standing in the middle of the street, talking to a woman who quite clearly did not belong in such a decrepit part of town. I hurried her inside my hovel and shut the door behind us, with the honest intent of convincing her to depart my scintillating company. Alas, women have always been drawn to me. Don't roll your eyes, my friend, your wife has been wet all evening just from staring at me. Feel free to ask her, she won't lie.

No sooner were we inside with the door closed than she had me pinned up against the wall with a knife of her very own so close to my neck she was practically shaving me. Now I'm not about to deny I have a particular attraction to strong women, and I believe it was right then that my determination to send her away crumbled along with the rising of a part of my anatomy.

Elize glanced down at the bulge in my trousers and smiled up at me and, at that moment, I loved her almost as much as a good brandy. "I've never met a man not afraid of the Guild before," she said in a voice like silk.

"That was not my first time robbing a Guild-protected establishment," I lied in a foolish attempt to impress the woman. As any man will tell you, we often do and say many foolish things to see what's under the covers.

"I want half," Elize said.

"Huh?" I responded as I desperately tried to look down her blouse. I have thought about this many times, and I am certain that this is the moment where it all went wrong. If only I had been thinking with my head I could have stopped it all before it began, but where a beautiful woman is concerned, I rarely think with my head.

"I want half of the take," she insisted, and I nodded along, "and half of the future takes."

Again I nodded, my drunken mind barely registering what I had just agreed to and a moment later my mind had no say in the matter anyway. Elize threw me to the floor and leapt on top, tearing at my clothing and mere moments later we were writhing around like ferrets in a sack.

It turns out she had already come up with the notion of robbing those establishments who paid protection money to the Guild but had never been able to act upon it as she realized the need for a partner in such a crime. I soon came to realize that, while Elize was smart and quick, she was not very learned. She honestly believed, having never seen an agent of the Guild, that they were as real as the Drurr, who she had also never seen. I should have known better as, even then, I had seen both apparent non-existences and knew just how dangerous the Guild could be when irked. Unfortunately, I was young, foolish, and in utter awe of the woman whom I had recently kidnapped.

We purchased a crossbow, a small and poorly made instrument, but it worked well enough to fire a bolt and could easily be hidden in the folds of a dress Elize liked; and a sword for myself as we decided it would look a touch more threatening than a knife, which looked more apt to buttering bread than ending a man's life.

Our first target was selected carefully and not just because of the subtle mark outside the door that decreed it was Guild-protected. It was a well-known bakery frequented by many of the local merchants or, at the very least, their servants. That meant it was also a rich business. It was exactly what we needed for our very first robbery.

It should have gone smoothly. Our planning had been perfect;

we waited until the last hours of business, just before dusk, and made our move on a dark and stormy night. The shop bell above the door jingled as we burst through the doorway hand in hand, laughing as though we had just heard the funniest joke ever told. The shop front was well lit, decorated by row upon row of stale bread and cakes, and smelled more wonderful than any brewery I've ever stepped foot in. The man at the counter was rolling out some dough and had dusty flour covering his hands, arms, and apron. He smiled as he saw us and mentioned some comment about the severity of the weather. I approached mouthing similar pleasantries, and as I reached the far side of the counter I laid my sword down and politely asked the man for every bit he owned. Elize, knowing her part well, produced her little crossbow from the folds of her dress and pointed it squarely at the man's chest with a grin somewhere between ugly and beautiful.

"I think there may have been a mistake," the man said calmly. "I'm all paid up."

Of course he was referring to the Guild, and why would he not be? Those who pay for protection believe in that protection and place their trust in the Guild. Fools. Placing your trust in thieves is no way to live your life, trust me. But the Guild of Acanthia has created quite a racket for themselves; folk pay them in order to stave off being robbed, which is in itself robbery only without the effort. The guards look the other way because as long as all crime is sanctioned by the Guild, then no crime is technically illegal and, therefore, the guards need rarely do anything to earn their pay. It is a brilliant system of well-balanced peace and Elize and I had set in motion a plan to disrupt it which, and I will stress that this is an entirely different story, caused ripples that spread into civil unrest for years and, to the best of my knowledge, the Guild has never fully recovered from that unrest. But, as I stated, that is most certainly another story because all Elize and I were attempting to do was rob a bakery.

The baker grumbled, as was his right, but he pursed up his bits and handed them over all the same. It was a good haul, enough to keep us in booze and food for many a day, but we were greedy and foolish, and the greedy always want more, and the foolish never know when to stop.

I believe it was a peal of thunder that covered the sound of the door opening. I'm afraid I was a little drunk and my recollection is hazy at best, but before we knew it there was another man in the room, well-dressed and smart and wearing the emblem of some merchant household. He gasped when he realized what was going on, and that startled us.

Now, my friends, I offer you a piece of advice freely and fervently. Never startle a woman holding a crossbow. Before anybody knew what was happening Elize turned, and the bolt flew. The man, who looked a lot like a servant come to order the next day's loaf of bread, found himself pinned to the wall and very much bleeding out his last.

For a moment everything was quiet and still as we all tried to adjust to what had happened. Well most of us tried to adjust, I'm afraid there's simply no adjusting to the development of finding a crossbow bolt where your heart used to be. It was a miraculous shot if truth be told, and I might have been proud if I hadn't already been horrified. Still, I'm a firm believer than when everything goes to shit, you might as well make it worse.

I grabbed Elize by the arm, she was in shock from having just murdered a man, and turned to face the baker one last time. "When you speak of this, and I know you will," I said, "tell them Ches and Elize send their regards." And with that we burst out of the door into the storm and away into the night.

Some people are able to distance themselves from their actions when it comes to hurting or killing folk, but not Elize. The murder changed her, made her tougher, more severe, and less forgiving. On a few occasions after the bakery, I found myself disagreeing with her and earned myself a savage beating for the effort. With my weakness for strong women, it only made me desire her more.

We ran, of course. It's the only sensible thing to do after committing both a murder and two robberies in a city policed by thieves and guards, and we would have both parties coming for us. On the road outside of Truridge we came across an old man and his son driving a cart full of ale. We stopped them, threatened them, stole their two horses and, unfortunately, the son decided to play the hero, and I was forced to wound him. I don't believe he died, it was a shallow wound, painful but not serious. Riding away with our newly procured horses we felt invincible, and it was only the start of our crime spree.

Our next stop was Eightrees, a shit-hole of a town, lying to the east of Truridge and on the border of the Great Desert. It was a tactical play on our part, or at least on mine. I figured we would make it look as though we were fleeing to the desert in the hopes of crossing the waterless expanse into the Five Kingdoms. Of course, we had no such intentions, but an insistent part of my drunken mind was aware of the fact that the longer we could confuse those who were no doubt chasing us, the longer we would stay alive.

We robbed a fancy liquor store in Eightrees, and the owner gave a similar reaction to the baker, insisting they were paid up and the Guild would not be forgiving. That theft went off without a hitch and, thankfully, Elize's crossbow didn't. We left Eightrees heading north with a considerable number of bits lining our pockets and two new horses better suited to a speedy getaway.

At this point the story probably seems a little romantic. Elize and I were young and in love and making our way in the world by stealing from those who thought they were safe and thumbing the eye of Acanthia's settled authority. We were rich and getting richer. We travelled the roads, slept under the stars, and fucked like horny rabbits.

Each new town or city we reached was a new place to explore, and we spent a few days in each, selecting our target. We robbed the place, changed direction, and rode away until we found another settlement. There were more deaths. Of course, there were deaths. I tried to avoid them wherever possible and, for my own part, I can swear to the Gods, any and all of them you can name, that I murdered no one… at least during that particular spree. Elize was another matter. With each robbery, she became more brazen and with each murder she changed more and more.

At the beginning, when we were getting to know each other, she used to compose poetry. Oh, she couldn't read nor write but she had me scribe them down, and they were beautiful. She loved sunsets more than sunrises, and to watch her dance in the rain was like seeing a child discover joy for the first time.

Yes, thank you, I'm well aware this is sounding like a soppy love story and you'll have to forgive me for a little romantic reminiscing. We were very much in love and in the middle of a crime spree the likes of which Acanthia hadn't witnessed in generations due to the Guild's *peace*.

Back to my point. With each murder she lost a little more of who she used to be and became more terrifying. To my count she killed twelve people in all, nine of whom were lawmen.

We made our way back to Truridge under the presumption that, as we had never hit the same city twice, the Guild would never expect us there. We were wrong, of course. We had caused enough chaos and presented our arses to the authority one too many times, and the real power in Acanthia was no longer willing to stand idly by. Looking back now I wonder why it took the Guild as long as it did to deal with us.

Having amassed a large fortune we had become used to some of the finer things in life. On the road, we slept under the stars but in civilization, we rented luxurious rooms at the finest inns, and we ate and drank well and tested out the bed nightly.

On our first night back in Truridge, and our last night together, we rented the largest room in *Bien'vlle's Parlour*, a truly ostentatious inn that served three-course meals, boasted no less than six different types of ale, and even sported its own bath-house out back. We ate our fill, I drank my body weight in alcohol, and retired to our room to disturb the neighbors.

Now anyone who enjoys the odd tipple like me will recognize the pain of waking in the middle of the night with such a pressing need to urinate that it is, in fact, painful to move. This was one such night, and it took all the willpower I possessed not to just release my agonizing bladder right there in the bed and, let me assure you, it would neither be the first nor the last time I had done just such a thing. But no matter what you may think of me at this point, I am not the type of man to piss on a lady, and Elize was still very much asleep.

I crept from the room, descended the stairs, and made my way, stumbling with every step, to the bathhouse where I promptly emptied my bladder and passed out.

Not the most noble of actions for a man of my prestigious birth, but it saved my life.

I woke again to an incessant tapping on my shoulder and, honestly, I would very much like to have ignored it, but the offending party became more and more insistent. Opening my eyes I saw a man, almost a boy, dressed in black with long dark hair and a dirt smudged face. He had a dagger in one hand and, I remember, a little clay gourd hanging from his belt. A strange thing to remember, you may think, but I have seen those gourds before and know what they contain, and I have always been partial to a sniffter of 'sinthe. Regardless, I managed to curtail my urge to steal the boy's drink and, instead, looked upon him with complete bemusement. It took me a good few moments to realize he was a member of the Guild.

"Stay quiet," the boy hissed. "Unregistered tappers upstairs. There might be some trouble."

I almost laughed. The boy, no doubt new to the Guild, had mistaken me for just another drunk passed out on a toilet.

"Head off to a tavern," the boy insisted. "Come back to your room in the morning. It'll all be over by then."

I thought about it. The lad's back was turned and my boot knife was sharp. It would have been an easy thing to silence him, rush back into the inn, and warn Elize. We would have to fight our way out and that would be dangerous, but we could maybe have made it. And I did love her. And I believe she loved me. It would have been an easy thing, but it was a much easier thing to simply walk away, and I do gravitate towards the easy way out.

Not so romantic now, I think you'll all agree, and you probably think me a right and proper cur. I could have saved Elize but… well… I'm just not the savior type, I'm afraid. Much more likely to lead astray which, with Elize, is exactly what I did. The Guild is not forgiving to those who subvert its authority and, though I do not know Elize's fate, I do not believe it ended peacefully.

To end my story, I shall say I ran. I made it to the docks where I spotted the *Fortune*, and I knew the ship's captain well. He picked me up, hid me in the hold, and that was the last time I saw Acanthia, and the last time I used the name Ches N'tt.

Perhaps this was not the swashbuckling jaunt you were expecting, but I hope you enjoyed my tale all the same. I know you did, sir, as you've been touching yourself the entire time I've been talking.

Now, who would like to buy me a drink?

TO THE END → 28

THE LORD COLLECTOR

Anthony Ryan

"WHERE ARE THEY, Varesh?"

Varesh Baldir was a tall man, somewhere past his fortieth year, thickset with a copious unkempt beard that partly concealed the weathered features common to those who eked a living from the shore. His heavy brows furrowed as he stared at Jehrid, eyes lit mostly with hate and fury, but also betraying a momentary flicker of fear.

"We counted near two score corpses on the beach after you lured that freighter to its death," Jehrid continued, sensing a fractional advantage. "I know the code as well as you. Blood pays for blood."

Varesh took a deep breath, closing his eyes and turning his face out towards the sea, hate and fear fading as his brow softened under the salted wind. After a moment he opened his eyes and turned back to Jehrid, mouth set in a hard, unyielding line, and his tattooed fists bunched, jangling the manacles on his meaty wrists.

Silence is the only law, Jehrid thought. First rule of the smug-

Illustration by OKSANA DMITRIENKO ▸

gler's code, drilled into him over many an unhappy year. *This is a waste of time.*

He sighed and moved closer to Nawen's Maw, an unnatural bore-hole through the rocky overhang on which they stood. Varesh's chain traced from his manacles to an iron brace set into the top of a stone resembling an upended pear, a wide rounded top narrowing to a flat base. It had been carved from the pale red sandstone that proliferated on the southern Asraelin shore and made the buildings here so distinctive. One of Jehrid's first acts upon assuming his role had been to hire a mason to fashion the stones, insisting they be at least twice the weight of a man and shaped so as to allow them to be easily tipped into the maw. When complete, he had his men arrange them in a tidy row atop the overhang; a clear statement of intent. He had begun with twenty, now only five remained, soon to become four.

Jehrid rested a boot on the stone, glancing down at the waves crashing on the rocks far below. The terns had already begun to gather, wings folding back as they plunged into the swell, eager for the fresh pickings below. This shore had ever been kind to scavengers. The diving birds were the only sign of the six men he had already consigned to the Maw, Varesh's kin: four cousins, a brother, and a nephew. Last of the Stone Teeth, a brotherhood of smugglers and wreckers that had plagued this shore for more than three generations. Before kicking each boulder, Jehrid had asked Varesh the same question, and each time the leader of the Stone Teeth had stood silent and watched his kin dragged to their deaths. Varesh's only child, a daughter of notoriously vicious temper, had fallen to a crossbow bolt when Jehrid led his company into the smuggler's den, a narrow crack in the maze of cliffs east of South Tower, crammed with sundry spoils looted from the Alpiran freighter they had enticed onto the rocks a month before. One of Varesh's cousins had allowed wine to loosen his tongue upon visiting a brothel in town the previous night, and Jehrid had always found whores to be excellent informants.

"My mother once told me a story of how the Maw got its name," he told Varesh in a reflective tone. "Would you like to hear it?"

"Your mother was a poxed bitch," Varesh told him, voice quivering with rage. "Who whelped a traitor."

"It's not natural, you see," Jehrid went on, his tone unchanged. "Nawen, or Na Wen to give him his correct name, was captain and only survivor of a wrecked ship from the Far West. A lonely old fishwife took him in, though he was quite mad by all accounts. Every day he would come here and chip away at the cliff with hammer and chisel. Every day for twelve years until he had carved a perfect circular hole through this overhang. And when he was done... well, I assume you can guess what he did next."

Jehrid stiffened his leg, tilting the stone towards the maw. "No one knows why he did it, for who can divine the mind of a madman? But my mother was wise, and judged it an act of revenge, a desire to leave the mark of man on the shore that wrecked his ship and killed his crew."

He gave Varesh a final questioning glance. "Life in the king's mines isn't much," he said. "But it is life. I know the Stone Teeth allied with the Red Breakers to wreck that ship. Things must have come to a desperate pass to forge an alliance between hated enemies. Settle some old scores, Varesh. Tell me where their den is."

Varesh spat on the rocks at Jehrid's feet and straightened his back. "If I find your mother in the Beyond..."

Jehrid kicked the stone, sending it tumbling into the maw, the chain rattling over rock as it snapped taught. Varesh had time for only the briefest shout as he was drawn into the hole, bones cracking as he rebounded from the sides, followed by a despairing wail as he plummeted towards the crashing waves.

"Make a note for the Royal Dispatches," Jehrid said, turning to his Sergeant of Excise, a squat Nilsaelin recruited as much for his facility with letters as his skill with a crossbow. "Varesh Baldir, leader of the gang known as the Stone Teeth, executed this day with six of his cohorts. Execution carried out under the King's Word by Jehrid Al Bera, Lord Collector of the King's Excise. Append a list of the contraband we recovered, and be sure the men know I'll check it against stores."

The sergeant gave a brisk nod, wisely keeping silent. Like most of those recruited to the Lord Collector's service, he had quickly gained an appreciation for Jehrid's intolerance of even the most petty theft. "You are paid twice the wage of the Realm Guard for a reason," he had told their assembled ranks the morning he flogged a former Varinshold City Guard for helping himself to a single vial of redflower. "Greed will not be tolerated."

"Rider coming, my lord," another Excise Man called, pointing to the north. The rider wore the uniform of a South Guard, a youthful recruit as many were these days. The new Tower Lord had been punctilious in enforcing the King's order that his command be purged of the lazy and corrupt, though it left him in sore need of guardsmen.

"Tower Lord's compliments, Lord Al Bera," the young guardsman said, reining in and bowing low in the saddle. "He requests your presence with all urgency."

"Another wreck?" Jehrid asked him.

"No, my lord." The guardsman straightened and gave a wary smile. "We have… visitors."

TOWER LORD NOHRIN Al Modral greeted Jehrid with an affable nod as he entered the chamber but failed to rise from his plain high-backed chair. Although they were technically of equal rank Jehrid took no offense at the absence of an honorary greeting. He had known this man as captain and, later, Lord Marshal throughout his years in the Realm Guard and was well acquainted with his former commander's disdain for useless ceremony. Also, Al Modral was only two years shy of seventy and his legs not so sturdy these days.

The plainness of his chair, and the mostly bare audience chamber where he received visitors, were a stark contrast to the previous incumbent. Former Tower Lord Al Serahl had maintained a richly decorated chamber and greeted visitors perched atop a tall throne-like chair, so tall in fact he required a ladder to ascend it. He had been a small man, narrow of face with a prominent nose, and Jehrid recalled seeing a resemblance to a suspicious parrot the day he and Lord Al Modral had walked in six months before, unannounced and bearing a warrant of arrest adorned with the King's seal. The full company of Realm Guard at their back had discouraged any unwise intervention from those South Guard present, despite the pleas of the unfortunate Al Serahl who screamed himself quite hoarse before tumbling from his lofty perch in a tangle of robes fashioned from the finest Alpiran silks. When Jehrid led him to the gallows, his clothing had been much more modest.

"It seems we have occasion to celebrate, Lord Collector," the Tower Lord said, gesturing at the three figures standing before him. "The Faith sees fit to lend aid to our cause."

Jehrid went to one knee before the Tower Lord before rising to survey the visitors. The tallest wore a sword on his back and the dark blue cloak of the Sixth Order, returning Jehrid's scrutiny with impassive pale eyes. His closely cropped hair was flecked with gray at the temples, and his features had the leanness typical of the Faith's deadly servants. Jehrid knew him from a best forgotten foray into Lonak territory, though he entertained no illusions the brother would remember the boy-soldier who stood staring in blank amazement as he cut down three Lonak warriors in as many seconds.

"Brother Sollis, is it not?" Jehrid greeted the pale-eyed man with a bow. *Deadliest blade in the Sixth Order,* he pondered as Sollis inclined his head. *Come south to battle smugglers. Does the King think so poorly of our efforts he begs aid from the Order?*

"This is Brother Lucin and Sister Cresia," Sollis said in a dry rasp, nodding at his two companions, both wearing the dun colored robes of the Second Order. Brother Lucin was a thin, balding man somewhere past his fiftieth year. It seemed to Jehrid that his apparently serene expression was somewhat forced, his features tensed as if holding a mask in place. Sister Cresia seemed to be little more than sixteen years old, honey blonde hair tied back from youthful features, her slight form concealed within robes worn with evident discomfort. Unlike Lucin, she felt no need for a false air of serenity, returning Jehrid's gaze with a barely suppressed scowl.

Second Order, Jehrid mused inwardly. *What use have we for missionaries here?*

"Our visitors come on a special errand, Lord Al Bera," the Tower Lord went on. "Regarding the Alpiran vessel wrecked last month. I was explaining you had the matter well in hand. You have finished with the Stone Teeth, have you not?"

"As of this morning, my lord," Jehrid replied. "Though the Red Breakers remain elusive. Perhaps another week of investigation will root them out. My agents are busy, promise of rich reward always stirs them to greater efforts."

"A week is too long," Brother Sollis stated. "With luck, our assistance will assuage any delays."

"The help of the Sixth Order is always welcome, brother," Jehrid replied before casting a pointed glance at the two missionaries. "However, I confess myself at a loss as to the aid offered by your companions. No offense, good brother and sister, but the hearts of the Red Breakers will not open to the Faith, regardless of how many catechisms you cast at their ears."

Sister Cresia's half-scowl twisted into a smirk, her voice betraying a faint note of contempt as she looked down, muttering, "Got more than catechisms to throw at them."

Brother Lucin gave her a sharp glance, saying nothing, but the severity of his gaze was sufficient to make her lower her head further, sullenness replacing contempt. "My apologies, my lord," Lucin said to Jehrid. "My pupil is barely a week into her first foray beyond the walls of our house and knows little of the world or, it seems, common courtesy." He glared again at Cresia who kept her head lowered, though Jehrid saw her hands were now clasped tight together, quivering a little.

This girl's no more a missionary than I am, Jehrid thought. *What do they want here?*

"The ranks of my Order are filled with varied talents," Brother Lucin went on. "The missions test our bodies as well as our Faith. I myself was a hunter before I felt the call to don these robes."

No you weren't, Jehrid surmised from the briefest glance at the brother's spindly arms and lined but unweathered features. *I doubt you spend one more minute out of doors than you have to.* However, he merely nodded as the brother continued, "Sometimes my brothers in the Sixth have occasion to call on my tracking skills, when their own talents are otherwise occupied."

"We need to see the wreck," Sollis said.

"There'll barely be anything left," Jehrid told him. "A month of tides will have cleansed the shore of timber, and the sands of tracks."

"Even so," Sollis said, meeting his gaze, pale eyes unblinking.

Jehrid had been a soldier for twenty of his thirty-three years. He had fought Lonak, outlaws, heretics and, though he preferred not the dwell on it, Meldeneans, and knew himself to be the equal or superior of most men he was likely to meet in combat. But this one was different, for he had never forgotten seeing him fight. Nevertheless, he had ever been a slave to his temper and resentful of those who sought to stir fear in his breast, a long dulled sensation, summoning ugly boyhood memories and unwise notions.

"May I ask," he grated, turning to face Sollis squarely, "what interest you have in this particular wreck?"

Sollis angled his head slightly, expression unchanged apart from a narrowing of his eyes. Jehrid felt his temper quicken yet further at the knowledge of being assessed and, no doubt, found wanting. Fortunately, the Tower Lord intervened before he could give voice to any anger.

"It seems there was a passenger aboard," Lord Al Modral groaned, levering himself out of his chair with difficulty, hand trembling on the heavy staff he was obliged to carry these days. Jehrid knew better than to offer assistance, the old man retained a surfeit of pride and had a temper of his own. "A passenger of some importance, eh brother?"

"Quite so, my lord," Sollis replied, blinking before switching his gaze to the Tower Lord. "One King Janus is keen to recover."

"Every soul on that ship perished on the rocks or drowned in the surf," Jehrid said. "The Alpiran merchants in town saw to the bodies and did what they could to glean names from their belongings."

"The passenger we seek was not among them," Lucin stated in an emphatic tone Jehrid found near as aggravating as Sollis's appraising gaze.

"They're all dead," Jehrid repeated. "You come here on a fool's errand..."

Lord Al Modral's heavy staff thumped onto the flagstones.

The old man's legs might be failing but his arm remained strong. The echo birthed by his staff resounded through the chamber for some seconds before he spoke again, "Brothers, and sister, the Lord Collector will be more than happy to escort you to the wreck and render any and all assistance required. Please leave us whilst we discuss other matters."

After the trio had made their exit the Tower Lord moved to the stained glass window set into the chamber's south facing wall. The window was the only vestige of the deposed Lord Al Serahl's love of expensive ornamentation, conceived to celebrate a battle, and an atrocity, he had taken no direct part in. It was a floor-to-ceiling wonder of expert craftsmanship, lead and glass of various hues rendered into an ascending narrative. At the bottom many ships sailed from a harbor, marked as South Tower by the lance-like structure rising above the docks. The middle panes depicted a vicious sea battle that failed to conform to Jehrid's memory. Most of the Meldenean fleet had been absent that day and the pirates hadn't been able to muster even a third of the ships ascribed to them here. Unlike the sea battle, the window's upper panes were entirely in keeping with Jehrid's memory: a city... burning. The late afternoon sun was clear of cloud today and painted the scene across the chamber floor in vivid detail, leaving Jehrid unable to escape its dreadful spectacle and the memories it provoked.

"More than ten years on," Lord Al Modral said, nodding at the window. "But it seems like yesterday sometimes. Then there are days when it's just a dim memory, like a fragment from a nightmare you can't quite shake."

"Indeed, my lord," Jehrid said, keeping his gaze lowered. He hated the window and had in fact petitioned for its destruction. The Tower Lord, however, had far too much respect for the arts to allow it.

"Before... this," Al Modral waved his staff at the burning city. "I recall a captain less inclined to anger."

"Ten years is a long time, my lord," Jehrid replied, resisting the impulse to close his eyes. Whoever had crafted the window had somehow managed to capture the exact shade of flame that had consumed the Meldenean capital, though fortunately, there was no art that could recreate the screams.

"Nevertheless," Al Modral went on. "I think the King would prefer his Lord Collector keep a clear and level head during this mission."

Jehrid blinked, forcing himself to focus on the Tower Lord. "Of course, my lord."

"They arrived unannounced, bearing missives from the Aspects of the Second and Sixth Orders, but no royal warrant. Curious, don't you think? Given that they come on royal business."

"Certainly, my lord. Sufficiently curious to require them to wait whilst we seek clarification from court."

Al Modral shook his head. "Life as a Lord Marshal taught me many lessons, Jehrid. Lessons you would do well to learn if, as is my fervent wish, you are to succeed me one day in holding this Tower. Today's lesson is twofold. First, the folly of obstructing the Orders, the Sixth in particular. Second, the value of information. I should like to know the identity of this passenger they seek, and the nature of their business on this shore."

Never reckoned him a schemer, Jehrid thought. *But the king gave him the Tower for a reason.* "I'll see to it, my lord."

"Good." The Tower Lord placed a hand on his shoulder as they turned and moved back to the chair, the old man more willing to accept aid now there were no witnesses. "And, if this passenger is still alive we know full well who holds them. With the Faith's help, mayhap you'll finally find what drew you back to this shore."

He settled back onto his chair with a sigh, his hand slipping from

Jehrid's shoulder like a limp rag. "Do you think it'll be sweet when you finally taste it, my fierce and implacable friend?" he asked. "They say vengeance can be bitter."

"It could be wormwood and I'd still drink until my belly bursts." Jehrid stepped back, dropping to one knee before rising to deliver an impeccable salute. "By your leave, my lord."

SHELTER BAY WAS a misnamed, rocky notch in the shoreline some thirty miles west of South Tower. It was formed of a hundred yards of beach flanked by tall bluffs. At high tide the sea became a fury of roaring breakers, churned up by the plentiful rocks lurking beneath the surface. They only became visible at low tide, a dark maze of jagged reefs making this such a favored spot for the wrecking gangs.

They had set out from South Tower the previous evening, Jehrid riding with twenty of his most trusted men. Brother Sollis rode with the two missionaries and a dozen brothers from the Sixth Order. They had camped in the dunes overnight before proceeding to the bay where, contrary to Jehrid's expectations, the tides had contrived to spare some vestige of the Alpiran vessel.

She had been named as the *Selennah* by the Alpiran merchants who came to lay claim to whatever cargo Jehrid might recover, an archaic term but within his grasp of Alpiran: *Voyager.* An old ship, but large and well captained, though not well enough to resist the lure of the wreckers' false lights. Jehrid assumed a junior mate must have had the watch when they neared the shore. A veteran sailor would have known better. Three of her arched beams rose from the waves like the bared ribs of some scavenged beast, all that remained of a freighter that had sailed the Erinean and beyond for three decades.

"And you found no survivors at all?" Sister Cresia asked, eyeing the wreck with little sign of the sullen frown she had worn throughout the journey.

"The sea is ever an efficient assassin, sister," Jehrid told her. "Though there were a few with their throats cut, fingers hacked off. Wreckers don't like to leave witnesses behind, or their jewelry."

Her features gave a twitch of mingled disgust and anger which Jehrid found himself liking her for. *Some sense of justice behind the scowl, it seems.*

"Best if we three proceed alone," Brother Lucin said, climbing down from his horse with a discomforted wince. "My… skills work best without distraction."

"The sand is bare, as I said it would be," Jehrid pointed out as Sister Cresia and Brother Sollis followed Lucin to the beach. The balding brother merely waved and kept laboring through the dunes. Jehrid watched the three of them approach the shoreline. For a time Lucin walked back and forth with Sollis and Cresia in tow, pausing occasionally to point at something on the sand before stroking his chin in apparent contemplation. Jehrid had never been one for plays, but he knew a performance when he saw one. *Tracker my arse.*

After some further mummery, Lucin came to a halt, turning his gaze out to sea. He stood still for some time, back straight and arms loose at his sides, seemingly uncaring of the waves lapping around his feet and dampening the hem of his robe. Abruptly, Lucin jerked as if in pain, clasping himself tight and doubling over. Sister Cresia came to his side in evident concern but he waved her away. Even from this distance Jehrid could see his hand was trembling.

"What is this, my lord?" the Sergeant of Excise murmured at his side, swarthy features bunched in suspicion.

"King's business!" Jehrid snapped, though in a low voice. "Still your tongue."

He watched Lucin say something to Brother Sollis before slumping with a weary shake of his head, kept upright only by Sister Cresia. Jehrid saw Lucin wipe at his nose before turning and raising a hand, now free of any tremble and pointing firmly west. It was too far away to tell for sure, but Jehrid could have sworn the brother's hand was stained with blood.

THEY FOLLOWED THE coast until the sky began to dim, Brother Lucin riding in front with Sollis at his side. Jehrid found it odd that Lucin barely glanced at the ground as he led them in apparent pursuit of the wreckers' trail. He had no guess as to where the brother was leading them; this stretch of coast was mostly bare of the caves or inlets beloved by smugglers, distinguished by tall cliffs and narrow stretches of shingle where only the most skilled or foolish sailor would seek to ground a boat.

Lucin and Sollis eventually came to a halt after ascending a steep rise over twenty miles from Shelter Bay. Jehrid trotted his mount closer as Lucin indicated a point a few miles ahead, a narrow channel cutting into the shore where waves broke on a series of tall sandstone columns, each shaped and honed by centuries of tides and wind so that they resembled a line of jagged swords.

"There," Lucin said.

"The Blades?" Jehrid asked, unable to keep the scorn from his voice. "You think the Red Breakers are sheltering in the Blades?"

"You know this place?" Sollis asked.

"Everyone raised on the southern shore knows this place, and they know to avoid it. It's completely unnavigable, even at low tide."

"The channel leads to a waterfall, does it not?" Sollis pressed.

"It does. Pretty enough place but the walls are too steep and damp to climb and free of caves, which is why it's of no use to the Breakers."

He saw the brothers exchange a glance before Sollis gave a small nod. "Not caves," Lucin said. There was a wariness to his voice, conveying the sense of a secret shared only through dire necessity. "Tunnels, built many years ago."

"By who's hand?" Jehrid asked.

"The Orders have a long history, my lord," Lucin replied. "And there are builders in our ranks as well as trackers."

"That farce you played on the beach," Jehrid grunted with a laugh. "Why not simply tell me of these tunnels back in South Tower?"

"We needed to be certain. And now ask for your discretion."

Jehrid glanced again at the Blades, the silent monolithic swords rising from ceaseless white fury. He recalled his first sight of them one frigid morning years ago, shivering at the rail as a large man pulled him into a warm hug and reeled off a list of foolhardy sailors who had ventured too close to this channel, among them his great uncle, dashed to ruin during a desperate gamble at evading the Lord's bounty-men. "That's how they kept law in those days," the large man had told him. "Put a bounty on our heads and set the scum of the fief on our tail. We fought a war to win this shore, boy, though you'll not find it in any history. Now we have a king, things are more civilized, but blood always pays for blood."

"What's in there?" Jehrid asked Lucin.

"Something that will remain hidden," Sollis stated before the tracker could answer. "With your assistance, for which the Faith will ever be grateful."

Jehrid had never been particularly scrupulous in his observance, but he had been raised in the Faith and the myriad dangers of a soldier's life had often found him holding to it with fierce conviction. Also, he had an obligation to honor Lord Al Modral's desire for information. "You know of a way in?" he asked Lucin.

WARY OF LOOKOUTS, Jehrid insisted they approach on foot and in darkness. This scarcely troubled the Brothers of the Sixth, who moved with an unnerving silence and sureness of foot, or his own men, well accustomed to finding their way across darkened country. Brother Lucin and his pupil, however, were not so attuned to stealth.

"Quiet!" Jehrid hissed at Sister Cresia as her foot contrived to find a rabbit hole, provoking a frustrated yelp. He saw her eyes gleam in the dark as she rounded on him, no doubt ready to deliver a retort, but a nudge from Brother Lucin was enough to still her voice.

Jehrid could hear the waterfall now, a low, steady rumble drifting across through the small copse of trees where they lay. The narrow but fast flowing river that fed the waterfall gurgled past fifty yards to their left, a clear track to their goal, but guarded. They were only the dimmest shapes in the gloom, wisely denying themselves a fire but well wrapped against the chill, four in two pairs on either side of the river, each hefting a crossbow and moving in tight circles, one never straying from the sight of the other.

"Easy targets," Sollis whispered at Jehrid's side, his bow already in hand, a gull-fletched arrow notched and ready.

"Wait," Jehrid murmured as Sollis turned to signal his brothers. "There's another. One you can't see. It'll be the youngest, small enough to be easily hidden. Kill these and he'll be blasting a horn a second later."

Sollis's lean features remained impassive, though a slight tightness in his voice told of a marked impatience. "This matter requires resolution," he stated. "One way or another."

"Their prisoner, if they truly have one, will die the instant that horns sounds."

"The matter requires resolution," Sollis repeated in the same clipped tone.

Not here to rescue, Jehrid realized. *Only to silence.*

He returned his gaze to the sentries, then scanned the surrounding grassland. This was not his usual hunting ground. Smugglers and wreckers tended to keep to the east, close to the main roads leading to northern towns. *Where would he have put me?* he pondered, eyes roaming the dim country. *The falls are loud enough to mask all but the strongest blast. He would need me close...* His gaze came to rest on a small mound near the edge of the spray-damp ledge next to the falls. It would have been easily taken for just a clump of grass in the gloom, but the shape was subtly wrong, the lean of the grass not quite the correct angle for the wind. *He grows careless with age.*

Jehrid turned to his sergeant, nodding at the loaded crossbow in his grip and beckoning him closer. He lay at the sergeant's side and pointed out the mound. "You have it?"

The sergeant braced the crossbow against his shoulder, settling his cheek against the stock, fingers poised on the lock. "Clear as day, milord."

"He'll stand when the others go down. Don't miss." Jehrid inclined his head at Sollis. "As you will, brother."

Sollis raised a hand to make a series of complex but rapid signs, seven brothers immediately rising in response and moving to the edge of the copse. They crouched in unison, arrows nocked and bows drawn, all without the barest rustle or creak of straining wood. There was no further instruction from the Brother Commander, he simply drew, aimed and sent his arrow into the chest of the left-most sentry, the man caught in mid-fall by another arrow before disappearing into the grass with barely a groan. Six more bowstrings snapped as one and Jehrid had a scant second to witness the demise of the remaining lookouts before a slim figure jerked upright from the tell-tale mound, a long sailor's horn raised, back arched as he drew breath. The sergeant's crossbow snapped and the slim figure had time for a spastic final twist before collapsing from sight.

Jehrid surged to his feet and sprinted for the falls, sparing a glance at the sentries to confirm none still moved and coming to a halt beside the one with the horn. His features were pale in the gloom, youthful prettiness rendered slack and ugly in death. There was something familiar about the set of his eyes, the smoothness of his brow stirring yet more unwelcome memories. *Aunt Tilda's eyes,* Jehrid thought, scanning the boy's body. *A good mother would have spared him this.*

"Just a boy," a voice whispered at Jehrid's back. He turned to find Sister Cresia staring at the corpse, eyes wide and face white. Something glimmered in her right hand, something sharp judging from the way it caught the meager light. She blinked, noticing his gaze and quickly concealed her hand in her robe.

Jehrid crouched and lifted the boy's limp arm, pulling back the sleeve to reveal two black circles tattooed into the flesh alongside three vertical lines. "Two wrecks and three kills," he told Cresia. "Youth is not the same as innocence, sister. Not on this shore."

Brother Lucin led them to a notch in the cliff edge where a series of narrow steps had been carved into the rock, so weathered and softened by the seaward winds as to be barely visible. The climb down to the ledge below was short but not without peril, the damp steps and gloom making for some unnerving slips, though luckily there were none in their company sufficiently clumsy to completely lose footing, a deadly mistake judging by the roiling waves visible below.

Sollis drew his sword and took the lead as they proceeded towards the falls, the cascade of water arcing down like a fluid glass curtain. The Brother Commander held up a hand to halt them in place and moved on alone, disappearing into the gloom behind the curtain. A second later came a faint sound of clashing steel then Sollis reappeared and beckoned them forward.

Behind the falls the ledge opened out into a grotto, much of it fashioned by hand judging by the worn but plain chisel marks on the rock. Sollis stood at the grotto's deepest point, running his hand over the rock as if in search of something. Another sentry lay nearby, sword in hand and blood streaming from a deep gash in his neck. Jehrid was impressed he had managed to draw a blade before Sollis cut him down.

Lucin moved to Sollis's side and peered closely at the rock, fingers probing for something. Eventually, he grunted in satisfaction and moved back, murmuring something to Sollis which Jehrid could barely catch, "Locks from the inside."

The older brother gestured at Cresia, leaning close to her as she came forward, his words too soft to hear above the tumult of the falls. Jehrid saw the girl give a reluctant nod before moving towards the rock, laying both hands against the damp stone, her form becoming still, face blank with concentration. She remained like that for some time, the two brothers standing by with evident impatience. Eventually Lucin moved to whisper a question at which the girl turned to him, face flashing anger as she voiced a harsh rebuke. Jehrid expected the brother to respond with some form of admonishment, but instead he merely sighed and moved back, gesturing for Sollis to follow.

"Our sister may be young," Lucin said, moving to Jehrid's side. "But is well versed in ancient lore regarding these tunnels. To open the entrance requires pressure in one particular spot. She'll find it soon enough."

Jehrid's gaze lingered on the girl, noting she had resumed the same statue-like stillness, her hands flat and unmoving on the rock. Abruptly she stiffened, leaning closer to the wall, eyes closed and head cocked at a slight angle. Her features betrayed a brief spasm before she stepped back, flexing her fingers, and a three foot wide section of rock swung inward to reveal a narrow passage. The sister stepped back, face paler than before though lit with a triumphal grin as she offered them a bow and bade them enter.

THE WIDTH OF the passage would permit only one entrant at a time and Sollis insisted on taking the lead. Jehrid ordered his Excise Men to remain and guard the entrance before taking his place at Sollis's back, expecting some objection. However, the Brother Commander merely glanced at him and drew his sword before disappearing into the passage. Jehrid followed with Brother Lucin and Sister Cresia at his back. He had suggested they remain with his men but they merely shook their heads and fell into line, faces tense but, to Jehrid's eyes, not so fearful as they should be. The passage was dimly lit with torches set into the walls every twenty paces, guttering in the breeze from the entrance. The walls were roughly hewn, displaying only the most workmanlike skill in their fashioning. Whoever had crafted these tunnels had displayed scant interest in artistry.

Sollis set a slow pace, keeping his steps soft to prevent any betraying echo. Jehrid noted a slight downward slope and a gradual but increasing curve to the walls, indicating they were following a spiral course deep into the bowels of the rock. The curvature of the passage became more pronounced the deeper they went, obscuring the way ahead sufficiently for Sollis to flatten himself against the wall and move forward in a sideways shuffle. He stopped at the sound of voices, softly spoken but echoing well in the tunnel. There were two voices, both male, engaged in some form of argument, the words indistinct at first but becoming clearer as Sollis began to inch forward once more, now moving in a crouch, sword-grip reversed so the blade rested against his back. He stopped when the voices became clearer, turning to Jehrid with a questioning glance.

Jehrid felt his hand dampen with sweat, knuckles suddenly white on his sword handle. Two voices, older men, one he knew, though it had been many years since he heard it.

"...speak to me of promises," it said, a rich voice possessing the broad vowels of the shore-folk, but colored by a faint note of scorn. "Promises were made to me also. Promise of gold and jewels. Instead, we risk much to scavenge no more than spices and silk. A tidy profit, to be sure. But hardly worth drawing the Lord Collector's eye."

"Gold will be forthcoming," the other voice replied. It was mostly toneless but with an odd accent, the vowels distinctly Renfaelin but the cadence similar to the harsh babble of Volarian sailors. "When you give me what I came for. And don't forget, without me you would have had no wreck to plunder."

Jehrid frowned in surprise as the other voice fell silent. *Since when did he ever fail to find a rejoinder?*

After a pause, the first voice spoke again, this time betraying a discomfort barely masked by angry defiance. "We've talked of this enough. She's mine. And she stays mine until you pay."

There came a sound then, so harsh and grating Jehrid took a moment to recognize it as a laugh. "What do you imagine you are, little smuggling man?" the second voice enquired when his mirth had subsided. "What cards do you think you hold? You are no more than a maggot feasting on the dead before the tide comes to wash you away. You have seen what I can do. Give me the woman unless you would like another demonstration."

A long frozen pause. *Now for blood,* Jehrid decided. The insult and the challenge were too great to ignore. Jehrid could picture him standing there, face stricken with fury, fist no doubt clamping hard on a dagger, his other hand clutching a cudgel. 'The Dance of Hard and Sharp' he had called it; the traditional smuggler's fighting style. In an instant all would be chaos and confusion. The perfect moment to attack. Jehrid inched closer to Sollis, readying himself for the rush.

So it was with no small amount of shock that he heard the frigid silence broken by the first voice. "Bring her."

He's afraid. Jehrid found he had to contain a gasp of amused realization. *He's actually afraid.*

Footfalls echoed through the tunnel then another long pause, silence reigning until they returned. "Ah," the second voice said, now tinged with a tense anticipation. "I was expecting someone... older."

"She carried the amulet you described," the first voice said, hard and sullen. "Worthless bauble though it was."

"Show it to me." Another pause, then a satisfied chuckle. "Worthless to you perhaps, but not to her." The voice switched to Alpiran, coarse and harshly accented, but still fluent enough for Jehrid to follow. "*Isn't that right, my dear? It must have taken a remarkable effort to earn Rhevena's Tear at your age. Most don't until they're nearing dotage. Is your gift so powerful? I imagine not, since you remain bound by this scum.*"

A female voice, tremulous but also defiant, the cultured accent contrasting with her interrogator's grating vowels. "*Free me, and I'll be happy to show you.*"

"*Don't trouble yourself, honored lady. I'll shortly discover its nature for myself.*" There came the scrape of a blade being drawn as he switched back to Realm Tongue. "Hold her still."

Brother Lucin came forward in a rush, his steps drawing a loud echo from the stone, the bleached concern on his face betraying a desperate urgency. "He will do it!" he hissed at Sollis. "We cannot delay."

An enquiring shout came from beyond the curve; Lucin's footfall had not been missed. Sollis straightened, reversing the grip on his sword and glancing at Jehrid. "Secure the woman and take her out of here. Leave the others to us."

Then he was gone, blue cloak trailing as he charged from sight. Jehrid surged after him, the multiple echoes of the brothers' boots like thunder as they followed. Beyond the curve, the passage opened into a large chamber, near twenty feet across with bunks covering the walls and several side channels leading off in various directions. Standing in the center were three figures, an olive skinned woman of perhaps thirty years of age, her arms bound behind her back, and two men. The man on the right was of middling years and unkempt appearance, his wiry frame clad in ragged, threadbare garb.

But it was the man on the left that captured Jehrid's attention. He was older, of course. Hair now gray and thinning when it had once been thick and dark, face clean-shaven and lined with age, though he stood just as tall as Jehrid recalled and his waist seemed as free of paunch as ever. As expected, he had armed himself with a cudgel and dagger, swirling to face the intruders in a crouching stance, lips drawn back in a snarl, one that faded as he caught sight of Jehrid.

"Cohran Bera!" Jehrid called to him as he charged clear of the tunnel. "Stand and await the King's Jus—!"

He ducked as one of the Red Breakers sprang from the shadows on the left, something fast and sharp cutting the air above Jehrid's head. Another appeared on the right, axe raised to swing at Sollis and falling dead a heartbeat later as the brother's sword delivered a single expert thrust to his throat. The Breaker confronting Jehrid was clearly a traditionalist, coming at him with a cleaver in one hand and a cudgel in the other, aiming well-timed blows at his head and legs. Jehrid sidestepped the cudgel, swayed back to evade the cleaver and brought his blade up and down to hack through the Breaker's hamstring before he could recover for another swing. This smuggler was not easily cowed though, despite being forced to one knee and yelling in pain, he managed another lunge with the cleaver before Jehrid's sword point sank into his chest.

Jehrid spun, sword levelled at Cohran Bera, now moved to the center of the chamber, eyes locked on his. "You've grown," he said in a low growl before turning and issuing a shrill whistle. Only a bare second's delay then a tumult of pounding boots, a dozen or more Breakers appearing from the side tunnels at a run, all armed. Four went down almost immediately, tumbling to the floor as the brothers' throwing knives flickered in the torchlight. Those who managed to get close enough to exchange blows were scarcely more fortunate, most falling in the space of a few sword strokes though the momentary confusion allowed their leader time to run for the nearest passage, three survivors at his back.

Jehrid shouted in frustration, a familiar red tinge coloring his vision as he started forward. It was the woman's shout that stopped his pursuit, his gaze swivelling towards her, now standing rigid and head drawn back, the wiry man's fist in her hair, his other holding a thin-bladed dagger to her throat. Jehrid had time to catch Cohran Bera's final glance, oddly somber and lacking in hatred, before the shadows swallowed him.

"Oh no!" the wiry man barked, addressing his words to Sollis as the brothers quickly surrounded the pair, closing in with swords levelled. He jerked the woman's head back further, the edge of his blade pressing hard against her skin. "I require your consideration."

Sollis held up a hand to halt the brothers, lowering his own sword to take a single step closer. Jehrid noted Sollis's free hand twitch as it caught something that slipped from his sleeve. "Release her," Sollis commanded in a flat rasp. "If your life has value to you."

The wiry man replied only with another grating laugh. Jehrid frowned at the genuine humor he heard in that laugh, and the lack of any real hostility on the man's face. For all the world he seemed no more than a man responding to a particularly well executed prank. "Ask him," the wiry man said, nodding to Brother Lucin emerging from the passage with Sister Cresia at his side. "What value does his Order place on life? Did they bother to warn you what you'd find here? I'll wager they didn't."

It was Brother Lucin who spoke, face grim and gaze steady as he regarded the wiry man, his voice now possessed of a cold, unwavering note of command. "Kill him."

"Brother..." Jehrid stepped towards Sollis but the brother had already begun to move. His left hand seemed to blur, something small and metallic catching the light as it flew free. Jehrid shouted in alarm, knowing a killing blow might cause the wiry man's arm to tense with dire consequences for his hostage. Sollis, however, had chosen his target well. The throwing knife sank hilt-deep into the wiry man's wrist, the knife falling from his spasming grip. The woman twisted, tearing herself free and falling to the floor. Jehrid quickly moved to her side, sword pointed at her now prostrate captor.

His gaze met Jehrid's for a moment, bright with pain and fury, then softened as it shifted to the throwing knife embedded in his wrist, and he began to laugh anew.

"Kill him, brother!" Lucin commanded in a yell, his voice suddenly shrill with panic.

Sollis moved to the wiry man, sword drawn back, then stumbled to his knees as the floor shuddered beneath his feet.

"You put too much trust in these deluded mystics, master," the wiry man said, blood now streaming in rivulets from his nose. "Far too much trust..."

A great booming sound shook the surrounding rock, a jagged crack appearing in the floor, stretching the length of the chamber. Jehrid saw Lucin grab Sister Cresia's arm and drag her towards the passage as the chamber shuddered again, the floor becoming a jumbled matrix of cracks, the brothers reeling from multiple fountains of shattered rock. The wiry man was laughing again, writhing on the shuddering floor in uncontrollable mirth, blood now streaming from his mouth and eyes. Sollis lurched towards him, sword raised for a slash at his neck... and the chamber floor exploded, stone shattering all around into a fog of dust.

Jehrid had time to catch hold of the woman before the floor gave way beneath them, air rushing past his ears as they plummeted, swallowed by the welcoming dark.

THE DOCKS ONCE again, his only reliable dream. It was always the same. The same pier, the same hour just before nightfall, every detail perfect and vivid even though the memory was over twenty years old.

He crouched behind a wall of stacked barrels in a quiet corner of the South Tower docks, peeking out at the end of the pier. There were people there, dim shadows glimpsed through twilight mist, four standing and one kneeling. The kneeling figure was bound, face concealed with a sack tied at the neck. Even so Jehrid knew whose face lay beneath the sack, knew without any shred of doubt the face of the woman who knelt with head bowed in numb expectation of her fate. Just as he knew the name of the man who drew a knife and stepped to her side.

He turned away then, knowing what was coming, reeling through the streets as his gorge rose to spill his guts on the cobbles. His treacherous ears caught the sound of a body tumbling into harbor waters, the splash carrying well in the clammy air. He ran, through the streets and the city gate and out into the fields beyond, blinded by tears, running until his lungs turned to fire and his legs gave way. He lay out in the fields until morning, and when the sun rose to wake him with its warmth, he got to his feet and started north. The road was long, and he grew to know hunger and danger as close friends for the wild country was ever rich in threats, but eventually, a thin, ragged boy staggered into Varinshold and sought entry to the Realm Guard.

"Has to be your real name, boy," the sergeant told him, quill poised over parchment, a somewhat wicked glint in his eye as he added, "King Janus wants only honest Guardsmen..."

He awoke to the taste of blood, iron, and salt stinging his tongue and provoking a convulsive retch as his senses returned. His dulled vision, hampered by eyelids that now seemed to be fashioned from lead, could see almost nothing save a faint impression of tumbled rock, though the sound invading his ears prevented any return to slumber; a muted but continuous, echoing torrent of rushing water.

"*Not alone after all,*" a voice muttered nearby, a female voice, speaking in Alpiran.

It took a moment before he made her out, crouching in the gloom, on her knees, arms still bound and eyes pinpoints of light behind hair hanging in damp tendrils over her face.

Jehrid paused to spit the blood from his mouth, tongue exploring where his teeth had left a ragged impression on the inside of his cheek. "*Nor, it seems, are you, honored lady,*" he replied in his coarse but functional Alpiran.

She straightened a little in surprise, then spoke in accentless Realm Tongue that put his Alpiran to shame, "Would you mind?" She turned, crouching to proffer her bound wrists.

Jehrid realized his hands were empty, his sword no doubt lost somewhere in the fall. He fumbled at her bonds, grunting in frustration at his shaking hands, forcing himself to draw a series of deep breaths until the tremble subsided, though the cause was obvious. *He laughed. He bled and he laughed... He did this. He brought down the chamber.* The mystery of it all was absolute, but for one signal and reluctant conclusion: *The Dark.*

The woman gave an impatient sigh and Jehrid mumbled an apology, shuffling closer to work on the binding cord. The knots were well crafted and it took a protracted effort before the cord came loose. She issued a loud groan of mingled pain and relief, slumping forward with hands cradled in her lap, a soft curse coming from her lips. The words were mostly unfamiliar but he caught the name *Rhevena* among them.

"Rhevena's Tear," he said aloud, remembering the wiry man's words. "Goddess of the shadowed paths, is she not? Protector of the dead."

The woman's posture became guarded, her hand moving unconsciously to her bare neck. "I thought your people had no truck with gods," she said.

"Knowledge does not equal worship." Jehrid took a moment to flex his legs, confirming the absence of broken bones or torn muscles, though they did ache considerably, and his hands bore several painful scrapes. He levered himself upright, taking a closer look at their surroundings. They were in a narrow passage, the walls even more crudely made than the tunnel under the falls, dampened by a constant trickle of water. He stood at the base of a steep gravel slope, formed no doubt from shattered rock and providing enough of a break in their fall to prevent a bone-crushing landing. To the right the passage was completely blocked by fallen stone, leaving only the leftward course, illuminated by a faint bluish light.

"Can you walk?" he asked the woman.

She nodded and got to her feet, ignoring or failing to notice the helping hand he offered. "Your comrades?" she asked, peering about.

Jehrid glanced at the wall of stone blocking the passage, then lifted his gaze to the black void above. *How far did we fall?* "I doubt we'll see them again," he said.

He took the lead, the dim luminescence growing as they followed the passage, the sound of rushing water increasing with every step. "You were held here for days," Jehrid said. "Have you any knowledge of these tunnels?"

"The route from my cell to the main chamber only. They were careful with me, my hands were always bound."

He found it odd Cohran would have exercised so much caution and restraint in confining her. Wreckers rarely took captives and the fate of those that did fall into their hands was never pretty. "*You are so dangerous then, honored lady?*" he asked, dropping into Alpiran once more.

She frowned and shook her head, gesturing impatiently for him to move on.

"*That man, back at the chamber,*" Jehrid persisted, halting to face her. "*He paid them to take you, didn't he? Paid them to wreck the ship carrying you. Why?*"

A mix of anger and grief passed over her face before she mastered it, meeting his gaze with stern resolve. "Did your father teach you Alpiran?" she asked, once again keeping to Realm Tongue. "You speak it with much the same accent. He told me he had been a sailor in his youth, learning many tongues and sailing to many ports. You have much the same face and the same bearing. He *is* your father, is he not?"

Jehrid found himself mastering his own surge of anger. "In name," he muttered, turning and continuing along the passage.

"And what is your name? You have yet to tell me."

"Jehrid Al Bera, Lord Collector of the King's Excise. At your service, my lady."

"Lord Collector… he spoke of you, said you would come one day. The thought seemed to make him sad. Now I see why."

Jehrid felt an abrupt need for a change of subject. "And your name, lady?"

"Meriva Al Lebra."

"Al Lebra is an Asraelin name."

"My father was an Asraelin sailor, obliged to forsake his homeland when he met my mother."

"Obliged?"

"She was a junior priestess to the temple of Rhevena in Untesh. Paying court to her required a certain… adjustment in his beliefs."

"He forsook the Faith for marriage?"

"For love, my lord. Has not love ever forced you to an extreme?"

There was a new note in her voice, clearly mocking but also gentle enough to remove any anger from his reply. "I have always found hate a better spur to useful action."

The passage soon grew wider and a dim glow appeared ahead, the pitch of cascading water deepening further. They found a body a few yards on, a slumped, cloaked bundle of twisted limbs. "May the Departed accept you, brother," Jehrid murmured, crouching to peer at the man's face, recognizing him as one of the archers who had taken down the sentries above. He was plainly dead, features drained of all color and his head pressed into his shoulder at an impossible angle. However, he had somehow contrived to retain hold of his sword.

"The Sixth Order," Meriva said, her tone soft but Jehrid could hear the fear it held. "You answer to them?"

"I answer to the King." He hefted the sword and held it up to the sparse light. *An Order blade*, he thought, seeing the tell-tale pattern in the steel, a facet of their secretive forging arts. *The strongest and keenest blades in the Realm. Doubtful they'll let me keep it.*

"Then why are you here with them?" she pressed.

Jehrid bent to remove the brother's scabbard from his back, a difficult task given the contortions of his body. "I came for the Breakers," he grunted, turning the corpse over and working at the buckles. "They came for you."

She made a small sound, half a laugh and half a groan. "To rescue me, no doubt."

"Their mission is their own." He tugged the scabbard free and buckled it on, around the waist rather than the back, sliding the blade in place. He straightened, staring at Meriva until she met his gaze, eyes shrouded and posture guarded, as if she might turn to flee at any second. "I will allow no harm to you," he told her. "But I will have the truth. Why do they want you?"

She sighed, her stance becoming a little more relaxed, though her gaze told of a lingering mistrust. "To hear the message I carry... or ensure my silence."

"You carry a message? From who?"

She looked down, clearly fighting a deep reluctance. Jehrid stood and kept his eyes locked on her face. It was a favored trick when dealing with reticent informants, stillness and silence always stirred the tongue better than outright threats. "From the gods to the godless," she said eventually, raising her gaze once more. There was still fear there, but also an overriding defiance. "I have said all I will say. Now, I suggest we move on. Unless you intend to stand and gawp at me forever."

He held up the only other weapon found on the brother's body, a hunting knife of good steel. "Do you know how to use this?"

She hesitated and reached for the knife, clasping it tight. "No. But I will, if needs must."

TWENTY PACES ON the passage opened out into a cavern, the ceiling lost to the darkness but the walls speckled with pinpoints of light, each no brighter than a match but combining to provide a clear view of the spectacle before them. A torrent of water arced down from the black void to continually replenish a broad pool in the center of the cavern. Jehrid saw there was a slow but definite current to the waters, his gaze tracking to the right where the cavern narrowed into another passage, water foaming as it was channelled deeper into the rock.

"There must be a fissure," Jehrid mused, gazing up at the cascade. "Siphoning off the river waters before they reach the fall."

He watched Meriva peer at the cavern wall, her fingers playing over one of the pinpoints of light, tracing dark tendrils across the surface. "Some kind of lichen," she mused. "Fed by the water and giving off light as a reward." She paused, then added something in Alpiran, voice pitched low in reverence as if she were reciting a catechism, "*May the goddess accept my thanks for her beneficence.*"

Jehrid was about to take a closer look at the channel on the right, assuming it led out to sea, and therefore might offer some avenue of escape, but paused when Meriva clasped his arm. She pointed at something in the pool, something limp and man-sized, trailing a blue cloak as it drifted in the shallows.

Jehrid plunged into the water and waded towards the body, heaving it over to reveal a lean face and graying hair. Sollis's eyes remained closed but his features twitched as Jehrid took a firmer grip on his shirt and began to haul him from the pool. *Still alive,* he thought with a certain grim resignation. *Of course he is.*

Meriva helped him drag the Brother Commander clear of the water and away from the damp rock fringing the pool. They rested him against a relatively dry patch of wall where Meriva pressed a hand to his forehead. "Chilled almost to the point of death," she said. Her eyes went to Sollis's right arm, his hand dangling from a twisted wrist. "And that's certainly broken."

Jehrid nodded agreement and reached for the brother's forearm, squeezing hard. Sollis came awake with a shout, trying to raise his right arm as it sought the empty scabbard on his back. He tried vainly to rise, ice numb legs giving way and leaving him flailing against the rock.

"It's all right," Meriva said, casting a reproachful glare at Jehrid as she placed a calming hand on the brother's shoulder. "We are friends."

Don't be too sure, Jehrid thought, watching the realization dawn on Sollis's face, the lean features tensing against the pain and a sharp calculation returning to his eyes.

"My brothers?" he said, gaze switching from Meriva to Jehrid.

"We found no others alive," Jehrid told him.

Sollis closed his eyes momentarily, face as immobile as the stone behind him. When he opened them again there was no grief, no sorrow, just firm decision. "I need a sling for this," he said, patting his broken arm.

Meriva tore a strip from the brother's cloak to fashion the sling and tied it in place, Sollis gritting his teeth against the pain as she pulled it taut. They helped him upright and moved to the channel at the far end of the cavern. Jehrid peered into the gloom beyond the foaming waters, seeing no ledge or other means of navigating such a treacherous passage.

"We could just jump in," Meriva suggested. "Trust the gods to see us safely free of this place."

Sollis gave a rasping grunt that might have been a laugh, drawing a scowl from Meriva. "They have preserved us this far," she said.

"Blind chance has preserved us," the brother replied, though his tone softened as he regarded the channel. "Though, in truth I see little option."

"The current is too swift," Jehrid stated. "And the course may well lead further underground before it reaches the sea. If we aren't dashed to pieces we'd most likely drown. And if we were to make it out, we'd find ourselves flailing amid the Blades in the dead of night."

He turned away from the channel, eyes roaming the cavern and finding a patch of dark a good way back from the pool where the glowing lichen didn't cling to the walls. He moved towards it, far enough until the shadows swallowed him. He could see nothing ahead, just blank emptiness, his hands finding only air as he reached out to explore the void.

"If we had a torch," he murmured. "A candle even. Just the barest flicker of light…"

And the black turned white. It was so sudden he found himself reeling, stifling a shout of pain and shielding eyes now streaming with tears. He blinked and cautiously looked again, finding the way ahead illuminated, a soft beam playing over the rock like a shaft of sunlight caught by a lens. The beam moved, revealing a tall, broad passage leading away from the cavern. Jehrid followed the course of the beam, tracking it back to Meriva, standing with her arm extended and light streaming from her hand, held out flat like a spear-point.

The Dark, he thought, feeling his mouth hang open in an appalled gape. *Free my hands and I'll show you… Light born of the Dark... this is impossible.*

His gaze shifted to Brother Sollis who seemed markedly less shocked than a servant of the Faith should be, standing back from Meriva with evident surprise but also a certain grave acceptance. *Perhaps he knew what he would find after all.*

Meriva walked towards Jehrid, arm still outstretched, the light beam bobbing as she moved. He saw a wary impatience on her face as she came to his side, avoiding his gaze and nodding at the way ahead. "I can't do this forever."

SHE KEPT A few steps ahead as they moved, a slim silhouette framed by the light she cast forth. It gave off no heat, no threat that he could see, and yet Jehrid found he had to force himself to remain close to her as Brother Sollis struggled on behind.

There can be no room for the Dark in a Faithful soul, he recited inwardly, recalling a sermon from a Second Order missionary his mother had once dragged him to. *The Dark, as practiced by the Deniers who lurk in our midst, brought the Red Hand down upon us. Never forget this, and always be vigilant. Only evil can come of the Dark.*

There is no evil in her, he knew, watching Meriva guide them on, her impossible light playing over the jagged vault of the passage. *So then,* he wondered, his gaze going to Sollis's hunched form. *What truth is there in the likes of him?*

Meriva came to an abrupt halt, shoulders sagging a little and her light flickering as she tried to hold it steady. "Something there," she said in a strained whisper. Jehrid moved to her side, his eyes tracking the faltering beam to some kind of mound. A mound that glittered.

Meriva issued a pained sigh and lowered her hand, darkness descending as her light died, though the glittering mound was still visible, lit by the faint orange glow of multiple torches.

"Give the brother your knife," Jehrid told her, stepping forward and drawing the Order blade. "Stay behind us."

He paused to meet her gaze, seeing a great fatigue there and a trickle of blood falling from her eyes. She held his gaze for a moment, then blinked and wiped the red tears away.

"Does it hurt?" he asked her.

She smiled faintly. "It… tires me."

"Wasting time," Sollis grunted, taking the knife from her and moving on.

They kept close to the passage wall, though Jehrid knew their presence would surely have been betrayed by Meriva's light. The glow of the torches revealed another chamber as they drew closer, a crafted place like the one from which they had fallen, the floor worked to a smooth surface and the walls shaped into a circle. In the center sat the mound, glittering metal clustered around a tall stone column. Moving closer they saw silver plate stacked amid bronze figures and tangled jewelery, here and there the tell-tale gleam of bluestone, all shot through by chains of silver and gold, shining like gossamer threads.

"Gold and jewels," Meriva said, plucking a necklace from the mound and holding it up for inspection, three rubies set in a gold chain. "And still he wanted more."

"He was ever a miser," Jehrid replied. "And what miser doesn't want more?"

However, it wasn't the riches that most captured Jehrid's attention, it was the seven-sided stone column about which they were piled. It rose from the center of the mound to a height of about twelve feet, etched all over with writing of some kind. Jehrid had learned his Realm letters at an early age, and could read Alpiran with sufficient effort, but these markings were unfamiliar, and the stone that held them clearly ancient. However, it did possess a form of decoration that made some kind of sense, a series of emblems carved into the top of the column on each of its seven sides. He began to circle the stone, finding each emblem to be different: a flame, a blazing sun, a book and a quill, an eye, an open hand… he paused at the sight of the sixth symbol, a figure holding a sword, deep holes where its eyes should be. *A blind warrior. Just like the one that sits atop the gate to the House of the Sixth Order, or the medallion every brother carries around his neck.*

"So the Faithful truly have builders in their ranks," Jehrid said, turning to Sollis.

Sollis said nothing, his stance unchanged and face as impassive as ever, though Jehrid noted he had managed to remove the scabbard from the knife. "There are six orders to the Faith," Jehrid went on, moving so he could view the final emblem, a snake and a goblet. "But seven sides to this stone."

Sollis merely returned his gaze and said nothing.

"These words." Jehrid jerked his head at the letters etched into the column. "What language is this? What do they mean?"

"It's Old Volarian," Meriva said. "The tongue spoken by the first Faithful to come to these lands."

"Can you read it?" he asked her, keeping his gaze on Sollis.

"It's been many a year since I had to." She placed a foot on the pile, dislodging a cascade of treasure as she leaned closer to inspect the letters. "The calligraphy is unfamiliar and the dialect strange. Far more archaic than any form I'm familiar with. But, I think…" She paused, lost in thought as Sollis and Jehrid continued to exchange stares.

"It's a narrative of some kind," Meriva said eventually, metal jangling as she moved to read more of the inscriptions. "Though it doesn't fit with any history I know, and much of the phrasing makes little sense."

"Read aloud what you can," Jehrid told her.

"'Armies clash beneath a desert sun… blood flows in rivers, spilt by lies... The One Who Waits will face the Hope Killer's song…'"

"Stop!" Sollis commanded in a flat rasp, now turned so that his good arm was closest to Jehrid, shoulders lowered into a crouch, the knife now gripped tight.

"My lady," Jehrid said, backing away, sword levelled at the brother. "Please get behind me."

Meriva hesitated for a second, then rushed from the pile, scattering trinkets as she placed herself at Jehrid's back.

"Something that will remain hidden," Jehrid said. "At what cost, eh brother?"

Sollis gave no response, moving to maintain the distance between them as Jehrid fought down the unwelcome memory of his skirmish with the Lonak all those years ago. *Sword against a knife,* he told himself, trying to stir a confidence he knew to be misplaced. *And him half-crippled.* But the memory was compelling, and still he backed away.

"What do those words mean?" he demanded, playing for time. "What is this place?"

"It's my home," a new voice cut in, rich and vibrant as it echoed about the chamber. "And you were not invited."

Cohran Bera stood perhaps twenty paces away, cudgel in one hand and long-bladed knife in the other. On either side of him stood two Breakers, perhaps the only survivors of his once fearsome band, both armed with crossbows. Jehrid whirled to face Cohran, nudging Meriva behind him, still painfully aware of Sollis's proximity but knowing this to be the greater threat for the moment.

"Fifteen of your cousins died today," Cohran told him. "You bring the Sixth Order to my door and destroy what took a lifetime to build. Have you no words of contrition, my son?"

"Fifteen wasn't enough," Jehrid replied, feeling a familiar, unwise sensation building in his breast. *The dim figures at the end of the pier, the sound of a body falling into the harbor…* "And don't call me that."

"Deny your blood all you want, *my lord.*" Cohran's face contorted as he spoke the title, like an ardent Faithful voicing heresy. "But I look at you and see no difference from that vicious little shit I pulled from a hundred dockside fights. The King chose well in you, a man who delights in slaughter and calls it justice."

"As opposed to a man who slaughters innocents to build a pile of riches he'll never spend."

"Riches." Cohran's voice softened a fraction as his gaze went to the mound of plundered treasure. "No. Power, boy. Power enough to buy a king's boon. He promised me, you see. Back when the wars raged as he built the realm. 'Soldiers need pay,' he said. 'Bring me gold, and there will be no more bounty-men. Bring me enough and one day, perhaps, I'll make a lord of you.' And, when he'd built his realm, paying his guardsmen with the riches plundered from this shore, what did he do? Have the Tower Lord spout empty promises at me for twenty years until he could send you."

Liar! Jehrid found the accusation dying on his lips as long-held suspicions tumbled into place. Al Serahl's lengthy and corrupt tenure in the Tower, tolerated far longer than anyone could have expected. The smugglers and wreckers able to buy immunity from the South Guard for years whilst in the north even the most petty corruption earned a swift execution. *The King took a loan from the shore,* Jehrid realized. *And now considers it paid, in me.*

"Doesn't have to happen, boy," Cohran went on, nodding at Sollis. "With this one gone, there are no other witnesses to gainsay whatever tale you choose to tell." He turned, gesturing behind him where the torchlight played on a series of irregular steps cut into the stone, ascending to a ledge far above.

"It's a steep and winding path," Cohran said, "but it'll take you out of here. Keep the woman, if you like. I suspect she'll have little to say about all this. You have secrets of your own do you not, my dear?"

Meriva moved to Jehrid's side, face set in a mask of determined fury. "Yes," she said. "I have secrets, but this one I'll share."

Her arm shot out, straight and true, hand once again like a spear point. Jehrid closed his eyes as the light blazed forth, birthing an instant scream. When he looked again he saw the man on Cohran's right on his knees, crossbow forgotten as he clutched at his eyes, shrill panic and pain issuing from his mouth in a continual torrent. The Breaker on the left gaped at his fallen cousin for the briefest second, then at Meriva, his crossbow swinging towards her in a fear-born reflex.

Brother Sollis moved in a blur, doubling over as the knife flew from his hand, swift as an arrow as it described a perfect arc ending in the Breaker's skull, the blade sinking in to the hilt. The Breaker remained upright for a heartbeat or two, mouth twisting around gibbered words and an odd, puzzled frown on his brow. Before collapsing, he managed to work the lock on his crossbow, the bolt missing Sollis by a clear foot before rebounding from the stone column and skittering off into the darkness.

Jehrid saw it all in the scant seconds it took him to close with Cohran. The Breaker chief was shaking his head in confusion, eyes moist and bleary, but some brawler's instinct provided sufficient warning for him to duck the slash Jehrid aimed at his head. He growled and whirled towards Jehrid, club and knife whistling, a large man of middling years moving with all the grace and speed of a youthful dancer. Jehrid parried the knife, ducked the club and knew in an instant Cohran was doomed. He was a killer and a fighter, perhaps the most deadly ever seen on this shore, but he wasn't a soldier. He had never faced a charging Lonak war band or hacked his way across a Meldenean deck. He fought for status or money but never truly for survival. He had never seen battle, until now.

Jehrid anticipated his next attack with an ease that almost brought a laugh to his lips, the knife slashing at his sword arm whilst the club arced up for a strike at his chin. An attempt to stun and disarm, not to kill. Jehrid leapt and kicked before either blow could land, delivering the tip of his boot to the center of Cohran's face, nose and teeth breaking under the impact. Cohran back-pedalled, trying to gain space for a parry. Jehrid slashed the knife from his grip with a quick swipe of his looted sword and drove a second kick into Cohran's guts, doubling him over. He tried a final, ineffectual blow with the club, Jehrid catching his wrist and twisting until he heard a crack, the club falling from useless fingers.

He stood back as Cohran stared up at him, face showing neither anger nor defeat. But pride. "Quite a dance, eh son…"

Jehrid drove the iron tine of his sword into Cohran's temple, sending him unconscious to the floor. "Don't call me that."

He turned at the sound of an echoing scream, seeing the blinded Breaker sprinting away into the darkness, his cries continuing to resound through the caverns until they were cut off by a faint splash. *He found the pool,* Jehrid surmised. *Carried out to the Blades, blind and mad. Nawen's Maw would've been a kinder end.*

He went to Meriva, now on her knees, shoulders sagging with exhaustion. He placed a finger under her chin and gently lifted her face, now so streaked with blood she might have stepped from a slaughter pen. "Will you be all right?" he asked.

Her eyes flicked to Sollis, now bending to retrieve Cohran's fallen knife. "*Will either of us?*" she whispered in Alpiran. "*This place, those words. They were not meant for our eyes.*"

Jehrid straightened, watching Sollis as he stood regarding Cohran's prostrate form. For once the impassive mask had gone, a somber frown creasing the brother's brow. "He taught you to fight?" he asked after a moment, his gaze still lingering on the fallen outlaw.

"Yes," Jehrid said. "But war taught me more."

Jehrid detected a faint note of regret in Sollis's voice as he spoke again, "The pupil always steps from the master's shadow." Abruptly Sollis raised his gaze, all expression fading from his features as he briefly glanced at Jehrid and Meriva before gazing up at the winding steps with a critical eye. "Dragging him up there will be impossible. We'll bind him to the column, send your men for him later."

Jehrid gave a wary nod. "As you wish, brother." He bent to take Meriva's arm. "Can you walk, my lady?"

She sighed agreement and began to rise, then froze, her gaze snapping to the pile of treasure as it issued a jangling rattle, displaced metal sliding as something stirred beneath it. "No…" she breathed.

Something exploded from the mound in a fountain of glittering treasure, something wiry and dressed in rags, revealing pale flesh marked by many wounds, a feral grin shining in a face caked in dried blood. It screamed as it stumbled free of the pile; triumph, rage, and madness filling the chamber. A tremor thrummed through the rock beneath Jehrid's feet, both he and Sollis pitched onto their backs by the force of it, powdered rock spouting as cracks rent the chamber floor from end to end.

Jehrid saw the blind Breaker's crossbow lying barely five paces away and lunged for it, shouting in alarm as the rock beneath him lurched anew. The ragged thing issued another peeling laugh as a fresh crack opened to swallow the crossbow. Jehrid saw Sollis cast Cohran's knife at the laughing wreck of a man, but the juddering floor made it an impossible task, the spinning blade missing its target by a handspan.

The tremor faded as the ragged thing staggered, eyes tracking over them in evident satisfaction before settling on Sollis. Blood flowed from its mouth in a thick stream as it spoke, "Sorry to lose you so soon, brother. I always did find your cruelty so… entertaining." He sighed and raised his arms, head thrown back and his smile blazing anew. "I will miss this g—"

Something small and sharp streaked down from above, moving faster than any crossbow bolt or arrow, issuing a small whine as it sliced through the air to spear the ragged man through the eye. He staggered again, head swivelling about in confusion. Jehrid saw something metallic embedded in his eye, a dart of some kind,. the needle-like point protruding from his skull as he reeled about, arms flailing like a drunk fighting imaginary foes. Another dart streaked down, a puff of red vapor spouting from the man's bony chest as it tore clean through his torso, drawing a piercing note from the floor as it rebounded and spun away into the shadows. The thing groaned and collapsed onto the mound, limbs soon slackening in death as blood streamed in rivulets across the gleaming metal.

Jehrid turned at a huffing sound, seeing Brother Lucin clambering down the crude stairway. Sister Cresia followed behind. "Brother," Lucin greeted Sollis on reaching the floor, a little out of breath as he moved towards the mound of riches, barely glancing at Jehrid or Meriva. Jehrid saw he wore a different face now, or more likely, felt no more need to conceal his true visage, free of any false serenity or deference. The face of a very serious man.

Lucin took a moment to survey the body slumped on the pile, eyes lingering on the blood-caked features though Jehrid saw no flicker of recognition. His expression grew yet more serious as he raised his gaze to the seven-sided column. "All too real," he muttered before turning away, addressing his next words to Meriva in Alpiran, no doubt assuming that Jehrid couldn't understand his meaning. "*You have a message for me, honored lady.*"

Meriva took hold of Jehrid's proffered arm and hauled herself upright, wincing from the effort. "*Yes,*" she said, voice heavy with fatigue. "*The answer is no.*"

Lucin lowered his gaze in evident disappointment before inclining his head at the column. "*You read that, I assume?*"

"*Some.*"

"*Then I hope it provided an inkling of what your refusal will force us to do.*"

"*The decision was not mine. I merely carry the message. The Servants have spoken. Your war is not our war.*"

Lucin merely shook his head with a sigh. "*It will be.*" He nodded at Sister Cresia, now standing at the base of the stairway. Jehrid's gaze was immediately drawn to the brace of darts clutched between her fingers, darts that were identical to those that had dispatched the ragged man, though he could see no device on her that could project them with such force. However, any doubts that she had been the author of his end vanished at the sight of her face, bleached white and gaze fixed on the body laying amid the bloodied treasure.

"The first is always the hardest," Jehrid told her. She stared at him with moist eyes, no sign of a scowl on her brow. He saw that her hands were shaking.

"Sister," Lucin said with a note of impatience. "This matter requires resolution."

"No." Sollis stepped in front of Cresia, though his gaze was fixed on Lucin.

Jehrid saw Lucin's throat working before he found the nerve to reply. "Our Aspects are in agreement regarding the import of this mission..."

"Do not make an enemy of me, brother." The words were softly spoken, little more than a whisper in fact, but they seemed to linger in the air, caught by the cavern walls and repeated until they faded to a hiss.

A new voice came echoing down from above, the words indistinct but Jehrid recognized his sergeant's Nilsaelin brogue. "Lord Collector! Are you well?"

"Your men were kind enough to escort us," Sister Cresia said, the darts now vanished from her fingers and a distinct note of relief in her voice.

Jehrid's eyes tracked from Sollis to Lucin, noting how the elder brother's gaze was now averted.

"Quite well!" Jehrid called back, glancing at Cohran's still unconscious form. "Get down here! And bring rope!"

COHRAN BERA STOOD gazing out to sea, a breeze stirring his thinning hair. It was a fine morning, barely a cloud in the sky and the rising sun a bright shimmering ball on a mostly becalmed Erinean. He favored Jehrid with a fond glance as he came forward, then offered a respectful nod to Meriva. She failed to respond, arms crossed tightly beneath her cloak, face rigid. Jehrid had invited her out of courtesy, as the wronged party she had every right to witness the proceedings, though he had hoped she might stay away. *She has seen enough blood.*

Sollis, Cresia and Lucin could be seen on the crest of a nearby hill, all on horseback. The Brother Commander's arm still rested in a sling, the bones set and bound tight by the Fifth Order mission in South Tower, though the scabbard on his back remained empty.

"I'll get another when I return to the Order House," he said when Jehrid offered him the blade he had taken from the dead brother.

"I can keep it?"

Sollis shrugged. "It's just a sword, my lord. We have many." With that he strode to his horse and mounted up. Jehrid surmised this was the only farewell, or thanks, he was likely to receive.

"Cohran Bera," Jehrid began in formal tones. "You stand convicted of murder, theft, piracy, suborning the Realm's servants, and evading the King's Excise. Accordingly you will be executed under the King's Word in a manner deemed fit by the Lord Collector. As you have profited from the deaths of so many by casting them onto this shore, such shall be your fate."

He stepped forward and rested his boot on the pear-shaped stone to which Cohran had been chained, gaze fixed on Nawen's Maw as he tried to summon a face from his memory, one he thought he would never forget, One he hoped would be witnessing this event from the Beyond. And yet, though he strove to recall the dim figures at the end of the pier, seeking to stoke a hatred he had nurtured for more than twenty years, today he couldn't find it. *Why won't she come? Surely she would want to see this.*

"At least look me in the eye as you do this, son," Cohran said.

For a moment Jehrid found he couldn't lift his gaze, as if some invisible hand gripped him in place.

"You must have questions," Cohran went on. "Ask me and I'll tell you."

"You will earn no reprieve," Jehrid told him, still unable to meet his eye.

"I know. But perhaps I'll earn my son's regard."

Jehrid closed his eyes for a second, his boot slipping from the boulder, a great weariness pressing down as he stood back. He forced his eyes open and faced his father, seeing the fearsome wrecker now vanished, leaving behind the man he recalled from childhood, the prideful shine in his eyes as he beheld his son.

"Why did you kill my mother?" Jehrid asked him.

Cohran's smile faded slowly, the depth of his regret plain in the sagging, weathered features. "She was taking you away," he said. "She had grown tired of this life of danger and distrust, and fearful of the future. For she knew one day you would become what I am. She sold us out to the Tower Lord's men, not knowing they worked for me. She thought she was buying a new life in the north, with you. You know the code, Jehrid. Silence is the only law. And so I killed her, because my kin expected it, and because I needed to keep you with me... But you left anyway."

Jehrid's gaze returned to the stone, though he found he had no strength to lift his boot.

"It's all right, son," Cohran said. "Truth be told, I'd rather it was you than any other. Blood pays for blood. Let's get it done."

Jehrid was aware of the eyes of his men, all gathered to watch their Lord Collector's nerve fail. But still he had no strength today. Not for this.

"The ship you wrecked was called the Voyager." Jehrid turned to find Meriva at his side, face pale but determined as she stared at Cohran, suffering no reluctance to meet his eye. "Crafted in the yards of Marbellis near thirty years ago, funded by the honorable trading house of Al Lebra. For many years it was captained by my father and, when he became too old to bear the hardships of the sea, by my brother. He was a good man, an honest sailor who rose to captain at a young age, respected by his crew and loved by his family. When word reached him that I must sail to this shore, he insisted it be the Voyager that carried me, unwilling to trust the task to any other."

She stepped towards the stone, placing her foot on it, gaze still fixed on Cohran as she grated in Alpiran, "*I watched your scum slit my brother's throat, you piece of filth!*"

Jehrid turned away as she shoved the stone into the maw, hearing the rattle of chains and the crack of breaking bones. But no scream. *No,* Jehrid thought. *He never would.*

He waited for the faint splash, then turned to his sergeant. "Return to the Excise House. Double rum ration tonight." He glanced at Meriva, now staring down at the Maw as if frozen in place. "I'll be along directly."

He paused to watch Sollis turn his horse and ride away without pause, although his two companions lingered a moment. Jehrid found he didn't like the way Brother Lucin's gaze rested on Meriva, sensing far too much calculation behind it and experiencing a sudden wild desire to seize the brother and see him follow Cohran into the maw. Fortunately, it seemed Lucin sensed his intent for he gave an inexpert tug on his horse's reins and quickly disappeared from view. Sister Cresia loitered a moment longer, Jehrid gaining the impression of a smile as she raised a hand to offer a tentative wave. He waved back and offered a bow, seeing her laugh before she too rode from sight.

"It wasn't truly a man, was it?" he asked Meriva. "That thing we left in the tunnels."

She shook her head. "In truth I have never encountered its kind before. But I suspect whatever humanity it once possessed withered away long ago, and the world is enriched by its passing."

He nodded and pulled something from the pouch on his belt. "I believe this is yours, my lady," he said, holding up a small amulet; a single bead of amber set in a plain silver mounting. "Cohran… my father had it in his pocket."

Her gaze finally rose from the maw, a small smile curving her lips as she took the amulet. "My thanks, my lord," she said, lifting the chain over her head.

"Rhevena's Tear," he said. "Am I wrong in assuming it to be worn by all those… similarly gifted?"

"Different gods have different servants, carrying different signs. Though we all endeavour to serve a common interest."

"An interest best served by refusing whatever the Seventh Order required of you?"

"Seventh Order? What's that?" He saw her smile broaden as she moved away, going to the horse he had lent her. "Will you escort a lady home, my lord?"

"Gladly. Though only as far as South Tower. I'm sure the Tower Lord will meet the expense of finding a ship to take you home."

"South Tower is my home now. At least for the time being. The House of Al Lebra has many interests here. It was my stated reason for coming. It would seem odd if I was to depart so quickly, don't you think?"

"Certainly." He mounted up and fell in beside her as they followed the clifftop trail towards the distant tower. "Tell me, have you ever heard the tale of how Nawen's Maw got its name…?"

Below the overhang the terns were already circling the spot beneath the maw, making ready to dive into the waves and claim the fresh bounty, for the southern shore had ever been kind to scavengers.

SUN AND STEEL

Jon Sprunk

THE AFTERNOON RAYS gleamed off the rusted sign above the Rearing Donkey. Crammed between a whorehouse and a *kafir* den, the tavern had the reputation as the worst dive in Pardisha. Jirom had only been inside once, and his decision not to return had been based mainly on a desire not to be knifed by one of the Donkey's prepubescent doxies who made their living rolling drunks and dumping them in the littered alley behind the tavern.

Three Moons had made the Donkey his newest home-away-from-home not long after the Company first arrived in Pardisha. Wherever the mercenaries went, their resident sorcerer was quick to put down roots, and that usually involved surrounding himself with a crowd of addicts and "free thinkers." And Jirom had been tasked with finding him.

He didn't want the assignment. He was a grunt at heart, but ever since he'd been promoted to squad leader his time was eaten up with even more responsibilities. He longed for the days when all he had

Illustration by ORION ZANGARA ▸

to worry about was himself and the men beside him, and this town didn't make his job any easier. Little more than a pile of limestone and dried brick, Pardisha was one of several dozen independent satrapies strewn across the deserts of Isuran. Its ruler, Amir Dazo He'Jahana, had hired the Company to protect him from his ambitious neighbors. Six nights ago the Company had successfully defended the town from two of the Amir's rivals working in concert. As far as most of the brothers were concerned the mission was over, but this morning one of their patrols had detected a force of Akeshians approaching from the north. Jirom wasn't privy to the details. He only knew there had been some debate as to whether their contract required them to defend the town another time. Yet, in the end, Major Galbrein had granted their employer an extension in return for a renegotiated bonus, to be paid when Pardisha was safe. According to the rumors, the amount was staggering—if they lived to collect it.

Bracing himself, Jirom opened the tavern door, and almost bumped into a Company brother coming out. "Hillup," he said.

"Sergeant." The tall corporal nodded. His eyes were bloodshot. "You come to see Three Moons?"

"Yes. You heard?"

"Unta told me. I was just headed to the east wall. The major wants every able body up there in plain sight in case scouts are watching the town."

"You can be sure they are. Keep a sharp eye up there."

As Hillup trotted off, Jirom pushed inside. He had to squint to see through the dense smoke lingering over the clutter of tables and benches. A few locals were passed out on the floor—their pockets no doubt already emptied. A short, squat woman in a shapeless dress sat at the end of the bar puffing on a thin cigar. Jirom nodded to her, and was ignored, as he went to the door behind the bar. He loosened his sword in its scabbard and pushed the door open.

A green haze filled the tavern's back room, which was almost as large as the front of the house. About twenty people lounged around on cushions and divans, while a bald-headed youth with kohl-lined eyes plinked on a zither. A naked girl lay sprawled on the floor, either asleep or dead.

Jirom's quarry sat in a tall chair against the back wall, surrounded by a group of young lovelies of both sexes. Three Moons wasn't much to look at—a short, scrawny man with lanky gray hair and droopy eyes the color of old dishwater—but the brothers held him in awe for all the times he had saved their asses. They scared new recruits with tales of his sorcery gone awry, like the time in Yermin he drunkenly set the barracks on fire, nearly killing the entire Company.

Jirom tried to get the sorcerer's attention from across the room, but Three Moons stared at the ceiling without blinking. The air reeked of burning leaves laced with powerful narcotics. Jirom took a step inside, but stopped as three young men in various stages of undress surged to their feet.

"Who you do think you are?"

"Nobody invited you, tinman!"

"Take another move, and I'll cut you up!"

The addict making the last statement waved a thin-bladed knife back and forth. Jirom frowned. This was precisely what he'd wanted to avoid. "I'm here to see Three Moons."

"He's busy," one of the youths replied with a sneer that showed yellow, slightly-crooked teeth.

"You don't want none of this, man!" the knife-wielder yelled, now making stabbing motions with his weapon aimed at Jirom's chest.

"I need to talk to him," Jirom said. "Get out of my—"

He stopped as the knife-wielder darted forward. The youth didn't look like much of a threat, but Jirom's instincts took over. He caught the knife-hand by the wrist, twisted it backward until the weapon fell free, then he twisted a little more until he heard a satisfying snap. His other hand gripped the youth by his ragged collar and heaved him into the air. The room's windows were covered by wooden shutters. Jirom picked the nearest one and sent the youth hurtling through it. The clapping of the shutters broke up the party. Everyone looked at him, including Three Moons.

"Sergeant Jirom!" the sorcerer said with a smile. "Welcome to my dream."

"I need to see you. Alone."

The sorcerer nodded. "Begone, my children. Out into the world once again. Return to me with tales of wonder. And a little more *kafir* wouldn't be amiss."

His entourage left in a shambling, groaning herd. Three Moons found a cup on the floor, sniffed it, and poured something into it from a flask. He held it out. "Drink, Sarge?"

"No. The major sent me to find you. We've got trouble coming."

He outlined the situation with the Akeshians. Three Moons finished his drink and dropped the cup back on the floor. "I suggest we pack up and get out after dark." After a long belch, he added, "Preferably with as much booty as we can carry."

"You're not the first to make that suggestion, but the major wants plans for how we can defend this place."

"How in the six hells would I know? You should talk to the sappers. Ridder and Hance will have some ideas."

Jirom stepped closer until he towered over the magician. "You aren't hearing me, so I'll speak up. The major sent me to find you. I guess he wants you to cook up some of your infamous nasty tricks."

Three Moons rubbed his chin, a wicked gleam in his eyes. "Hmmm.

Give me some time, and I'll see what I can come up with."

"We don't have time. Grab what you need and come with me to headquarters."

"Well, I don't know—"

Three Moons reached for his flask but Jirom snatched it away and threw it through the open window.

"Now," he said, putting some growl into his voice. He had his own reputation among the brothers, and it wasn't for playing nice.

The sorcerer came along without any trouble.

A HAND SHOOK him out of a dream. "Sarge! You need to get up."

Jirom blinked and looked up. Longar stood over him. The light coming through the shuttered windows of the barracks house was pale gray. He'd been up half the night readying the town's defenses, which mostly meant patching the gaping holes that time and neglect had eaten into the outer walls. Given a few more months and access to a decent quarry, he might actually accomplish something. "What hour is it?"

"Almost second bell. The major's been asking for you."

He got up, buckled on his body armor and sword-belt, and looked around for something to wash the sticky dryness from his mouth. After a minute, he gave up on the drink and left the barracks.

Major Galbrein was waiting in his office, surrounded by the Company sergeants. "Did you find Three Moons?"

Jirom bit back a curse. "He didn't come find you? I put him to work on the problem. I assumed he would report in."

"Never mind that now. The Amir has demanded that we march out to meet the enemy."

Sergeant Skawl chuckled. "You've got to love this asshole. He figures if we get ourselves killed, he won't have to pay up."

"Are we?" Jirom asked. "Marching out?"

Major Galbrein shook his head. "Our mission doesn't include mass suicide. The latest scouting reports are in."

Jirom looked over the sheets of parchment handed to him. "'Twelve hundred infantry. Six hundred light cavalry. Two hundred archers.' Sir, we can't handle this many."

"I know, but we're committed now." The major stood up. "I have to get back to the palace. Where are we on the town's defenses?"

"Not very far," Jirom replied. "But I'll go check on it."

"Good. Focus on the reinforcing the gates. The Akeshians won't wait long before launching their offensive."

His words proved prophetic. The Akeshians made their first assault an hour after full dark, aided by the full moon. They hit the northeast and west sections of the walls simultaneously. Jirom stood atop the southern gate with half of his squad. The other half was below piling stones against the gate's timbers in anticipation of an attack. Longar and Furuk stood next to him, watching the approaches.

The desert spread out beneath the walls in all its barren glory. Nothing but sand and rocks, and yet there was something hauntingly beautiful about the dunes at night with the moonlight dappled across their ridged slopes.

"We won't see the fucking sand-fleas until they've crawled right up our asses," Furuk muttered.

Furuk was the only one in the Company who actually hailed from this part of the world, and he was less tolerant of its natives than anyone.

Longar chuckled. "Sounds like you're talking from personal experience, Sweetness."

"Kill the chatter," Jirom said.

He turned as Three Moons climbed the stone stairs to the battlements, huffing with every step.

"Where's the major?" Three Moons asked.

"Probably on the north wall overseeing the defense, which begs the question: why are you here?"

Three Moons unslung his bag and set it at his feet. "Because this is where they'll attack next."

"Sergeant," Furuk said, pointing.

Jirom turned back to the wall. It took him a few heartbeats to see them, a column of shadows coming over a dune to the southeast. Moonlight glinted off helmets and the points of spears marching toward the town at a fast clip. "Elsig, go tell the major we've got company. Three Moons, what can you…?"

The sorcerer pulled a small wooden box out of his bag and set it on the wall. He opened the box and took out a tiny wooden post, which he attached to the top of the lid. Hanging from the post was a thin membrane resembling a leaf or a slip of brown parchment.

"What's that?" Jirom asked.

"Just watch."

The sorcerer leaned close to the little apparatus and gently blew. The leaf-thing flittered and made a humming sound. Minutes passed, but nothing else happened except that Three Moons kept blowing and the Akeshians kept marching closer. They got within catapult range, but the south wall only had one working siege engine, a relic from Jirom's grandfather's time. It made a loud *thwunk* as it fired, launching a fifty-pound stone into the night air. A few seconds later, a cloud of sand kicked up in front of the advancing enemy. The Company sappers cursed at each other as they loaded the arm for another shot.

Jirom was about to check on the preparations below when he noticed a dark cloud in the southern sky, highlighted by the moon. Dread inched up his backbone as the cloud moved *against the breeze* to follow the enemy column. When it got over the Akeshians, it dropped like a swooping hawk. Distant cries rang out over the dunes. Three Moons broke into a victory jig.

Jirom tried to piece together what he'd seen and heard. "Locusts?"

"Wasps," Three Moons answered with a guffaw. "Big, angry suckers. I wouldn't want to be those—"

The sorcerer stopped dancing and clutched the wall. Out on the dunes, a pillar of inky smoke rose from the enemy force. The cries of outrage had ended. A few moments later, the Akeshians emerged from the smoke, once again marching in formation toward the town.

"What happened?" Jirom asked.

Three Moons opened his mouth, and then ducked behind the battlements. Jirom lost his balance as the entire wall rocked like it'd been struck by a fleet of battering rams. A few seconds later, the catapult exploded in a shower of broken timbers. After he sent Longar to organize a medic detail, Jirom propped up the haggard-looking sorcerer.

Three Moons grimaced. "They've got a heavy-hitter out there, Sarge."

"Another wizard?"

"And not just any hedge wizard. Akeshian war-magi are bred to sorcery and trained up in fancy schools."

"So what are you saying? You can't handle him?"

Three Moons slid down on his haunches. "He's wielding High Magic, son. Not the backwater bayou stuff I learned at my grandpa's knee. The next time I pop off, he's liable to squash me like a bug."

Jirom rested a fist on top of a merlon. The enemy had advanced to within bowshot. Company archers sent a flight of arrows sailing into the column, but without much effect against the heavily-armored infantry. He didn't see scaling ladders or siege equipment with the enemy, but it was dark enough that he couldn't be sure. And he didn't have enough men to protect the entire wall. He estimated they could hold the gate for an hour, perhaps two, but he needed...

Marching footsteps echoed down the street behind the gatehouse. Jirom turned, and almost couldn't believe his eyes. A small unit of troops in blue-dyed armor approached from the city center—the Amir's personal guard. Jirom could have hugged them all. He started mentally placing the new arrivals at different spots along the wall to shore up the defenses. He hoped they had brought some crossbows, which would put a dent in the Akeshian advance.

Three Moons leaned over the battlements. "What the hell?"

Jirom was turning as a clash of steel erupted in the courtyard below. He looked down in time to see one of the new arrivals split a brother's skull with a battle axe. The Amir's bodyguard had surged forward to envelop his men at the gate. Spears and javelins flew in the darkness, painting the street with blood as they slammed into flesh.

Jirom drew his sword and ran to the stairs when a titanic explosion, like the cracking of the world's foundation, burst behind him. His weapon dropped from his senseless hand as he hurtled through the air. He saw a bright green flash of light, and then darkness closed around him.

DAWN'S RAYS STRETCHED across the cobbled square at the heart of the city. Its golden fingers walked across the row of bodies lining the western edge of the courtyard—Akeshians and Company men and locals all laid out together like family.

A bead of sweat ran down Jirom's forehead into his right eye, blurring his remaining vision; he couldn't see out of his left at all. After the explosion, he had awakened in the dark to find himself pinned under a pile of armored bodies. The gate was gone, completely destroyed except for its charred bronze hinges. He had been trying to pull himself free when a party of invaders had found him, bound him, and marched him here where a group of his brothers awaited, similarly tied and kneeling on the cobblestones.

As morning came, Jirom saw Major Galbrein arrive, escorted by a squad of enemy soldiers. The Company commander had a bloody compress around his head and one arm in a field sling. Every brother straightened up as the major stepped into the square, and Jirom joined them. If he was going to die today, he would die like a soldier.

The Akeshian command staff arrived with the major. A dozen tall men in shining mail, their scarlet scarves blowing from their necks. Jirom didn't see anyone who resembled a sorcerer, but then again he'd never known one before Three Moons. And where had Three Moons gone anyway?

Dead, probably.

A column of Akeshian crossbowmen entered the square from the north, escorting a big red-and-gold palanquin. An uneasy feeling crept into the pit of Jirom's stomach when the Amir got out of the litter and greeted the Akeshian commanders with polite enthusiasm.

Jirom tested the leather restraints binding his wrists. He had a knife hidden in his right boot, but waited as Major Galbrein was taken to meet the big-wigs. Jirom couldn't hear what was being said, but he saw the controlled rage written across the major's face. He wasn't surprised when the Company commander knocked the Amir on his ass in front of the assemblage, nor when the Akeshians dragged the major to a wooden block which had been set in the center of the square.

While the mercenaries shouted and cursed, they were forced to watch the beheading. The narrow two-handed sword of the Akeshian leader cut through the warm morning air, and the major died with as much dignity as a decapitated man could manage. This had all been for nothing.

Shouts broke out as a pair of brothers, Quarren and Skawl, broke free of their restraints. While they grappled with their captors, Jirom yanked his arms apart. For one terrifying moment, the cords held fast. Then, with a snap, he was free. He drew his knife and leapt to his feet. Many of his brothers had risen up as well, many fighting with their hands still tied. Jirom shouldered his way through the melee, his gaze locked on his target beside the execution block.

An Akeshian infantryman stepped in front of him, but Jirom spun around the point of the man's spear, slid the edge of his knife under the soldier's coif, and kept moving through the crowd with fresh blood running down his fingers. He drew back his arm as he reached his prey. The man turned, mouth agape, and Jirom drove the knife forward with all his strength. The blade punched through the mail shirt and sank to the hilt.

The Amir gasped as he glanced down at the handle protruding from his chest. Jirom smiled at him, and then lunged forward. He caught the nobleman's nose in his jaws and yanked back, tearing the flesh loose. Blood filled his mouth. A moment later, a hard blow landed on the side of his head, and the world tilted.

Gazing up from flat on his back, Jirom took a deep breath. The sky was a flawless azure blue. He grinned at the brown faces leaning over him. He was ready to die now. After fighting and scrapping for most of his life, a respite would be nice. If the gods were kind, he'd spend eternity under the shade of a nice fruit tree. Maybe he'd see his brothers again. Strong hands lifted him to his knees.

Blinking back against the pain in his temple, Jirom saw the Akeshian commander approach like a god of war with his beautiful two-handed sword. Jirom spat out the pieces of the Amir's nose at his feet.

"I am impressed, outlander," the Akeshian warlord said in a reasonable semblance of the local mercenary argot. "You fight like a lion.

No fear at all. Nothing matters but the kill, eh?"

He looked at the rest of the Company brothers, once more back in custody, and lifted his sword. "All of you may have death, if you wish it. Or you may take the iron collar and live as a slave."

Akeshian soldiers armed with swords and collars went down the line of mercenaries, offering each the choice. The sounds of death and hammering iron echoed through the square. Jirom swallowed and wished he had a drink. The day was getting hot already, but with a cold drink in his hand a man could face anything. He started to laugh. It was only a chuckle at first, hardly even a sound, but it grew with each passing moment.

Then a shadow fell over him as the soldiers came to his turn.

THE SUBTLER ART

Cat Rambo

ANYTHING CAN HAPPEN in Serendib, the city built of dimensions intersecting, and this is what happened there once.

The noodle shop that lies on the border between the neighborhood of Yddle, which is really a forest, houses strapped to the wide trunks, and Eclect, an industrial quarter, is claimed by both, with equally little reason.

The shop was its own Territory, with laws differing from either area, but the same can be said of many eating establishments in the City of a Thousand Parts. But the noodles were hand shaved, and the sauce was made of minced ginger and chopped green onions with a little soy sauce and a dash of enlightenment, and they were unequaled in Serendib.

It was the Dark's favorite place to eat, and since she and Tericatus were haphazard cooks at best and capable of (usually accidentally) killing someone at worst, they often ate their meals out. And because

Illustration by ORION ZANGARA ▸

the city is so full of notorious people, very few noted that the woman once known as the best assassin on five continents on a world that only held four and her lover, a wizard who'd in his time achieved wonders and miracles and once even a rebirthed God, were slurping noodles only an elbow length's away at the same chipped beige stone counter.

Though indifferent cooks, both were fond enough of food to argue its nuances in detail, and this day they were arguing over the use of white pepper or golden when eating the silvery little fish that spawn every seventh Spring in Serendib.

"Yellow pepper has a flatness to it," the Dark argued. Since retirement, she had let herself accumulate a little extra fat over her wiry muscles, and a few white strands traced themselves through her midnight hair, but she remained the one of the pair who drew most eyes. Her lover was a lean man, sparse in flesh and hair, gangly, with long capable hands spotted with unnatural colors and burns from alchemical ventures.

"Cooking," said another person, newly arrived, on the other side of her, "is an exceedingly subtle art."

"Cathay," the Dark said, recognizing the newcomer. Her tone was cool. Cathay was both acquaintance and former lover for both of them, but more than that, she was a Trickster mage, and you never knew what she might be getting into.

Tericatus grunted his own acknowledgment and greeting, rolling an eye sideways at the Dark in warning. He knew she was prone to impatience and, while Tricksters can play with many things, impatience is a favorite point to press on.

But the conversation Cathay made was slight, as though the Trickster's mind was elsewhere, and by the time the others had tapped coin to counter in order to pay, most of what she'd said had vanished, except for those few words.

"A subtle art," the Dark repeated to Tericatus, letting the words linger like the pepper on her tongue. "It describes what I do, as well. The most subtle art of all, assassination."

Tericatus leaned back in his chair with a smile on his lips and a challenging quirk to his eyebrow. "A subtle art, but surely not the most subtle. That would be magery, which is subtlety embodied."

The Dark looked hard at her mate. While she loved him above almost all things, she had been—and remained—very proud of her skill at her profession.

The argument hung in the air between them. So many words could go in defense of either side. But actions speak stronger than words. And so they stood and slid a token beneath their empty bowls and nodded at one another in total agreement.

"Who first?" the Dark asked.

"I have something in mind already, if you don't care," Tericatus murmured.

"Very well."

SERENDIB HAS NO center—or at least the legend goes that if anyone ever finds it, the city will fall—but surely wherever its heart is, it must lie close to the gardens of Caran Sul.

Their gates are built of white moon-metal, which grows darker whenever the moon is shadowed, and their grounds are overgrown with shanks of dry green leaves and withered purple blossoms that smell sweet and salty, like the very edges of the sea.

In the center, five towers reach to the sky, only to tangle into the form of Castle Knot, where the Angry Daughters, descended from the prophet who once lived there, swarm, and occasionally pull passersby into their skyborne nests, never to be seen again.

Tericatus and the Dark paid their admittance coin to the sleepy attendant at the entrance stile outside the gate and entered through the pathway hacked into the vegetation. Tericatus paused halfway down the tunnel to lean down and pick up a caterpillar from the dusty path, transferring it to the dry leaves on the opposite side.

The Dark kept a wary eye on the sky as they emerged into sunlight. While she did not fear an encounter with a few Daughters, a crowd of them would be an entirely different thing. But nothing stirred in the stony coils and twists so far above.

"This reminds me," she ventured, "of the time we infiltrated the demon city of S'keral pretending to be visiting scholars and wrestled that purple stone free from that idol."

"Indeed," Tericatus said, "this is nothing like that."

"Ah. Perhaps it is more like the time we entered the village of shapeshifters and killed their leaders before anyone had time enough to react."

"It is not like that either," Tericatus said, a little irritably.

"Remind me," she said, "exactly what we are doing here."

Tericatus stopped and crossed his arms. "I'm demonstrating the subtlety with which magic can work."

"And how exactly will it work?" she inquired.

He unfolded an arm and pointed upward towards the dark shapes flapping their way down from the heights, clacking the brazen, razor-sharp bills on the masks they wore.

"I presume you don't need me to do anything?"

Tericatus did not deign to answer.

The shapes continued to descend. The Dark could see the brass claws tipping their gloves, each stained with ominous rust.

"You're quite sure you don't need me?"

A butterfly fluttered across the sky from behind them. Dodging to catch it in her talons, one Daughter collided with another, and the pair tumbled into the path of a third, then a fourth...

The Dark blinked as the long grass around them filled with fallen bodies.

"Very nice," she said with genuine appreciation. "And the tipping point?"

Tericatus smirked slightly. "The caterpillar. You may have noticed that I moved it from one kind of plant to another...?"

"Of course."

"And when it eats jilla leaves, its scent changes, attracting adults of its species to come lay more eggs there."

"Well done," she said. "A valiant try indeed."

THE HOME FOR Dictators is, despite its name, a retirement home, though it is true that it holds plenty of past leaders of all sorts of stripes, and many of them are not particularly benign.

"Why here?" Tericatus said as they came up Fume and Spray and Rant Street, changing elevations as they went till the air grew chill and dry.

"It grates on me to perform a hit without getting paid for it," the Dark said, a little apologetically. "It feels unprofessional."

"You're retired. Why should you worry about feeling unprofessional?"

"You're retired too. Why should you worry about who's more subtle?"

"Technically, wizards never retire."

"Assassins do," the Dark said. "It's just that we don't usually get the chance."

"Get the chance or lose the itch?"

She shrugged. "A little of both?"

Tericatus expected the Dark to go in through the back in the way she'd been famous for: unseen, unannounced. Or failing that, to disguise herself in one of her many cunning alterations: an elderly inmate to be admitted, a child come to visit a grandparent, a dignitary there to honor some old politician. But instead she marched up the steps and signed her name in bold letters on the guestbook: THE DARK.

The receptionist/nurse, a young newtling with damp, pallid skin and limpid eyes, spun the book around to read the name, which clearly meant little to him. "And you've come to see...?" he said, letting the sentence trail upward in question as his head tilted.

The Dark eyed him. It was a look Tericatus knew well, a look that started mild and reasonable but which, as time progressed, swelled into menace, darkened like clouds gathering on the edge of the horizon. The newtling paled, cheeks twitching convulsively as he swallowed.

"Simply announce me to the inhabitants at large," the Dark said.

Without taking his eyes from her, the newtling fumbled for the intercom, a device clearly borrowed from some slightly-more-but-not-too advanced dimension, laden with black-iron cogs and the faint green glow of phlogiston. He said hesitantly into the bell-like speaking cup, "The, uh, Dark is here to see, uh, someone."

The Dark smiled faintly and turned back to the waiting room.

After a few moments, Tericatus said, "Are we expecting someone?"

"Not really," the Dark replied.

"Some thing?"

"Closer, but not quite," she said.

They glanced around as a bustle of doctors went through a doorway.

"There we go," the Dark said.

She tugged her lover in their wake and up a set of stairs where they watched the doctors gather in a room at the head. An elderly woman lay motionless in her bed there.

"The Witch of the Southeast," the Dark murmured. "She's always feared me, and her heart was as frail as tissue paper. Come on."

They drifted further along the corridor. The Dark paused in a doorway. A man in a wicker and brass wheelchair wore an admiral's uniform, but his eyes were unseeing, his lips drawn up in a rictus that exposed purple gums.

"Diploberry," the Dark said. "It keeps well, and just a little has the effect one wants. It is a relatively painless means of suicide."

Tericatus looked at the admiral. "Because he heard you were coming?"

The Dark spread her hands in a helpless shrug, her grin fox-sly.

"And you're getting paid for all of them? How long ago did you plant some of the seeds you've harvested here?"

"The longest would be a decade and a half," she mused.

"How many others have died?"

"Three. All dictators whose former victims were more than willing to see their old oppressors gone."

Tericatus protested, "You can't predict that with such finesse!"

"Can I not?" She pointed at the door where three stretchers were exiting, carried by orderlies in the costume of the place; gold braids and silver sharkskin suits.

She smiled smugly. "Subtle, no?"

Tericatus nodded, frowning.

"Come now," she said. "Is it that hard to admit defeat?"

"Not so hard, my love," he said. "But isn't that Cathay?"

The Dark felt another touch of unease. You never know what a Trickster Mage was getting you into. And there indeed stood Cathay at the front desk, speaking sweetly to someone, a bouquet of withered purple blossoms in her hand, more of them in her hair, exuding a smell like longing and regret and the endless sea.

The Dark murmured, "She always loved those flowers, and yet did not like contending with the Daughters."

Tericatus said, "She had lovers here, I know that. No doubt she has five inheritances coming."

Cathay turned and smiled at them. The Dark bowed slightly, and Tericatus inclined his head.

"BUT," THE DARK finally said into the silence as they walked away, headed by mutual accord to the bar closest to the noodle shop, "we can still argue over which of us exercises the second most subtle art."

TO STEAL THE MOON

Rebecca Lovatt

THERE WERE MANY ways Willem Al'Caryth had pictured the night of his betrothal going. Many included feasting, dancing, drinking, and most of all, spending the night with his bride-to-be.

Incidentally, none of them included being sent across the world, in the blink of an eye, to steal the moon. It was odd, how these things seemed to happen. All part of being a fae prince, he supposed.

From his rooftop perch, he watched over the palace grounds, studying the guard patrol and learning the layout. The guards down here were simple, well-trained, and stuck to their pattern. Twenty-five steps, eight seconds, turn, walk back, meet with another guard, praise the Mother and the Empress. Repeat. Those on the rooftop would be a bit more of an issue. By his best guess there were four, but they stuck to no discernible pattern he could make out from his perch.

When it came down to it, getting in would be no issue. If he so chose, he could simply walk through the front doors and none would question him. He was of the Third Honor, only half a step below the empress herself, outranking all others within the palace. No, getting in was no problem, it never was. Getting out without starting a war was an entirely different matter. He was going to need to be quick, if he were to have the mask of darkness as an advantage, he would have to get in and out before Haeyn and the seven sisters rose. He would need stealth, cunning. With a short yell, he slipped off the top of the low rooftop and fell, landing in a painful heap on the grass below.

Amber light spilled toward him, and the sound of movement in the long grass drew closer and closer. He groaned, heart racing as he crawled and hid in the alcove beneath the hut's window, hiding deep within the darkness. Light from the crystal torches swept across the field, thankfully deepening the shadows in which he hid.

"You hear something?" one called to another.

"Thought so, might have just been a coon though. Couldn't hurt to check it out," another voice, this one deeper, responded.

Minutes passed as the dark figure with the crystalline torch moved warily through the field, at times only an arm's length away from Willem's huddled figure. With the blood pounding in his ears, he hardly noticed the guard moving away and calling that there was nothing to be found. Already though, Haeyn was beginning to peek about the horizon, Talyn with it. There was no more time to waste. If he was to do this tonight, he needed to do it now. With a grunt, Willem ran across the short stretch of grass, pressing himself against the palace's stone wall, bruised limbs screaming in protest. His Night Cloak wrapped around him, masking his form. Soon though, with the light of the sisters and Haeyn, it would be too bright for the cloak to be of any use.

To his luck, the first he had seen of it this night, none of the guards had noticed the strange blur that moved across the field. Though, it was equally likely that if any had seen him, they had assumed it a trick of the light. *Now,* he thought with a grin, *was when things would truly get interesting.* All ground floor entrances were guarded, even the servants' entrance, and while he was sure there were secret passages, they were likely blood-bound, or masked by some other magic. Stolen magics, he reminded himself. Tiana had made it clear that any and all magics were property of the fae. Else it was considered stolen. He didn't quite agree, but well, he was clearly exempt to that rule now… and really, the lady probably knew best. If she wanted him to steal the Moon, well, by the seven sisters, he would.

Eventually, as a low cloud obscured some of Haeyn's light, and the night's darkness once again deepened, he climbed. The rooftop above was manned, though not by many. The precaution seemed odd to him, despite the fact that he was going to do what they were there to protect against. The land was at peace, and the doors of the palace were open to any, at all hours of the day and night. Only a fool would choose to climb up a stone wall when an open door invited. Only a lovesick fool.

HANDS RAW FROM the climb, and surrounded by four armed guards, Willem supposed his situation could have been worse. He could have fallen to his death halfway up the wall, he could have been killed on the spot, or well, he could already be on his way to the prisons. All in all, standing there, unshackled and notably not dead, was an extremely fortunate turn of events. There was a disturbing lack of places to hide up here anyways, so it was best to get it over with.

"Stranger, I will only ask this once more. What is your purpose this night?" said the guard in front of him. A nervous youth, the guard was younger than Willem by a couple summers, he couldn't have been older than eighteen years.

"My purpose?" Willem said lazily with a smile. "I think the true question is, dear lad, what is your purpose? Is the palace not public?"

"Yes, but—"

"So, are you not then wrongfully questioning me? I am of the public, mostly. Though, my fiancée might disagree."

"All visitors are required to state their business and purpose for visiting the palace at the gates, by order of the Empress," the guard said, running his hand through his sandy hair, but staying true to his training. Willem could respect that in a man, even if it was a useless sentiment.

"Kid, what's your name?" he asked, still ignoring the enquiries, and the other three guards surrounding him. The kid looked to the other three, who, he presumed, shrugged. "Jakum, Lieutenant of the Thorn Guard."

"Well, Jakum of the Prickly Guard. If you and your men were wise, you would take this opportunity to stand down. I'm busy, and you're beginning to annoy me. You may leave now, and your transgressions will be forgotten." The guard blanched visibly, but again, to his credit, held his ground. *By the light, these people were stubborn.*

"I will have your name, sir." Jakum sounded nervous, and unsure of himself. That was good. Already, he would be feeling his authority diminish. Perhaps, if he was lucky, Willem wouldn't have to kill them.

"You may call me Willem Jael Al'Caryth. I am he who is fool enough to tame the very forces of life and chain himself to them. I am the betrothed of High Lady Tiana Caryth of the fae. You have no authority over me, and you will leave." In what he hoped was a casual gesture, he put his left hand in his back pocket, feeling for the sachets hidden there, contemplating the men and their reactions. He fingered one of the packets, toying with taking it out and making quick work of the men. *A simple sleep dust,* he thought, *would be more than enough to do the trick.* Having the men be caught asleep at their posts would be enough to discredit any tales they might spread. Nodding to himself, as the men exchanged looks, he pulled the small leather sachet out of his pocket, unfastening it.

The man in front of him dropped, a puddle of dark blood pooling out of the man's back, staining his shirt and dripping onto the rooftop. *What in the world?* He only had a moment to think before the three stunned guards drew their blades and moved on him. *Wonderful. Just bloody wonderful.* He drew his dagger and spun, stepping over the dead man's body and faced the guards.

"Fae. A bloody fae," one of them, with a nasally voice, spat as he caught sight of Willem's eyes.

"Nah, he's a runt. Mostly human, I'd reckon," responded the guard with the hooked nose.

"Don't matter. Fae, human, both bleed. He'll pay for what he did to Jakum," the first said, the second nodding in agreement.

"Sir," the third, who had remained silent up until now, spoke. His voice had a much more commanding air to it than the others. "Under the Empress's authority, I place you under arrest for trespassing and the murder of Jakum. You *will* submit, or you *will* die."

"I'm quite sorry," Willem found himself saying, "but I really won't."

Feeling the warmth of the pooling blood begin to soak through his cloth shoes, Willem raised his hand in response, slowly, as to not arouse suspicion. Then, he leaped forward and threw the powder from the leather pouch into the faces of the guards, willing the winds to work in his favor. Dancing back and holding his breath, he held his knife out at the ready, watching, waiting.

The first man came forward, falling into a defensive stance as he approached, keeping steady even while treading through his friend's blood. His movements were calculated and precise, keeping to a well-practiced form. Willem found himself doubting the man had ever faced an opponent out of the training field. Closing the distance, Willem jumped in, parrying the guard's sword to the side with his dagger and driving his fist into the other man's chin. The guard collapsed into a heap, joining his fallen comrade.

Looking up at the two still standing, the effects of the sleeping powder were starting to take hold, but were yet to take complete control. Likely, their thoughts were beginning to cloud, but their minds were still their own. He sighed as they approached. It would be a shame to kill them, he had hoped the powder would take more immediate effect.

Hooked Nose rushed him, Nasal Voice going around in an attempt to flank him. He ducked underneath the tall man's slash, driving his pommel into the guard's gut. The man fell back to recover, giving Willem a moment to turn and face Nasal Voice.

"I don't want to hurt anyone," he said one last time. By the light of the world, all he wanted was immortality and a shiny gem for his lady. Was that so hard? A quick glance over his shoulder showed that the authoritative guard was nowhere in sight. He'd have to worry about that one later.

"Shoulda thought of that before you came here and murdered Jakum," Nasal Voice spat, eyeing his dead friend.

"I didn't." His words fell on deaf ears though, as the man rushed forward. He sidestepped, careful not to slip on the blood that littered the ground. Dancing around the guard's blade, knocking it aside with his, Willem waited. Within moments, the man's efforts grew wearied, until he too slumped to the ground, unconscious.

"You, my dear, were taking way too long." Willem spun, lowering his blade and looked to where the final guard lay. On his chest sat a fair-skinned woman with ageless features. A devilish grin split her face in two as she rose to her feet, using her sword that was embedded in the man's back as a support.

"You're losing your touch. I'm almost disappointed," Tiana said in a sultry voice, as she casually pulled her bloodied blade free and walked to the unconscious guards and, in turn, killed them.

"They didn't need to die." Anger boiled inside of Willem, threatening to consume.

"Oh, hush now. That's no fun at all. They're humans. Mortals. That's what they do. Die." She eyed him, before closing the distance and placing a hand on his cheek. His hands twitched to grab her and push her away, but he forced himself to stillness. "Willem, a life is a life. You will learn, their lives end in a blink of an eye, to cut it short by a breath is hardly a tragedy. They rest now in the mother's embrace, think upon it no more." She smiled, though, her eyes looked sad. Was she seeing that same mortality in him? Thinking that he, too, shared this fatal flaw? By the seven sisters, he *would* have his promised immortality.

"Now, come my dear. We have a moon to catch." She walked toward the door of the closest tower, stopping only once to turn and wink at him, before shadows enveloped her leather-clad form.

With a prayer for the dead men, and a promise to never become as cold as she towards life, he raced after her, letting the shadows welcome him into their embrace.

THE PALACE WAS empty. Or so it seemed. It was hard to reconcile this with the court of an empress after Willem's years surrounded by the fae. Where they were always engaged in feasts and festivities, here, no music was to be heard, no cajoling or merrymaking carried through the halls to greet them as they entered into a side passageway. Occasionally, a soft echo of conversation would be heard as they passed doorways. Not even guards were posted in those corridors.

As they made their way to the main halls, where brighter lights and sound began to reach them, Willem pulled Tiana to the side.

"If we're going to do this, we're going to do this my way. If you want to argue, leave. No blood spilt, no lives ended. Nothing. We get the Moon pearl, or any other valuables, and leave." The bodies of the innocent men above haunted him. He could imagine the halls of this palace running red with blood. Tiana's eyes, large and violet, studied him. Her lips pursed.

"They must pay a price for their thievery. It cannot go unpunished."

"No killing," he said firmly, pushing it as far as he dared to. "We're here for the Moon, not to start a war." She looked at him, an unreadable expression crossing her face, and in that moment his blood ran cold. Finally, she shook her head, pushing his hand off her. "Think what you want, just get me that moon. I will check her private chambers, and return here. She will either be there, or in the throne room below. If you find her... do what you want, just do *not* fail me. The Moon will be *mine*." Her slender form flitted away, soundless, and seemed to fade into invisibility as she sank into the shadows, but for her drawn blades as they glinted in the light of the crystal torches.

Taking one last look down the wood paneled hallway, with the rich auburn walls, Willem went with an entirely different form of invisibility. Removing his Night Cloak, he stepped into the middle of the long hallway and began to make his way to the throne room.

Tiana hadn't said it, and in ways, she hadn't needed to. Starting a war was exactly what she wanted. Perhaps it was the true purpose of their presence here this night. Who was he to deny her that? Married to her, he would become a prince, but for now, he was still a mortal man. Even if he didn't go along with it, there would still be war. This way, though, he would get to live. He knew which side would win the upcoming battles, and by the seven moons, he would stick to the winning one.

Striding purposefully, with his back straight and his head held high, he was never stopped. Not by guards, not the emperor-consort, not by any of the other assortment of individuals he passed. While he may not have had the fae's ability to bend light and disappear, he had something that worked just as well: rank. The best way to get anywhere was to blend in, and in a palace, the best way to do that was to strut about like you owned the place. He ignored salutes, bows, and curtseys. The first few times he passed the palace guards in their leather armour, he had fingered the pouches in his pockets. One for pain, one for death, and one to forget. None of which would help him now. All he could do was continue moving.

He passed rich tapestries and paintings, ornate statues and fixtures, pocketing a few small trinkets that caught his eye. Any other time, he would have stopped, ran his hands along the art, and admired the craftsmanship required to make them. Now, though, he had a place to be. The railing along the curved staircase was like polished vines, intertwined, and smooth. They seemed alive to the touch. It seemed magical, true magic, not the glamours that the fae surrounded themselves in.

He approached the great doors that lead to the throne room. They were parted, slightly, and though he could not see beyond them, he knew the empress would be there. He felt at the pouches one last time. His plan had been to simply send her into a dreamless sleep, find where she hid the Moonstone, and leave. That option was gone now.

If he truly wanted to start a war, pain and death would be his friend. To kill in cold blood would be to embrace the sentiment Tiana had shared, that to cut short a life by a breath was no great travesty. It was not a choice he would willingly embrace. A war would leave this palace, this temple of life, in much the same state as the dead men on the roof. Bloody, decaying, and fly-ridden.

What of forgetting, though? How much would she lose? The evening? The War? Her very identity? Her love and her family? Would it be a mercy to sentence her to a life without memory, or to cut it short, allowing her to have the solace of memories in her last moments? A third, darker option flitted across his mind: *betrayal.* He ignored it, dismissing the thought. Instead, he forced a smile, straightened his posture and pushed through the door, entering the throne room.

It was a room of life. The room seemed to have been forged by the forest itself. The throne, on a raised platform seemed to be made of living trees, roots and vines intertwined to form a chair. Tiny white flowers sprouted upon it.

Dispersed throughout the room, noblemen and women stood clustered, chatting, in small groups. Surrounding it all was a melody that seemed to dance from the harpists' fingers. It expanded out from the center of the room where a woman stood. She was tall, her figure accentuated by a blue and green floor-length gown that wrapped around her. Even in the grand chamber, which seemed to contain the essence of life itself, she stood out like a rose in a field of snow.

There was no room for doubt in his mind that this woman, with her almond hair and dark skin, was Empress Anyada, ruler of the so-called Civilized Lands, the most powerful human in the world. He took a step into the room, straightening his jacket. He gave his name to the portly doorman and waited. The man cleared his throat and, at once, the assembly of dark-haired nobility turned to inspect the newcomer.

"Sir Willem Jael Al'Caryth of the Third Honor, future prince and envoy of the Island Fae seeks private audience with her Lady Anyada, Empress of the Civilized World," the doorman said, in a booming voice which seemed to echo back upon them.

A wave of whispers went through the large chamber room, the words inaudible to Willem, but the shock and curiosity was not.

The empress eyed him, her large brown eyes locked onto his, seeming to scrutinize his very existence. Eventually, she raised her hand and the whispers died down, all looking to their ruler. Even the harpists in the far corner cut short their song.

"You all may leave me now. I will be available for public audiences with the rising of Laya in the morning." Lowering her hand, she nodded to him. "You may approach." At once, in a flurry of movement, noblemen and women in a variety of hues of green, blue, and gold exited the room. The men with their short hair, and the women with silver brocades in their woven hair, all watched Willem with obvious interest. He ignored them. They were his issue no longer, provided they stayed out of his way.

He stepped further into the room and gave a sweeping bow to the empress. Just because he was here to steal from her, and potentially assassinate her, wasn't any excuse to be disrespectful. He took a moment, with the last of the nobles leaving, to scan the shadows. No sign of Tiana. Was she really just waiting for him upon the rooftop? Images of her murdering the resident nobility flashed through his mind, followed by ones of her doing the same to the empress. He would be glad for her absence. It would give him time. He would think about her later.

"Greetings, Lord Willem of the Third Honor. To what do I owe the pleasure?" The empress looked to be about thirty. She was pretty, not yet with the mature mask to her features that time would bring. Still, there was an undeniable air of authority to her. Her eyes, though warm, were sharp and calculating.

"I was informed that I should come to meet you. It is only in this past day that I've risen to my rank and honor." She examined him, much as he had her.

"You are mortal, are you not? To be a fae prince and not of them is unheard of."

"I am, yes, though mortal for not much longer, and I'm not yet a prince either."

"I see. Answer me this, if you have only just come to your rank and betrothal this past day, why are you here? Where is your beloved? Do her people not celebrate?"

He smiled in what he hoped would pass for a sheepish grin. "The fae are ever partying, and as you stated, I am mortal still. They won't miss me this night. I thought it best to get to the official duties and delegations."

She nodded, her eyes narrowed and thoughtful. "You will give up your mortality, the very thing that makes one human?"

"Who hasn't dreamt of living forever? Divorcing ones ties with death, to see the coming and going of ages?" he spoke nonchalantly, shrugging, and looking around the room. This place would burn when war came. With no magic to save these people, they would be destroyed.

"It is an evil thing, immortality. At least, in the hands of once-mortal men." Her words rang through the halls, and he remained silent, sensing she had more to say. "If one lives through the ages, what happens to the value of a life? When the rise and fall of empires, peoples, and species happen in a day?" Her voice was not harsh, instead, it was questioning. "What is war then, but the snuffing of candles?"

Tiana's words echoed in his mind, '*You will learn, their lives end in a blink of an eye, to cut it short by a breath is hardly a tragedy.*'

What if he didn't want to learn?

"I carry with me the weight of immortality every day. The power would consume my mind. It would change me, rewrite my existence to make me what it sees as perfect. It would deny me the mother's embrace, it would deny me the last trip through the veil and to the lands of our forefathers, if I allowed it." She looked at him, pulling a chain from beneath the neckline of her dress. From it, coiled in gold wire, was the Moon. It was a white sphere, milky, and it seemed to glow. It seemed a perfect replica of Theia, the smallest but eldest of the Sisters. It called to him, whispering, yearning to be used. *To burn.*

"This is your purpose, is it not? I feel it calling for you." He tore his eyes away from pearl and looked back up at her. "The woman you are to marry, how many millennia has she lived? She cannot possibly love you."

He stepped forward, feeling the pouches in his pockets as he moved.

One for pain,

One for death,

And one to forget.

"Immortality is my right, Anyada. It will be mine."

"You fool."

Tiana waited for him upon the rooftop. She sat upon the parapet, legs dangling over the side of castle. She didn't look up as he approached, didn't acknowledge his presence, though she knew he was there.

He sat, swinging his legs over the edge and clasping her hand. After minutes of looking over the forest haven she turned to him, wide eyes pensive.

"You have changed."

"Starting a war does that to a man," he said in a low voice. His words felt hollow in his own ears. He didn't turn to meet her gaze, nor tighten his grip upon her hand as she did his.

"Is she dead?"

"No." She took in a sharp breath at that, but he continued. "If their lives are nothing but the blink of an eye, allowing them to live but a breath longer should be no issue." He could feel her eyes, questioning, curious, boring into the side of his head. Still, he did not turn to her.

"You have my Moon?"

"No." Why was his heart not racing? Not pounding with fear, adrenaline? His stomach not turning with dread? Instead, only a cold, icy power washed over him as he sat next to Tiana, Princess of Fae.

"You failed." Her voice was cold, harsh, and… childish?

"No. There will be war, as you wished, and the Moon is no longer in their possession, but neither is it yours." Bringing his feet under him, he stood. Standing on that ledge, there were three options to him. To fall forward; death. To deal with the raging tempest beside him; pain, and quite likely, also death. To leave, to step down, walk away, and forget? No, that wasn't an option.

"You have it. Give me the Moon, Willem. I made you into who you are. I can undo all of that," she said, her teeth becoming fangs, her eyes into slits.

"You can't, though. She has spoken to me, and has accepted me as her own. In exchange, she grants me her power."

She sniffed. "Very well. I will allow you to hold it for me. Come, we will go home. There is likely a feast we are missing."

"No."

This time he did look at her and caught her arm as she moved to strike him. "Never again. I am a mortal man."

"You are weak," she spat, her voice venom and her eyes fire.

"I am mortal, that is far from being weak. It is stronger, in fact, than any power an immortal might have." He stepped down, onto the flat surface on the castle's roof, and moved toward her. She twisted and rose to meet him. Like this, the fire in her eyes, the petulance in her voice, he began to question why he had sought out her hand from the king and queen of the court. For all that she was ageless and beautiful, she was a child.

Tiana stepped off the wall to stand at eye-level with him.

"You would betray me, now? After all that my kin have done for you?"

"I did say there would be war." She looked at him, eyes searching, exploring, and uncertain. He memorized that image, when both fury and curiosity were at battle with one another across her features. He used that moment, when she seemed entranced in discovering the dark recesses of his mind, to reach behind his back. He looked over her features, soft and delicate, with silver hair that reached down to her shoulders, her plump lips which parted delicately, and then in shock as his dagger pierced her flesh.

It would not kill her. Killing an immortal was much more difficult than that. It would accomplish what he needed, though. Pain. Pain and forgetting, as the powders upon his blade penetrated her flesh. Sliding his blade free, and wiping the blood on his trousers, he picked her up, her frail body convulsing with pain and terrors beyond his imagining.

Light of the Moon, grant me admittance to the other realm.

The world seemed to peel away from him as he stepped through the veil. Ghosts, imprints of the living, and a haunting melody played through there, the dark and twisting realm. Too long here, and he would slip away, the physical realms forever lost to him.

He stepped through to the other side.

Tiana's screams pierced the cacophony of the fae court. Revellers and musicians stopped mid-twirl and mid-track, all to look at him, their prince-to-be, and their bloodied princess. Dropping her to the ground, he squatted and retrieved a couple of items off her body.

"I'm afraid I'm going to have to decline the betrothal. The princess and I had a bit of a spat," he said as he stood, pocketing a few jewels. "I'm sure she won't mind me taking these. You know, for the trouble." He winked at his audience, ignoring the stunned fae folk in front of him.

"Well, can't exactly say it's been a pleasure, so, how about this: the Moon belongs to humans. Keep to what is yours, and we will to ours. Any actions will be seen as an act of war. It will not go well for you."

Once more, Willem Jael Al'Caryth let the veil of worlds part, and felt himself slip into the ethereal darkness. All that was left to him was death, stolen jewels, and the powers of immortal divinity.

WHAT GODS DEMAND

James A. Moore

THE SA'BA TAALOR have very few rules. First among them, however, is never disobey the gods. That would never happen with Swech.

Swech Tothis Durwrae served all of the Daxar Taalor—the gods of the Seven Forges—without hesitation. She had her favorites, of course. Paedle, who believed that wars could be won without the use of warriors, and Wrommish, who believed that the body was the finest of weapons.

She agreed with both of the gods, and she served them as loyally as any child has ever served a loving parent. Though if the truth were to be completely revealed, she could have done without her current predicament.

She was standing on a rooftop in a foreign town that she barely knew, stalking one of the men walking below her, and wearing the wrong body. She bore the flesh of a different woman; it was only her spirit that remained unchanged. With a thought she could even change

Illustration by OKSANA DMITRIENKO ▸

her memories—as if she were moving behind a veil and watching the world through someone else's eyes. Swech remained in charge of the body at all times, the other woman was dead, killed by Swech when she took the form—but she had access to a lifetime that had nothing to do with her own. It was an enlightening experience.

The Daxar Taalor liked to challenge their followers, to sharpen them as a whetstone sharpens an edge, but there was a part of her that wondered about the wisdom behind their actions.

The city was Canhoon, often called the "Old Capitol." In appearance Canhoon was much like Tyrne, the Summer City. As Tyrne had been designed to look as much like Canhoon as possible that was not surprising.

Canhoon was a vast place that was ancient well before Swech was born. The city was, in fact, one of the last remaining cities left from the time of the First Empire, which had been destroyed ten centuries earlier. There was history in every stone building and in the timeworn statuary that lurked near every building and often atop the older structures. She moved among those frozen forms, flittering from one shadow to the next as she eyed her potential targets.

There were six men down there, and they moved together, but not for much longer she suspected. A few of them were armed, dressed in clothes that spoke of function, not wealth. Two, however, were dressed in finery, and of those two neither looked capable of fighting. One was old and heavy and walked with a pronounced limp, supporting a good deal of his weight in a walking staff. Her lip curled at the sight of him in an involuntary sign of disgust. Weakness was repugnant to her. Not the physical frailty of the man's form, but that he leaned on the staff as heavily as he did and that, likely, the four men dressed for fighting were there to defend him from any assault.

The Sa'ba Taalor learned to walk by the time they were six months of age. They were offered shelter and food and learned to speak at a young age. Not much later the training began on how to make war. There were seven gods in their land and all of those gods believed in war in its myriad incarnations.

Physical weakness was not something that could be avoided. In time all flesh fails. But mental weakness and emotional frailty were flaws that were either cut away or costs beaten out of the flesh as flaws are pounded from forged metal. The Sa'ba Taalor did not abide the weaknesses of the spirit.

"Do not make enemies you cannot defend yourself against." She whispered the words. Now was not the time to attack.

Swech ran her tongue over the back and then the front of her teeth, feeling the differences in the terrain of her mouth. These teeth were fine, she supposed, but they felt wrong. They were in just off from where she expected them to be. Her body was either resting in the heart of Wrommish or it had been incinerated when she threw herself deep into the volcano at the request of her god. She had been reborn into the new body, and it was sufficient, of course, but still not quite right. There were few scars on her body to tell tales of her previous combats. The Sa'ba Taalor were warriors, and each scar told a tale. The gods made demands and she listened, but the skin she wore now was almost unmarked. There were few scars and none that spoke of combat so much as they spoke of clumsiness. A scar on the hand where a knife has cut is not the same as a scar where a sword had kissed the flesh.

Her first name meant "soot hair," and it was a name that had always suited her appearance. Her tresses had been dark gray more than black for her entire life and she never much gave them any thought. Now her hair was a different color. She liked it well enough, she supposed but, like her teeth, the hair felt wrong.

Her hands were strong, lean and well muscled, with good joints and properly callused, but they looked wrong just the same, and her skin was unsettling pink in comparison to the light gray she had long since grown accustomed to.

The winds blew hard from the north and promised cold weather. Swech glanced in that direction but it did her little good. There were clouds gathering, a promise of storms to come. To the south Tyrne was gone, taken in a massive eruption of fire and molten rock only days earlier. Between the two towns a stream of refugees was makings its way to Canhoon by land and river alike, most carrying whatever they could and praying it would be enough. Swech had left a week before the destruction, warned away by her gods.

A great mountain rose where the city had been, birthed from the very fires that bled from it even now. She looked at it and smiled. Durhallem rose from those ashes. One of the gods of her people was now in place. She knew what would come next, what Durhallem would offer to the world around them, and she was pleased by that knowledge.

The world was changing and, as the Daxar Taalor demanded, she aided in that transformation.

The heat of the volcano mingled with the cold of the encroaching winter and gave birth to clouds.

The rains were already there, and as she blinked against the breeze she felt the first light droplets falling from above. The rooftop she stood on was at an angle. She made it a point to adjust her stance as the rains started in earnest.

Below her, in the streets and narrow alleys, people either ran for shelter or pulled up their hoods as they prepared for the rains.

"Which one?" she asked. Her eyes looked down on the crowds and Swech prayed for an answer from her gods.

What does distance mean to gods?

She closed her eyes and listened.

Wrommish and Paedle answered her together.

Sometimes the gods are kind.

"OF COURSE THE world is changing, you old fool." The words were spoken without any enmity. "We've lost the new capitol and now the refugees from Tyrne overwhelm our town and fill the streets with their filth. If that isn't a sign of bad times ahead I don't know what is."

Lirrin Merath was an opinionated jackass, but he was also a powerful man. He had wealth and he had influence. He also had no intention of surrendering either, simply because the new empress was coming to live in Canhoon.

The man prattled on, waving his fat hands about and trusting that his hired guards would be enough to keep the beggars away. The gold on his fingers would have purchased a small house, but that hardly mattered. The important thing, as far as the old man was concerned was that he kept what was his.

Walking next to him, Arlo Lancey would have gleefully slapped the man senseless if he could have, but he was wise enough to know not to press his luck. Lirrin was an ass, but he was also the minister of land in Canhoon and as such he was a very powerful figure, even without his money and his guards.

Just of late land had become the most valuable commodity known to anyone.

"Lirrin, my friend, the refugees have only started." Arlo was not a minister. He had his own sources of power, but an appointment by the Council was not one of them. "We have a few of the Roathians, but only the start of them. When the people who escaped from Tyrne show up, the city will change, whether we want it or not."

"You don't need to tell me." Lirrin snorted the words as if trying not to laugh at a particularly fine quip. "I've already seen the desperation in some people's eyes. Tyrne is gone, but hardly forgotten." He scowled. "Her refuse is coming in like a tide of backed up sewage."

The winds picked up and Arlo raised his hood just before the faint drizzle became a proper downpour. They could have sought shelter, but nether of them much wanted to be where they could be easily heard, and so they continued on in the rains, preferring the added sounds to confound any who would listen in on their private conversations.

It was best not to discuss murder when others could hear the words spoken. The rain hammered down on their shoulders in a thousand tiny drumbeats. Arlo squinted against a rude droplet as it tried for his eye.

"I am for secrecy, Arlo, but we have reached a limit." Lirrin very nearly had to yell to be heard over the rains. He pointed toward the door to a tavern and Arlo nodded his agreement. There could be no discussion if they could not hear themselves speaking.

Within moments they were inside and grateful to be free of the deluge.

The Broken Oak sported a painted sign of a vast oak tree split in half, with four shields around the base and seven swords rammed though the tree itself. There was a legend about those very things, but Arlo couldn't remember it and didn't have time for childish tales in any event. The tavern was a larger place than they'd expected, reaching deep into the building and sliding far enough back that the back wall was lost in shadows and smoke. Between that shadowy depth and the front entrance squatted a collection of well-used tables and, at most of them, a few people sat locked in their own conversations.

Lirrin moved into the place as if he owned it, and headed for a table that sat hidden well in the murk of the large room.

The owner nodded in their direction and otherwise ignored them for the moment. There would be time for serving them after they'd made themselves comfortable.

Lirrin sat and gestured for his four bodyguards to stand close by but not too close. The four men managed to look suitably intimidating as they surrounded the table.

"Are they truly a necessity?"

"The lads? Of course they are. There are plenty hereabouts that would see me dead. I am not a popular man, Arlo. I am well hated by those with whom I do not do business. And right now that list is very long indeed."

Arlo already understood that, of course. The minister did not control the cost of land, but he did handle the paperwork involved in the sales. There were normally fees involved and he dictated what those fees might be. While he could not forbid a person from selling land, he could make the notion a very expensive one.

Currently, Lirrin was living a life of luxury and doing so gladly, but he also knew it might not last long now that there was a new empress and especially now that she was coming to Canhoon to live.

A flash of a coin and the barkeep came and took their order personally and then brought them their ales. When he was gone, Lirrin continued as if there had been no delays. He spoke and jabbed his fat fingers into the polished wood of the table to emphasize his words. "I have families coming here—entire families, mind you—that have nowhere to go. The messengers from those families have been coming to me and nearly demanding that they be allowed to purchase the houses they'll need, as if I have control over how quickly buildings rise."

"Well, they're desperate."

Lirrin shook his head and his jowls wobbled sympathetically. "No, they are scared and angry. And they think that coins alone will cover the cost of finding them new homes. The fact is that there simply aren't a thousand buildings waiting to be filled."

Arlo managed not to say anything that would have caused tension. There were ways around the problem, of course. Though there were few buildings waiting around empty, a few could have been found without too much trouble. Not enough, true, but for some of the wealthier families exceptions could be made.

Almost as if he could read minds Lirrin made a comment, "Not even a fortnight ago there were several lots that I could have used, but they were all purchased." He waved a hand. "Had I known then what was happening I could have charged a levy large enough to make the price impossible to handle, but the woman came through and made the deals before there was any reason to wonder about the future."

Arlo shook his head and made a face. There were reasons he was dealing with the old man across the table from him and mostly those reasons revolved around gold.

"Do you have a name for this woman? With a little persuasion, perhaps she could be convinced to sell the lands again. I have stonemasons waiting to start building as soon as the word is given. I have carpenters and a workforce that could be building even as we speak."

"Of course she has a name." The man's fat face twisted into an ugly mask of annoyance. "I don't recall it at the moment, but of course she has a name." Sometimes Lirrin played at being absentminded and sometimes he was sincere. For a few coins he would remember in the former. Arlo knew Lirrin's expressions well enough to know he sincerely could not recall.

A stray breeze caught the candle and lamp flames throughout the room and brought in a wave of fresh, cold air. Arlo looked toward the doors but saw no one cross the threshold.

He looked around the vast tavern again as he gathered his thoughts. There were four large men around them and he was grateful for that.

The shapes around them were shadows, mostly, hulking shapes that loomed and fed themselves on mutton stew, or chunks of roasted meat. They were only people, and Arlo knew that, but as they spoke of dark things and deeds best not considered, those forms seemed more sinister than they should have.

Dark thoughts bred dark fears.

"Could the papers be lost?"

"Certain copies could be misplaced. Hers, however, are in her possession." Lirrin stared at Arlo as if he might be daft.

"A name, Lirrin. But give me a name and I can make this all better. You can have your higher levies and the families that pay the best can have their homes within a few months at the most."

Lirrin chuckled, his face taking on a particularly gourd-like symmetry as he did so. "Unless things change and drastically, we might not have to worry about that. These gray people everyone is talking about will see to it."

The Sa'ba Taalor. The name made Arlo's skin shiver. He'd not seen them, of course. No one had. But there are always rumors, aren't there? Giants. Invaders who were indestructible in combat from all he'd heard. One traveler he'd spoken to briefly told him they'd destroyed the Guntha by themselves, a hundred of them taking on over a thousand and winning. Actually, the man had said ten had done the job, but both agreed that had to be a case of the man mishearing what was told to him originally. If one of the monsters could kill a hundred soldiers, the empire was already doomed.

"That is a river I should rather worry about crossing when the time comes. Until I see these giants, I will continue with the daily business."

"Well then," The shadows spoke, soft and feminine. "You should wait no longer."

SWECH WATCHED AND listened and waited. The Daxar Taalor had told her who she should eliminate, but she waited just the same. There was no hurry and she had a constant desire to know more.

The two men were soft, both of them dressed in finery and perfumed. The older one she knew. She had dealt with him when Wrommish told her to buy the lands around the area. Four days ride into Canhoon, one afternoon spent counting coins, and four days back to the home she'd made in Tyrne before the gods decided it was time to destroy the city. Hardly an effort at all, but the Daxar Taalor wanted the land, and she claimed it silently in their names.

What the gods demanded, Swech was glad to do.

When she knew enough, Swech stepped from the shadows and made herself known. Her hair was pulled back, leaving her face free, but as had been the tradition when she first met the people of Fellein, she was wearing a veil that covered most of her face. In this work the shadows were her comrades and she intended to keep it that way.

Her attire was all dark, mostly black, with loose sleeves and leather breeches. She'd slipped free of her cloak and stood before the men in attire they surely thought better suited for a man.

"You are a Sa'ba Taalor?" The younger of the men was the one asking, but the four paid fighters immediately came to attention at the question.

The man sounded skeptical.

"I am."

The older man laughed, but there was no humor in the sound. "I know you. I would know a northerner's eyes anywhere and yours are lovely enough. You're the very woman I was speaking of. You are the one who purchased so much land."

If he was trying to woo her with words his compliments were weak.

The younger one immediately smiled. "Truly? Perhaps we can

reach an accord." Dogs ran for table scraps with less enthusiasm. He had a smile that showed many teeth, and too much of his gums. The Pra-Moresh smiled much the same way before they bit down and killed.

"The land is not for sale. Nor will I be paying extra fees."

The young man grew annoyed with her words. His smile wilted and became a confused scowl. He was pretty enough and likely expected her to swoon when he gazed in her direction. That was a problem with many of the people she'd met since coming to Fellein. They thought pretty faces and perfume made them attractive.

"There you have it, Arlo. The land is not for sale." Lirrin was the older man's name. He was old, and soft enough that he hired others to fight for him should the need ever arise. She resisted the urge to sneer again.

The other, Arlo, shook his head. "What a pity."

She knew their kind. They spoke lies and dressed them in pretty deceptions. Perhaps there were some among the Sa'ba Taalor who would not know the difference, but the god Paedle taught the purpose of lies, and how best to see them. Sometimes the finest battles were won with words as the weapons.

Other times....

"I have told you the land is not for sale. Was there anything else you needed to know?"

"Just your name." The younger one, Arlo. "Just that, so I can try to convince you again."

"You have no desire to convince me." She studied him carefully. "You prefer to know where I am staying and what name I use, the better to send your hired killers to take what is mine in the night."

Arlo blinked, and for one moment his true face was revealed. He was stunned by her direct words. The man was used to a certain level of respect accorded to his station, and thought himself too pretty to be so easily read.

"That's simply not true." He spoke softly and slid from his seat.

Behind the veil, Swech allowed herself a very slight smile.

"You would have me dead and take the deeds. The cost is less for you. Then you and your fat friend would make arrangements that profited both of you and left me a rotting corpse."

Lirrin made a disbelieving noise. She did not like him.

"You cannot speak to Arlo that way."

She didn't look in his direction, but kept her eyes on the pretty man. "I just did."

Lirrin spoke again and snapped his fingers. "I've a mind to teach you a lesson in proper behavior." As his fingers moved, so too his guards, who moved in a loose circle around Swech and eyed her without expression. All save one. The man to her right was trying not to smile and failing. He liked the notion of beating on a woman and likely felt it would be his place to do whatever he wanted with her when he was done.

"You would have your hirelings teach me a lesson? Or you would do it yourself, old man?"

She finally looked his way and Lirrin's face wobbled as he scowled. "I'll have it both ways, perhaps." His tongue licked across his lips. "I'll have my lads handle you, and I'll teach you a few lessons in civility when they're done."

The younger one actually seemed surprised by the comments. He was, perhaps, a little less likely to have others do his work for him.

Swech took a long stride to the left and brought her elbow around behind her, spinning her body to follow. The elbow struck the first of the bodyguards across his jaw and she felt the bones and teeth shatter under her assault. As the man was falling she grabbed the dagger he had at his side and pulled it from the sheath.

The man hit the ground and groaned as his broken face struck the floorboards.

The eager one came for her, bulling his way across the short distance. He had a few scars on his arms and though he was bearded she could see the remnants of an old wound on the side of his face.

As he reached for her, Swech dropped low and drove the dagger in her hand deep into his inner thigh. He yowled and staggered and tried to stand. She dodged to the left and drove her heel into his knee, forcing it to bend in the wrong direction. His screams grew louder as he crashed down, unable to stand on the ruined leg.

Blood flowed like water from the wound in his thigh. He would be dead before he could teach himself to walk again.

The third hired man shook his head and tried to back away, but Swech had a point to make. She reached for him and rammed stiffened fingers into his throat, feeling the cartilage in his neck collapse. In moments he was gagging and his face reddened as he tried to breathe through a ruined windpipe.

The fourth drove a fist into her side and Swech moved with it, feeling his heavy knuckles scrape across her ribs and drive into her stomach with bruising force.

Her arm came up from under and behind his elbow, and captured his forearm. He looked toward her, surprised by the move and then horrified as she bent her body and forced his arm to follow suit. For one moment he almost got away, but she turned her hip and felt his elbow break like a twig.

He could not make a noise. The pain, she knew, was far too large to allow him the luxury of a scream. Down he went, onto his knees, mouth open in a silent shriek of pain. She captured his head with one hand and brought her knee up into the side of his temple. When he fell the rest of the way to the floor his head was the wrong shape.

When Swech looked back at the table the old man stared at her with wide, frightened eyes and his hands clutched at his chest.

"What lesson will your men teach me?"

Arlo very carefully sat back down.

Around them the activity of the tavern had come to a complete halt, save for the moans of the broken and battered around Swech's area. Every person in the place was looking, and Swech shook her head. She could not understand these people. In the Taalor Valley a fight was not a spectacle very often.

"I—" Lirrin looked at her and shook his head. His eyes remained wide and stuck to her gaze, unable to look anywhere else apparently.

"You killed them!" Arlo shrieked. He looked at the bodies around her with a shaken expression and trembled where he sat.

"No. Some will live." She stepped away from table letting the two men contemplate both their actions, and the dead and wounded around them.

ARLO TRIED TO keep his eyes on the woman but she faded away into the shadows of the tavern.

He also tried to breathe, but found he could not drink in enough air to help him.

Beside him Lirrin was pale and trembling, his eyes doing their very best to look everywhere at once. "Is she gone? Did she go away?" Five decades or more to his life and the bastard whimpered like a child having nightmares.

Arlo took comfort from the other man's fear. It balanced him and soothed worries.

Around them several of the patrons were staring at the dead and dying surrounding their table. Some looked upset, but less than he would have expected. This was a place where people came to talk and not be seen. The mess at their table was exactly the sort that guaranteed people got seen more than they wanted.

"We have to go, Lirrin."

"Go?" The calm surface was gone and the man trembled visibly. In all of his years of posturing it seemed the official had never seen bloodshed on that scale. It was possible, likely, even, that he'd thought himself safe from it, insulated by his hired swords.

"Yes, go. The City-Guard will be coming soon. We should not be here when they arrive."

Lirrin's thick fingers clutched at his sleeve and the man's round face wobbled as he shook his head.

"She might be anywhere, Arlo. We can't leave here. We have to wait for the guard. They'll protect us."

When he spoke his voice was cold and much calmer than he actually felt. Someone needed to take control of the situation. "We came here to discuss matters best not heard by the City-Guard or anyone else, Lirrin." He pulled his sleeve from the fat man's clutch. "We need to leave here. Now."

"What if she's still out there?" Lirrin nearly wailed the words and Arlo stepped away from him, embarrassed for himself and for the man he'd never respected but had at least considered a man.

"Come out of this, Lirrin! You're behaving like a child!"

That did it. Lirrin's head rocked back as surely as if he'd been slapped, and the wild fear in his eyes was crushed down.

For one moment Arlo thought he'd pushed the minister of land too far. The heavy jowls still quivered, but with a different expression on the mewling mouth buried in that face. His teeth were bared in anger for a moment before he calmed himself down.

"You're right. Thank you for that, Arlo."

"We must leave here. Now."

"Of course." Lirrin hauled his considerable bulk up and leaned heavily on his walking staff as he maneuvered around the dead and wounded. "Time to be elsewhere."

Outside the sounds of approaching figures could be heard past the closed door. They did not hesitate, but instead took their chances in the torrential rains.

If anything the storm was worse. The waters fell in sheets and the winds threw those sheets sideways, slapping open cloaks and making any attempt to stay dry a laughable failure. The City-Guard were stomping up the street, looking for any sign of who might be a danger. The man in the lead was unknown to Arlo, but he had the look of a seasoned veteran and his expression when he eyed the two of them was uninterested at best.

Arlo felt a slow bloom of shame in his chest. Even the City-Guard, who made less coin in a year than he did in a fortnight, looked at him with no real interest. He would have to look into hiring someone to train him in the finer points of using a sword. He had not so much as practiced since he'd done his required service to the Empire. He had just seen an unarmed woman ruin four men in a matter of seconds, and the sword at his side was never even considered as an option. It was an ornament to him, a sign of his status and nothing else.

He had to change a few things about himself, if he ever got the chance. The woman behind the veil, Lirrin said he knew her, that she was the one he wanted to deal with. She said she was one of the Sa'ba Taalor, the unholy terrors he'd heard about before. After watching how quickly she took down four trained men, he was beginning to doubt his earlier assessment of the assault on the Guntha.

The rains continued and Arlo had to shout to be heard over the constant deluge. "Did she seem like that when you permitted the land sales, Lirrin?"

"What?" The man was distracted, looking around at every alley as they moved along the wet cobblestones and sought a place where they could, once again, continue their conversation.

"The woman. Did she seem so damned... competent?"

"She was just a woman. I thought she was attractive enough. What did I care?" He shook his head and then went back to looking at every darkened corner. "As I said, I had no notion of what she was up to until it was too late."

Lirrin was crumbling again. Arlo could see it. Now that he was no longer among the public the fear was coming back and pressing down on the man. "We have to get inside! We have to find a safe place!"

They had chosen to meet in Old Canhoon, at the heart of the city, because many of the shops were closed at night and the chances of running across people who could identify them were slimmer when they were away from their homes. Now that choice played against them. The rains had come along unexpectedly and driven most of the City-Guard into hiding. The cut-purses were gone as well, but there was no place for them to easily hide, and they would be walking and exposed for longer than Arlo liked before they reached his home and safety.

He walked faster and then forced himself to slow down when Lirrin whimpered. The old bastard was lame, but he was also important enough that Arlo had to remember him.

Lirrin puffed along, his staff tap-tap-tapping along the cobblestones at a pace that was nearly frantic in comparison to his usual plodding steps.

Arlo bit back a demand that he move faster still, the words fading away as the now familiar sound of hard wood striking stone suddenly stopped.

He was ahead of the minister and he felt a deep and abiding cold creep through his flesh that had nothing at all to do with the rain.

He did not want to turn around. He was terrified by the notion. He did not want to see the older man dead or dying, but he had to see, he had to know, because until he checked he could not be certain if he was safe or in danger.

He turned and cursed under his breath.

Lirrin stood where he had been, his eyes bulging from the folds of fat around them. His face was red and growing redder and his hands reached out imploringly. The staff he'd been holding wobbled as if surprised, and seemed determined to stand on its own. Without the support of the old man's hand, however, it fell victim to gravity. The sound when it clattered to the street was loud enough to hear past the falling rains and the maddening winds.

Lirrin strained his arms forward but the rest of him did not move.

"Lirrin?" Arlo's voice was too small to be heard from more than a few inches away. "Lirrin what is it? Are you ill?"

The man dropped forward. He collapsed first to his knees, which gave a much louder crack of sound than his staff had, and he winced at the pain of impact even as his body shuddered.

Suddenly shorter than he had been, it was far easier to see the shape of the veiled woman standing behind him.

Even lost in shadows and rain, Arlo could see that she was a strong woman, her body well muscled, and almost as tall as he was. Arlo knew that he should have been able to take her in a physical challenge.

Should have been able to. His hand was only inches from his sword's hilt but he did not reach, did not attempt to draw the blade. He was far too scared for that. She had killed five men before his eyes and he had never killed even one in his life.

She was holding what looked like a fine metal thread in her hands.

The thread spun into two metal rods, one held in each hand, the color of the metal ran from silver on either end to a deep red in the center.

Lirrin's neck vomited blood as the man tried to breathe and failed.

"You have walked away from your safety, Arlo." The woman's voice was muted by the rain, but not lost to him. "I was told that you should possibly live. That you might have value. What do you think of that notion?"

"Oh, yes!" His vision bobbled as he nodded vigorously, doing his best to keep a solid eye on the woman in front of him as Lirrin fell face first into a puddle among the cobblestones. The water around his head formed a reddening halo. "Yes! I can be very useful to you, I swear it!"

Her hands moved and the reddened metal strand wrapped around one of the rods in her grip. Her eyes never once moved from him.

She did not move closer, but the stance she took, the way she looked at him, carried a level of threat that nearly made Arlo soil himself. "My gods have said you could be useful to me. They have also said the choice is mine as to whether or not you survive. So tell me. How are you useful to me alive?"

"Lirrin was the minister of land! I'm in line to take his position should he die and—" He gestured at Lirrin's corpse. The halo was dispersing now, washing into a faint pink corona that bled down between the stones. "As you can see, he is very dead."

"You will take his place as minister?"

"Yes! Yes, of course! I would be his replacement!"

"And how does that help me, Arlo?" She was closer now. He didn't remember her moving but she was closer, her body in front of the corpse of dear, dead Lirrin. Arlo managed not to scream but it took an effort.

"I can help you buy more land, and keep your secrets! Yes! I can keep your secrets!" His voice had gone shrill again, but he could not stop himself. He could not make his voice be strong and confident when he was so certain he was about to die.

"I have already kept my secrets. You do not know my name and the only man who could have told you is dead." He listened to each word from her with a growing dread. She was right, of course. Lirrin was dead.

"Everyone needs allies. I can be your ally. Please let me show you how useful I can be to you."

She did not speak, but instead closed her eyes for a moment.

He raised one foot.

"If you run, I will kill you."

Arlo set his foot firmly on the ground.

THE DAXAR TAALOR were gods. It was exactly that simple. They had been a part of Swech's life since she first breathed and likely even before that moment.

They were the beginning and the end of everything that mattered in her world. When she was asked to throw herself into the heart of Wrommish, the fiery volcanic pit that pulsed with its own rhythm, she did not question the request, she simply obeyed.

Her body plummeted down into fire and she felt her skin and hair ignite. There was pain, of course, but there is always pain in life. She accepted the pain and was rewarded for her faith when she rose hundreds of leagues away from where she had been in the body she now occupied. Great Wrommish could ask anything of her and it was given. That was the way of the Sa'ba Taalor.

She looked at the pitiful man standing before her. She had warned him not to move and then she had waited with her eyes closed and listened to her gods.

He trembled. He stood before her and shook, his eyes wide and wet in the continuing rain. His hand scant inches from his sword and he never reached for it.

Had she not met members of the Fellein Empire capable of fighting, she would have been even more disgusted.

"Where I am from, you would be dead if you had not attacked me when you had the chance."

Arlo blinked and shook his head. "But I don't want to die." She read his lips as much as she heard him speak. The words were lost in the rain.

"When I come to you again, and I will come to you, you will do as I say. Do you understand?"

"Yes. Oh yes. Whatever you need." He looked so grateful she almost believed him.

"You say that." She stepped closer and he shook again. She was close enough she could have kissed him or bitten him and either way he would not have been able to stop her. Swech smelled his breath: it was as sour as the way he made her feel.

"You say that," she continued," and I know you think you mean it. You will change your mind later." Her hands moved quickly and caught his left hand in a strong grip. He flinched.

"No! I swear to you!"

"Do not swear to me. Swear to your gods."

"I don't have any gods."

Her smile was as cold as the rain.

"Listen to this name. Know it. Understand that to recite it means your life to me. Wrommish. Say it."

He looked at her for a long moment, puzzled. "Wrommish?"

"That is correct. Wrommish. Know the name. Keep it in your breast and keep it closely. If you do not repeat it to me when I see you again, I will kill you. Do you believe me?"

His sickly white face grew paler. "I do."

"Say the name again."

"Wrommish?" So weak a voice, so frail.

"Louder."

"Wrommish."

"Pray every night. Before you go to sleep, you must pray to Wrommish. Do you understand?"

"No."

"Before you close your eyes tonight, pray to Wrommish." She moved closer still, until the water that dripped from her veil fell across his lips as she spoke. "Thank him for your life. He is the only reason I have not killed you. Wrommish says you have not lost your usefulness."

"I will." He nodded his head slowly, but with very strong conviction. "I will. I swear it."

Her thumbnail scratched the top of his hand hard enough to scrape flesh and drawl a thin stream of blood. He was wise enough not to pull back.

"Before that heals, we will meet again." Swech let his hand go.

"I… Your face is covered. How will I know you if I can't see your face?"

"Look at my eyes. You will know me."

He nodded.

"You will say the name of your new god. Every night and when we meet. If you have not said your thanks to him every night, I will know. And you will die. Do you believe me?"

"Yes. Of course I do."

"This is good."

She stepped back from him, moving easily over the cooling corpse of the former minister of land.

"Now, Arlo. Go to your home."

He couldn't have run much faster. He turned from her and pelted his way up the road, panting and puffing after only a dozen strides. He was handsome enough in form, but he was soft and weak. A child of eight years could kill him with ease. At least if that child were of the Sa'ba Taalor.

"I have spared him, Wrommish. As you have asked. But he is so very weak."

Swech looked around carefully—always be aware of your surroundings—and then moved slowly away into the night. The rains would continue for the next few days, she knew that well enough.

For now she had to get to her home.

There was much that had to be done, and time was short.

Thunder rumbled from where Tyrne had once stood, a beautiful city crushed under the fury of Durhallem.

The gods made their demands and she obeyed without question.

A LENGTH OF CHERRYWOOD

Peter Orullian

JASTAIL J'VACHE CROUCHED behind a thick patch of scrub oak and watched the woman washing clothes in the river. She hummed a tune as she worked, alone, unaware of him or his highwaymen hiding in a rough circle around her. Beyond the thinning trees stood a wagon, a hundred paces away. Too far for anyone to be of immediate aid. Jastail put a hand in his pocket, running his fingers over grooves in a short length of cherrywood. A reminder. Then, quite casually, he stood, revealing himself. "Greetings, my lady."

The woman's head snapped up. Her eyes wide.

"I've alarmed you." Jastail began to skirt the low brush, moving toward her. "My apologies. It's something of a hazard in my line of work, I'm afraid."

Insensibly, the woman gathered in the wet clothes and got to her feet. Jastail offered a wan smile at that. Such value for clothes belonged to the exceptionally poor. She began to back away from him, in the direction of her wagon.

Illustration by ORION ZANGARA ▸

"Come, don't fret yourself. This needn't go hard between us." He stepped into the shallow river, crossing directly toward her.

Just as she turned to run, he raised a hand and his men stepped from their concealments. The woman skidded to a stop, fell, and dropped the wet clothes.

Jastail reached the other side of the river as she scrambled to her feet and turned to face him.

"There, much better." He put on a smile of reassuring approval. "I think we have an understanding."

The woman glanced down at the clothes between them. He followed her gaze. The clothes . . . belonged to children.

Lawry, his newest man, laughed. "A neat prize. The lady and her loinfruits, besides." He nodded in the direction of the wagon.

Panic entered her eyes, and she shook her head. "No. No! Marcus! Highwaymen!"

The alarm echoed through the woods around them. And a moment later the sound of hurried feet came pounding through the brush.

"Oh, my lady." Jastail sighed. "If you'd only had a bit of patience. Now we've a hero to deal with. Let's hope he's sensible."

Jastail maneuvered around her, putting himself between the woman and her would-be rescuer. He drew his sword, holding it at an unthreatening angle. This Marcus came into view, and caught sight of the woman surrounded by Jastail's men.

The man held a smith hammer and a shoeing knife—he'd probably been tending his horse—and slowed as he surveyed the odds.

Good, at least he can do math. "Let me explain what you're seeing," Jastail began, planting his sword's tip in the dirt and leaning on it. "Your lady here was washing clothes in the river. Not usually a dangerous task, I'll admit. But today, it's bad fortune for you that *we* are here." He gestured with his other hand at his men.

"You won't be taking her." Marcus flipped his knife into a backhand grip—a pit fighter's grip.

Why couldn't I, just once, meet a man who sews or bakes?

Jastail bent and lifted a pair of trousers from the pile of wet clothes. "And who's going to watch the owner of these while you fight for your woman's honor?"

Worry crossed the man's face, and he cast a glance back toward the wagon.

"Dead gods," said Lawry, "let's get on with it."

Jastail's new man—first time on the road—started off to gather the little ones.

"Hold there," Jastail ordered, then fixed his attention back on the woman. "I need your help," he said with endless patience. "Marcus here is about to do an honorable thing. He wants to protect you from us. Perfectly understandable. In his place, I'd want to do the same. Love makes fools of us all. It blinds us to our real chances. It blinds us to the harm our heroism might do to others." He shook the wet trousers in emphasis.

"You want me to tell Marcus to let you take me." The woman's voice came with the monotone of the beaten. "You want me to tell him not to fight. Then you'll leave my family alone."

"Jastail?" It was Lawry, incredulous at the suggestion being made.

"I don't take more than I need," Jastail replied, and dropped the pants. "And remember we have a specialty." *Women—"wombs"—who can breed.* The little ones were both boys. He knew it by the clothes at his feet.

"The hell with that," Lawry exclaimed. "There's thirty full marks a head sitting back there. Easy pickings. If *you* won't take them, *I* will."

"Excuse me," Jastail said, raising a finger to the woman as he slid past her toward his new man.

He gestured for Lawry to join him in a short walk away from the others. Twenty paces removed from the rest, he turned to face the man. "It's your first time on the roads."

"I don't see what that has to do—"

Jastail put his knife into the man's stomach with a short powerful stab, and yanked up, severing several internal organs. Lawry's eyes widened in surprise and pain before he dropped into the brush. Jastail wiped his blade clean on the man's shirt. Men who argue don't ever stop arguing. And they don't obey. With such men, he'd learned long ago to cut quick. Saved lots of pain later on.

Still, he paused long enough to offer over the body a line from one of the dark poets he'd learned to appreciate as a boy. "Each of us is walking earth, upright dust, consuming breath in ignorance."

Black verse. Like a good cool wine.

Jastail nodded a goodbye, and returned to the others, wearing his casual smile.

"Now," he said, taking a deep breath, "what will it be, Marcus? Can we be done with threats and heroism today? I'd really like to be on my way."

Marcus looked at the woman. "Jaryn?"

She returned a tortured gaze. Tortured, Jastail knew from experience, for her loved one. Not for herself. She'd already weighed the stakes and folded her cards.

Then Marcus shifted his gaze to Jastail. "If you take her, I'll follow. And I'll bring help."

"Of course you will." Jastail nodded to the fact with good humor. "And you'd have time to get your little ones someplace safe, so you can make an unencumbered rescue attempt. Quite practical."

In all the time Jastail had lain this type of ambush, only one man had ever successfully reclaimed the woman Jastail had taken. Good odds. And he didn't mind the game of it when a husband had wit and skill.

Marcus lowered his knife and hammer.

Jastail smiled apologetically—a touch of theater on his part. Then he put his hand on the woman's arm and began leading her northward. Their horses weren't far.

Marcus stood still as Nichols, Jastail's most seasoned man, passed by him. Then the would-be hero brought his shoeing knife up in a swift motion and plunged it into Nichols' kidney. A pit fighter's move. Debilitating. And lethal. Nichols cried out and fell.

Medi, one of Nichols' good friends, lunged at Marcus, blade and dagger slicing through the air.

Marcus shuffled back, avoiding the blades. He then closed fast, dropped low, and brought his hammer around hard on the side of Medi's left knee. The bones crunched as Medi's leg bent at an impossible angle and he fell. Marcus pounced, driving his hammer down on the man's throat, silencing his cries of pain.

Jastail pulled the woman away, clearing the area for the fight. *He has real skill.* Jastail nodded with approval, and smiled with eagerness.

The rest of his band formed a circle, caging Marcus in. But the man seemed unconcerned, keeping a fighter's crouch, and turning constantly to meet every eye. When he came last to Jastail, he showed a cold, reasoning expression.

"You won't harm her. She's your prize." *Good wit.* "And you're content with just the woman, which means you're a womb trader. You don't care for trafficking brats." *Damn, but I like this fellow.* "And I've a bit more skill than changing a horseshoe. I'll take my chances here, since I don't like them once she's gone."

A gambler, too. Jastail must have looked like he was beaming to his fellows, since he never could have imagined so good a contest coming on a minor highway in the south of So'Dell.

Jastail raised his sword. "You and I, then. For the lady's honor."

Marcus flipped the hammer up, spinning it twice, and caught it again. He nodded.

The two began to circle, each feinting several times. Finally, Marcus stepped in with a clever combination of stab and swing. Jastail didn't fall for the dagger strike, anticipating the hammer from the other side. Good way to get an arm broken.

When the hammer came around, he wind-milled his sword and cut Marcus' upper arm deep. Blood soaked the man's sleeve with a spreading crimson.

Jastail hoped it wouldn't be so easy, and switched hands with this sword, shuffling his feet to a right-handed stance. His weaker side.

Marcus adjusted his grip on his knife, taking a standard hold. And did something surprising. Instead of circling in, he took half a step back and threw the dagger with a quick, flip of his wrist.

Jastail had no time to evade the attack. The knife sank into the meat of his upper chest. If he hadn't been ducking, it might have struck his heart or lung. He stumbled backward, as Marcus leapt forward, bringing his hammer down in a vicious arc.

Jastail spun, just escaping the blow, and brought his sword around with his momentum, forcing Marcus off-balance. As the two faced each other again, Jastail pulled the knife from his body and smiled. He loved to be surprised. And he loved to surprise others. He slowly tossed the knife back to Marcus handle first. The man caught the weapon and stared back in confusion.

"Again," Jastail said, and started forward.

Marcus crouched, looking more a pit fighter than before. Jastail rushed, feigning a sweeping overhand stroke, then lowered his sword fast and came in under Marcus' guard. The move put the man off-balance, and Jastail kicked him to the ground.

Before Marcus could roll, Jastail had his blade at the man's throat. A simple stab and the man would die.

"No, Da!"

Jastail looked up and saw two faces peering through the brush at the edge of the trees. But it wasn't mercy that kept him from killing their father.

"Let go your weapons," Jastail ordered.

Marcus looked at him a long time. Pride and defeat battled in the man's face. But not worry. Jastail wanted to meet more men like this. Marcus finally obeyed, and Jastail kicked the knife and hammer away.

"Thank you for the contest," Jastail said, bowing slightly. "A pleasant surprise. It hardly changes things for you, as it turns out. But you should feel good about your effort. And, of course, you can still come looking for us once you see to your little ones." Jastail bent, and quite earnestly confided in the man, "We're heading north and east to the river. I hope you'll take your chances again."

Sparing no concern, and ignoring his fallen men, Jastail left Marcus there. He paused only to take an article of clothing from the woman's wash—a child's sock. Then he gathered her with a gentle hand and led her from her wet clothes and family.

THE RIVERBOAT RANG with laughter and the sounds of dice and odds-makers calling numbers. Tobacco smoke lazed in the air, thick and sweet. Beneath it the sharp tang of brandy—the drink of choice—rose from countless cups and goblets. Serving men went shirtless, and could be bedded for a full realm mark. Serving women wore a bodice so thin they might as well not have bothered, and could be had at the same price. Gamblers' hands roamed to the delicate parts of servers and other gamblers as liberally as the drinks flowed. In the far corner of the riverboat's third deck, Jastail took a seat at the table of the boat's proprietor, Gynedo.

Back in this corner, behind a low wall, the din eased a bit. Gynedo smiled as he shuffled a set of plackards, and stared at Jastail from beneath a broad-rimmed hat.

"You think you're ready for this game, my young friend? You understand the rules?" Gynedo set the plackards aside and prepared himself a long-stem pipe.

Jastail nodded.

"We're not betting on coin value, you understand," Gynedo explained again.

It was a new game, something the gambling boss had conceived when money stakes ceased to hold his interest. That suited Jastail fine. More than fine.

Gynedo struck his pipe alight and eyed their third player, a raven-haired woman of perhaps twenty-five, whose smile suggested carnal appetites that involved instruments. She wore a black hat from which cascaded a thin curtain of black netting. The net-holes were wide, making her easy enough to see, but the black mesh gave her an air of menace and deceit. Lovely.

"Not even slave-stock," Gynedo said. "I have more men and women for the blocks than I can trade as it is. And that's messy, besides."

Jastail took a long drink of his brandy. "Wagers for this game are about the emotional loss of a person. Suffering, you might say." He grinned at the thought.

"And we bet a token of that suffering for each round we wish to stay in the game," the woman finished. She turned to Jastail. "Since Gynedo hasn't the manners to introduce us, I'm Fleur."

"Jastail," he replied. "Pleasure."

She held out her hand as a noble might, expecting a kiss on her knuckles. Jastail took her hand and made a slight bow.

"Just so," Gynedo confirmed. "I'm still working out a system to place emotional value on the items. For now, we'll take it by instinct and agreement at the table." He smiled around the stem of his pipe. "Three rounds, I think. Escalating value. Game will be Suits."

Suits was a simple three plack draw. Placks of the same suit could be added together to get a total point value. All cards were kept face down, and turned one at a time, in turn. Very little strategy, but a serviceable game given their purpose and wagers tonight.

Gynedo dealt out three placks to each of them.

Jastail turned first. A hawk with eight feathers showing. He then gently pushed a folded piece of parchment into the center of the table.

"And what do we have here?" Gynedo asked, a glimmer in his eyes.

"A letter," Jastail explained. "Written by a man awaiting execution for a crime . . . a crime that *I* committed."

There were false gasps from his table-mates.

"I orchestrated a bit of misdirection, and got him pegged for it." Jastail waved a dismissive hand. "Somehow, I was taken for his friend, and given the letter to deliver to his wife."

"What does it say?" Fleur asked, leaning in with anticipation.

Jastail looked at the letter, smiled. "It's filled with regret. Apology for petty wrongs. Declarations of love." He paused, considering. "It carries the sad realizations of all the things this man will never see or do again. He wanted to say all this to his wife, but they wouldn't let her visit him. The letter is all they'd allow."

Gynedo offered a low chuckle. "You should have saved this for a later round," he observed. "You realize, of course, that this token isn't just the suffering of the man. You've also prevented his wife from hearing his last, dearest thoughts and declarations of love. Your bet is double." He patted the table in appreciation and acceptance of the wager.

"You're a lovely bastard," Fleur declared. Her hand snaked beneath the table to cup his manhood. Jastail nodded thanks and gently put her hand back in her own lap. He knew the art of carnal distraction in a game of chance.

"My turn, then," Fleur said, turning her plack—a grey jay with twelve feathers up. She removed an emerald ring from her gloved left hand and placed it in the center of the table.

"There's a story behind this, I'm assuming," Gynedo said with good humor, "since I couldn't give a tinker's damn for a ring."

"Well, of course." Fleur cleared her throat dramatically, her face reminding Jastail of a young girl receiving her first kiss. "One of my former husbands ran a shipping trade. Profitable. Very profitable. Despite pirates and storms, we turned coin as though we minted it ourselves. A Soren Sea squall took one of our larger ships down. As an act of compassion, my husband not only made good on the lost freight with his customers, but gave to me 100 full realm marks for each crewman who died. I was to take that money to the spouses and families of those lost. 'You have decorum,' he said to me. I bowed gravely to the compliment, and went into the city and bought myself with that money this ring. It's lovely, don't you think?"

She smiled wickedly at Jastail and Gynedo.

"Suffering by omission," Gynedo mumbled, seeming to sort through the value. He was still refining his new game. "Those left behind had no breadwinner and no compassion money from their loved one's employer. I say it's good." He looked up and tapped the table again.

Fleur sat back, looking pleased with herself.

Gynedo turned his plack—a pine sparrow with three feathers.

He reached into this pocket and produced a single, thin plug. He examined it a moment, as if he might not like to part with it. Then he solemnly placed it with the other tokens, making a show of it by doing so painfully slow.

Gynedo sat back. "Men and women stroll on to my boat every day," he began. "They come in two stripes. One has bags full of coin. And if this type leaves empty-handed, it means nothing to him. The other sort boards my boat with desperation in his heart. He hopes for a bit of luck. He hopes to turn a meager stake into meat and rent money, because not doing so means people who depend on him will go without."

"Then you must have bags full of coins like this," Fleur observed, leaning forward and fingering the coin.

Gynedo nodded. "But this one . . . this is one I took myself. And I took it with a cheat. The man had me cold with a high hand of triple draw. But I hate to lose. And it sets a bad precedent for me to be seen losing to a dock worker, of all things. So, I made a simple card exchange." He paused, his eyes distant. "The look in the man's face when he lost . . . I could see the ache of it. I could see those who depended on him losing a measure of hope."

Jastail stared at the coin, thinking of a line from one of his dark poets. "I'd have saved *that* for a later round."

They exchanged glances, silently agreeing that they'd all bought another turn. Jastail didn't hesitate to turn up his second plack. Another hawk. Ten feathers. He now had a suited pair. And he promptly produced a child's sock—the one he'd earned just a few days prior when he'd taken a woman by a quiet riverside. He shared the story of the article of clothing.

"Lovely," Fleur said.

Gynedo tapped the table again.

They continued around, each turning a plack, each offering a token. Jastail had the high hand when the third and final round came. But it was clear that both Fleur and Gynedo had dropped more suffering into the pot. He gave them both a long look, then reached into his inner pocket for his length of cherrywood. For perhaps the last time—should he lose tonight—he fingered the groove marks in the short stick. Then, he pulled it from his pocket and placed it with the rest of the wagers.

Gynedo eyed the token. Fleur looked aflutter with eagerness to hear the story.

"In Sever Ens, where I grew up, there's not much for a woman if she's not a soldier's wife." He smiled at dark memories. "My mother was *not* a soldier's wife. She wasn't a wife at all. And she couldn't tell me who my father was, because she didn't know."

"The wood belongs to your mother?" Gynedo asked.

Jastail shook his head. "Money was hard to come by. She was fifteen when I was born, and she struggled along until the day came I could help her earn a coin. I was six."

Gynedo sat forward. "Jastail?"

Fleur made a sound of delight at the story.

"Like anyplace, Sever Ens has its whoreboy trade." Jastail said it matter-of-factly. "But those are usually gangs of runaways, orphans, or snatched sons brought into the city from far places." He shook his head. "My mother started asking me to take meals with strangers who came by our shanty. 'A full, warm meal,' she'd say. 'Be grateful,' she'd say. And sometimes there was, in fact, a meal. But they were bugger meals. And just as often, the bugger bought me nothing."

He looked up at his two table-mates, and flashed a wicked smile. "After the first time, I found something to hold in my teeth when these meal-men set to their sport. It kept me from screams, which only ever earned me angry fists anyway. It helped me . . . suffer through."

Fleur removed her gloves and picked up the cherrywood, fingering the bite marks. Her expression held fascination and a glint of something Jastail had only seen in a woman at the peak of orgasm. She handed it to Gynedo, who wore a serious look as he studied the token.

Making the bet felt like pulling a knife slowly through one's own palm. It burned. Seared. But it exhilarated him to have the will to do something so personally painful.

He'd hate to lose the cherrywood. But he played to win.

Gyndeo placed the stick back at the table's center, knocked the table once rather weakly, and the round continued.

Gynedo won. He gathered in the pile of tokens, placing them gently into a felt bag. Fleur stood to go. As she passed Jastail, she bent near him, placing her face gently against his neck, and took a deep breath through her nose. *She's smelling me.* Then she ran the tip of her tongue over the delicate folds of his ear—a clear invitation—and returned to her room below-deck.

"It's an interesting game," Jastail remarked, as Gynedo settled him a firm stare.

"It's rough yet, but it'll smooth out." Gynedo gestured for Jastail to follow him into the small quarters just behind his rear-room table.

Once inside, the man closed the door, dimming the riverboat noise to a low roar. He came around to face Jastail square, and held out the length of cherrywood. "Take it."

"I lost." Jastail shrugged. Then he grinned. "Unless you cheated."

Gynedo returned a wry smile. "Not this time, I didn't." The smile fell away. "But I won't keep this."

"Why? Tender heart?" Jastail tried to push the length of wood away.

"You and I, we're not tender men," Gynedo said. There was no lament over the fact for either of them. "But a man who carries something like this is a man who has unresolved quarrels with his past."

"You sound like a priest. It was a wager, Gynedo, not a confession." Jastail thought a moment. "And certainly not a plea for help. I have my poets for that." He offered a mild but genuine laugh.

"Then it wouldn't bother you if I burned it." Gyendo strolled to a lamp and removed the glass windbreak to expose the flame.

Jastail felt a tug of panic low in his gut. "I rather thought I could win it back at our next round of the game."

Gynedo began lowering the cherrywood toward the flame. "Snatching travelers from the road and selling them as stock on the blocks has grown tiresome, hasn't it? Oh, it's profitable, but hardly thrilling anymore for you or me."

Jastail spoke fast. "You think my holding onto the wood speaks of a weakness. A sentimentality, perhaps." He laughed. "Did I tell you I've completed my first stock sale to Bar'dyn out of the Bourne. Dead gods did that pay well. But, to your point, the risk was quite a thrill. One of every two men *die* trading with the Bar'dyn."

Gynedo looked unimpressed, and continued to lower the cherrywood. It was a hand-length from the flame now.

"Your new game has raised the stakes, too," Jastail quickly added. "You're right. I don't think much anymore about the wombs I gather for Bar'dyn buyers, though I like walking that line of uncertainty every time I meet with the beasts. No, when I'm collecting wombs, I think about what small token I might find to wager at your table." He gestured toward the gambling deck, where they'd just concluded their round of the new game.

Gynedo kept lowering the wood. "You should have won tonight," he said. "You lost because you put up a personal token. I'll modify the game rules to disallow it. Or maybe that'll be a separate game." He showed Jastail a moment's sympathy. "But I don't like to see a gambler with your potential chained by his past. It makes you weak. And if I know your weakness, I'll win every time." He stopped the wood's descent to the flame. "And you see, I'm a rather selfish bastard. I want the game to have real sport to it. I want to know I *could* lose. And unless you do something about this gods-forsaken wood, I'll find a way to beat you no matter what we play."

"I'm not quite sure how you'd manage that," Jastail said, smiling.

"Trust me." Gynedo lowered the cherrywood into the flame.

"Fine!" Jastail blurted, more loudly than he'd intended.

Gynedo smiled and pulled the wood away from the lamp with only a slight black sear. He tossed it to Jastail.

After a brief inspection of the scorching, Jastail placed the stick back in the pocket against his chest.

"Even bastards like us need to make peace with the past," Gynedo remarked, smiling conspiratorially, "or we'll never have the cool to play chances the right way . . . with the necessary indifference. Especially at high stakes."

Jastail returned the wisdom with a mock salute and shook his head, smiling, intending to heed every word the gambling boss uttered.

"And I'd stay out of Fleur's bed," Gynedo added. "She's a biter. She'll leave teeth marks in you like that wood you carry."

Well, maybe not every *word.*

JASTAIL DIDN'T BOTHER to knock. He simply went into the home of his childhood. Such as it was.

It looked precisely as it had seven years ago, when he'd finally run from this place. He'd decided he wouldn't let his mother send him with men anymore for a *meal.* The room closed in tight. Suffocating. It was warmed by a fire over which a pot of beans was always simmering.

Cow bones were tossed in for flavor—whatever could be scrounged from the butcher's waste barrel. And under the smell of the overcooked beans was the stench of armpits and unwashed skin.

In her chair beside the fire sat his mother, Lona. Her face told of a recent beating. She wasn't above *bedwork* herself if it came to that.

"My dying gods. Jastail," she exclaimed. "Come to your senses, have you. Returned home."

Jastail closed the door and took a seat opposite her near the hearth. Closer here, the beans smelled burned. He could also now see the small table beside her with its second shelf beneath. Lying there, covered in years of dust, was a volume of poetry by Tawl Tawminh. It was Jastail's book. One he'd forgotten when he fled this place. One of his dark poets. A line rose in his mind: *I hear secret convulsive sobs from young men, at anguish with themselves, remorseful after deeds done.*

"A visit is all. I'm not staying," Jastail said. He looked her over. Aside from the bruising, she didn't appear ill or underfed. "You look well."

She produced a coin bag hung down between her breasts on a leather strap. She jangled the coins within. "No complaints."

"You working alone?"

"Let's talk about you," she said, avoiding the question. "I've heard you ply the roads. Take folk and sell them on the blocks. That's gainful work. I imagine your purse is a might heavier than mine." She smiled, exposing a missing tooth. "I deserve some credit for that, you know. What you learned of *human wages* you learned from me." She eyed him. "Might even entitle me to a cut of your take."

Jastail laughed out loud. "I don't whore for you anymore, mother."

"Oh, lad. It wasn't like that." She waved a hand at him, as though he were talking foolish. "Each of us does what we must to get by. If you can't swing a sword or keep a ledger, you do what's left and be grateful to those who pay."

Jastail gave a politician's nod of agreement. "You're wise beyond your years. Survival is more important than . . . well, than love."

"I see, you think I didn't love you. That it?" She put the bag of coins back into her blouse. "You come all this way to hear me say it. It'll make you feel better, I suppose, if I tell you I didn't want no baby when I was fifteen. Or that no good mother makes her little boy take a meal with a grown man who expects a little kindness in return for his generosity. Is that what you'd like to hear?"

Jastail glared at her. A hundred vicious things entered his mind. But he held his tongue until he found his smile again, and flashed it brightly. "You're a high breed bitch, all right."

She winked conspiratorially. "That I am, my boy. That I am. No one gives a good gods damn about me, and I give back the same."

He decided a little honesty wouldn't hurt. "I did love *you.* At first, anyway. You knew it. And you used it to convince me that I needed to go with that first meal-man. You said he'd want some kindnesses from me, and pay me for it." Jastail fell deeper into the memory. "You said that I'd do it if I loved you. Because we were starving, and we needed the scratch to buy meat. You sent me out with him, and a hundred more like him, asking me to do it because we were all each other had. Needed to do hard things to make our way, you said."

She nodded to it all, her eyes distant, wearing that particular frown of one hearing something entirely sensible. "Rough times in the beginning." Then her eyes focused again. "But look how far we've come, eh?" She grinned a wicked grin. "You doing hard trade on the road and no doubt flush with coin. And me? Well, I do better than most. Learned a thing or two, besides."

Rough times.

He regarded her for several moments. Damn hells how he'd looked forward to this. "Tell me these things you've learned. Educate your son."

She gave a coarse laugh, and rocked forward in her seat to share her secret. "A crew of five I have working the taverns and bedhouses. Young waifs. I pay one strong-hand to keep them from running, and to keep them safe from the kill-sex types. And I pay a second man to be sure the first doesn't get no ideas about taking my girls."

"Girls then?" Jastail said, feigning surprise.

Her devilish grin widened. "That's just what I call them. I offer the company of both lads and lasses. Payer's choice," she said proudly. "And I keep the crew small. No permanent home, neither. That way, I slide under the lawguards, who make examples of madams who set up expensive brothels with baths and lace. Hells," she laughed, "a few of my best patrons are lawguards. They get their turn free."

Jastail listened. All this he'd learned already for a few coins in a nearby tavern.

A silence settled between them. Just the low crackle of fire and warm smell of beans.

"You must have lost a few drabs, to learn that you needed protection," Jastail observed.

"Precisely."

"It's a good thing, then, that in all those times you sent me with buggers, none of them damaged me so badly I couldn't keep taking *meals*."

"Unavoidable risks, really," she answered, with a proprietor's tone. "I had no money for a strong-hand then."

"And you've operated all this while without any real challenge." Jastail sat back, speaking as though he truly marveled over her prowess and ability. "Until now."

She eyed him with suspicion. "How's that?"

"What I mean to say is, I've taken ownership of your working waifs." He flashed his grin again, mocking and bright.

His mother stared back a long moment, dumbstruck. Then her own devilish smile rose on her bruised lips. "A game? You're all grown up, and come to see if I can hold my own."

She produced a small knife with a serrated edge.

Jastail chuckled low over the threat.

"Don't think because I'm your mother that I won't use this." She spun it over the top of her hand in a deft movement he hadn't seen before. "Or that I don't know how. Now, what's the game?"

Jastail leaned forward, elbows on his knees, and spoke with dripping earnestness. "No game. Just doing what I must . . . to get by."

"You're an ungrateful whoreboy." She waved her dagger threateningly. "What you done back then ain't hurt you none. And it gave us coin to struggle through the lean years. What's wrong with that?"

He reached into his inside pocket and drew out the length of cherrywood. He stared at it a moment, then tossed it at her. She caught it with her free hand, and looked it over. Realization slowly bloomed in her face.

"What do you call it, mother? A 'bugger's bit'?" Jastail saw in his mind a rapid stream of men, their wanton nervous smiles, the sweat on their upper lips, their white puckered flesh.

Any bit of guilt or regret slipped from her face. "Poor boy. Carrying his little piece of wood around all his life. Thinks he had it rougher than most." Her expression hardened. "You're going to return my drabs, or I'm going to open you like a fall pig. Don't test me, Jastail." An idea lit her face. "And better yet, you and me, together. We could run quite a crew of drabs. You pluck 'em from the highway, I'll keep 'em on their backs."

Jastail shook his head and offered her an incredulous grin. "You're a high breed bitch, all right."

He leaned back and drew the curtain away from the windows once and let it fall back. A moment later, four of his men quietly entered the shanty house, steel drawn.

She stared at each man in turn, her eyes coming to rest again on Jastail. "What then? You going to kill me, take over my operation?"

Jastail noted that she hadn't lowered her knife. He shook his head as one might to shush a complaining child. "Absent gods, no. I'll be selling them to clients from the Bourne. They pay well for young girls." The boys he'd likely cut loose, leave them to their odds.

His mother shot him an angry frown, her lips drawing into a snarl. "That's bad business. I can earn a hundred times their sell-price in a few years, making them work the taverns." She calmed herself, adopting a negotiator's tone. "Let me keep on as I have. And I'll cut you in for one coin in three. That's more than fair. Hard to turn down a deal such as that."

He marveled at her tenacity. Maybe he'd gotten a bit of that from her. Again he leaned forward in his chair, to watch her face when he shared his next bit of news. "You won't have time for this nonsense anymore, mother. You see, the Bar'dyn prize something even more than *young* girls. Pay well for it."

He paused. The fire hissed beside them.

She'd already begun to nod, understanding, when he explained, "Wombs, ma. They pay handsomely for wombs. Girls will grow into their use. And you," he pointed between her legs, "bless you, you pushed me out at a tender age. There's still good bearing years in you."

He was almost too slow when she lashed out with her knife. Almost. He swayed back in the chair, and brought his arm around in a swiping motion to push the blade away. She recovered fast, and stabbed quick at his belly. He kicked out and knocked her down beside the pot of beans.

Casually, his men came forward, their blades pointing at her.

"Does selling me off make your ass hurt less, whoreboy?" She still held his length of cherrywood, and wagged it at him. "You're a weak mule. Here, take your bit. You're going to wear it all your days." She barked a single bitter laugh.

To his own surprise, he took the cherrywood from her hands, then motioned for his men to take her out. She thrashed for a moment, then put on an air of dignity that looked preposterous in her little shanty.

They exited quietly, leaving Jastail beside his boyhood hearth. He sat staring into the embers of the fire a long while, a strange mix of peace and hollowness in his chest.

He didn't hear the knock at the door. Or rather heard it distantly. The third time the knock came it was cracking loud, urgent. He got up to answer it, pulling the door back to see an overweight man in a leather smith-apron calling on his mother's home late in the evening.

Jastail's gut tightened. "Can I help you?"

The man didn't fidget from foot to foot. He didn't lick his lips or need to wipe sweat from his brow. He was altogether comfortable. This wasn't his first time calling at this door. He only looked at Jastail, then past him when the patter of feet came from deeper within the shanty home.

Jastail turned to see a boy, maybe six, maybe seven. The lad had a careworn look in his eye. A bit of fear, too. And he looked, for all the gods-forsaken world, like a young Jastail. *A brother. Did she have another child to replace me?*

The boy's face showed a hint of confusion when he saw Jastail, but a heartbreaking familiarity when he saw the man at the door. He glanced toward the hearth. "Where's mother?"

Jastail fingered the grooves in his length of cherrywood, feeling like he might lose his own moorings. He considered the words of one of his dark poets, but left them alone.

Instead, he stepped into the doorway, near the caller, and stared him dead in the eye. Just above a whisper, he said, "Don't ever come back here. If you do, I'll find you, and I'll use your own tools to brand the words 'boy bugger' on your forehead."

The big man managed a momentary look of defiance, but must have seen something in Jastail's eyes. He nodded once and scurried away.

Jastail went back into the shanty home, and quietly closed the door. The boy was staring at him, still looking confused, but now worry also showed in his young face.

Jastail shook his head. "There'll be no more meals with strangers. You don't owe anyone that sort of kindness anymore."

The boy's eyes filled with tears. He hung his head, and quietly began to sob.

THE FIRST KILL

Django Wexler

IT WAS AN hour before dawn, and the heat was already stifling. Andreas stared at the water-stained plaster of the ceiling, gray and shadowed in the grimy light filtering through the curtains. His pillow was damp with sweat.

Damn the Deslandai, he thought, *for building their God-damned city in a swamp.*

He was suddenly eager to be moving, in spite of the early hour. The bedsheets were already in a tangled pile on the floor, the night too hot for even thin linen. Andreas rolled off the scratchy mattress, hit the floor in a noiseless crouch, and padded silently to the window. It was cheap glass, bubbly and yellow in an iron frame, and the latch squeaked as he tugged it open and pushed the panes wide.

The air outside wasn't much better. A trifle cooler, perhaps, but what it lacked in temperature it made up for in smell. The little room, on the fourth floor of a crumbling brick apartment block that catered to thieves, whores, and rivermen, overlooked one of the Free City of

Illustration by OKSANA DMITRIENKO ›

Desland's famous horse markets, and the stench of the by-products of thousands of nervous horses was omnipresent. Even Andreas, no stranger to foulness, found himself wrinkling his nose.

The only virtue of the place was that it was anonymous, somewhere no one would remark on two foreigners staying for a few days. If, as he'd been warned, the Komerzint really was on guard, they would be unlikely to peg the poorly-dressed travelers as Concordat assassins.

There was a murmur from the bed as Beth rolled over and sat up, woken either by the squeal of the window or the pervasive stink. She yawned, her dark hair puffed around her head like a frizzy halo.

"Sir?" she said. "Is something wrong?"

"Just the heat," Andreas muttered, turning away from the window. "Is it time?"

"We've got another hour. Go back to sleep, if you like."

"Too hot to sleep." Beth flopped back on the bed, staring at the ceiling. "Are you nervous, sir?"

Andreas glared at her. She was just past her twentieth year, a compact, graceful woman whose small size belied a surprising amount of muscle. She'd been assigned to him for her final training for the last six months, the latest in a string of apprentices the Last Duke had given to him when they were finally ready to get their hands dirty. He hadn't asked to her to climb into his bed as well, but she'd taken to it as eagerly as to her official duties.

"Nervous?" he said. "Why? We don't even know the job yet."

"About the meeting. The Gray Rose."

The Gray Rose. Andreas had been trying not to think about that. *Am I nervous?*

After a moment of self-examination, he decided he was, a little. It was an unfamiliar feeling, but not an entirely unpleasant one, a tingle of anticipation in the pit of his stomach, like the best moments just before a kill.

After all, there was no way around it. The Gray Rose was a legend. The greatest agent in the history of Duke Orlanko's Ministry of Information; a spy and assassin absolutely without equal. Some of the stories told about her in the canteens of the Cobweb veered into the absurd: she could walk through walls, kill men with the merest touch, disguise herself as anyone from a beggar-child to the King of Vordan.

Andreas had taken pains to find out the truth, or as much of it as was in the archives, and it was almost as impressive. Orlanko turned to the Gray Rose when a mission required daring, skill, and ruthlessness, and she had more kills to her credit than any other Concordat agent. Most of the techniques the Cobweb now taught to new recruits, the Gray Rose had invented. She'd been with Orlanko almost since the beginning, since he'd taken over the moribund Ministry of Information and converted it into the most feared secret police on the continent, and her hands were drenched in blood.

And I will meet her in an hour. No one he knew at the Ministry had been afforded that singular honor. Andreas stood staring a moment longer, staring through the horse market as though it were a curtain of fog.

He turned, abruptly, and went back to the bed. Beth raised her head.

"Sir?" she said. "I'm sorry if my question offended. I thought—"

His hand slid across her skin, up from her ankle and along the curve of her inner thigh.

"Oh." Her small chin lifted in response to his touch. "Are you sure—?"

"We have," he said, kissing her breast and feeling her give a little shiver, "an hour."

Beth raised no further protests. As she gasped and wrapped her arms around his shoulders, Andreas closed his eyes and thought, *The Gray Rose. At last.*

THE RIVER VELT, lifeblood of the Free Cities, flowed broad and deep through Desland. Above the city, the river narrowed as it descended from higher ground, the rushing water providing power to the city's innumerable waterwheels. The wide, flat stretch just below the rapids was as far north as deep-bottom ships could come, and Desland had grown up as the gateway between ocean-going traffic and the ox-drawn barges that plied the waters upstream.

The east bank of the Velt was higher here, and so the business of loading and unloading cargo stayed on the west side. The opposite heights were lined with the houses of the wealthy, square three- or four-story stone mansions belonging to merchants and city burghers who'd grown rich off the river trade. They were lined up like soldiers on parade, facing the river with broad terraces and enormous windows to take in the view. At the base of the crumbling red stone cliff, private docks jutted out into the water, with the pleasure craft of the quality tied up beside them.

Andreas sat on the west bank, across the river from these fortresses of privilege, studying them over the tin rim of a coffee cup. The coffeeshop was only a wooden stall surrounded by a few rusting cast-iron tables and chipped wooden chairs, the whole thing ready to be stacked on the back of a wagon and hauled away at a turn in the weather. The owner had set up on a stretch of muddy grass flanking a brick warehouse, only a few yards from the riverfront. All around was the business of the city, just getting into full swing now that the sun was well and truly risen, a chorus of shouts and rattling wheels and the sounds of horses.

A shadow fell across the table. Andreas didn't look up.

"Hello." A woman's voice. "Three-aye-five-one."

"One-dee-three-seven," Andreas said. Today's code, memorized from the table printed in tiny type on a scrap of foolscap sewn into his breeches.

"Hello, Andreas," the Gray Rose said. "Welcome to Desland."

"Thank you," Andreas said. "Please sit down, ah ..."

"Call me Rose." There was a touch of humor in her voice. She pulled out the chair across from him, which creaked in protest, and sat.

Andreas had carefully schooled himself to have no expectations regarding her appearance. Rumor had it, of course, that she was a great beauty, but he'd known better than to believe that. The woman facing him was plain, unremarkable. She had dark hair, tied back and coiled behind her head, and a thin face with a hatchet of a nose. He guessed her age at thirty, or a little past. Like him, she had looks that would not draw attention in a crowd and would be easily forgotten. She wore a dark brown dress with brass buttons, and could have passed for a local, a dockworker's wife or a fisherwoman.

"It's an honor to meet you," Andreas said. He had to concentrate on keeping his tone casual.

"Still telling stories about me in the canteen, are they?"

"They are. I didn't know what to believe, so I went looking in the archives."

Her eyebrow went up. "And what did you find?"

"A lot of missing files. But enough to know how good you are."

Rose chuckled. "And I, in turn, have read the files on you. The Duke thinks very highly of you, you know."

"I'm honored by his grace's trust." He couldn't help a slight smile. "And what did *you* find?"

"I found a man who seems to enjoy his work." Her tone didn't make it clear whether she approved of this or not. "The girl in the blue dress. Your partner?"

"My... assistant. I'm training her." Beth was acting as lookout at another table, behind the coffee stall.

"Well, tell her there's not much point to standing sentry if she makes it obvious by staring at everybody."

"I'm sure she'll appreciate the feedback."

"Are you two ready to move?"

"Everything is in place." He'd spent the last week accumulating the tools he might need and securing an escape route for a quick getaway; standard procedure for a mission in unfriendly territory. "We can go on your word."

"Good." She scraped her chair halfway around the table, until she was sitting beside him and they could both look out at the river. "See the house with the blue marble, second from the left?"

"I see it." Andreas sipped his coffee. It was a three-story manor house, much like the others. A huge semi-circular balcony jutted out from the second floor, supported by stone buttresses sunk into the cliff face.

"It belongs to the Baronet di Ninevah, and he has a special guest tonight. The Secretary-Treasurer Sepulveda of the Knights of the Far Shore."

Andreas nodded slowly, taking in every detail of the building.

"The Knights have considerable business interests in the far east," Rose went on. "They are expanding their concern westward, and negotiations have been ongoing with several potential partners. One of them is the House of Nachten, out of Hamvelt."

While not an expert on commercial dealings, Andreas recognized the name. The Nachten were one of the High Families of Hamvelt, the elite who supplied the commercial and political rulership of the mountain city. He cleared his throat.

"I take it that the Duke would not approve of this partnership."

"Emphatically," Rose said. "His grace has several times suggested more suitable arrangements to the Knights, and they seemed amenable. Nevertheless, we discovered the Secretary-Treasurer had come here, in what he believes to be all secrecy, to meet with Hamveltai representatives. His Grace is not pleased. You are to visit Secretary-Treasurer Sepulveda and make this absolutely clear."

"Exactly how displeased *is* His Grace?"

"Extremely displeased. His instructions to me were, 'tell Andreas the leash is slipped.'"

Andreas fought back a grin. "I *see*. Very well. Tonight?"

"Tonight."

"Will you be joining us?"

"Only if something goes wrong. Otherwise, I will be...watching."

So this is a test. He'd guessed it was something of the sort. The mission was no doubt real—it wouldn't be much of a test if it wasn't—but there was more at stake than an order of puffed-up old windbags and their ambitions. Orlanko and the Gray Rose wanted to see what he could do. He felt his pulse quicken. *I'll show her what I can do.*

"Understood," he said.

Under the table, he felt the touch of her fingers against his hand, and she passed him a folded sheaf of paper.

"That's what we know about the layout and the guards," she said. "The Knights have brought a few people with them, but nothing serious. If there's real opposition, it will come from the Komerzint. There have been some hints that they're keeping an eye on this."

The Komerzint—Commercial Intelligence—had once been a private firm supplying information to highly placed Hamveltai concerns. In the last few decades, it had grown into the *de facto* clandestine service of the Hamveltai state; only natural, in a city where business and political interests were so intertwined.

"Any particular instructions as regards the Secretary-Treasurer himself?" Andreas said.

"Nothing elaborate necessary. The message will be received in the right places." Rose pushed her chair back and got to her feet. "Good hunting. His Grace looks forward to your report."

Andreas grinned. "His Grace will not be disappointed."

A LESSER MAN might have been disappointed at not being given the opportunity to work side by side with the Gray Rose, but Andreas decided it was better this way. *She'll be watching me.* That was enough to make his heart beat faster, and it meant that he could work without risk of being overshadowed.

What *was* disappointing was that the first step in the proceedings was up to Beth. He didn't like trusting his apprentice with crucial matters, but she was smaller and lighter than he was, and a better climber. *And there's always a backup plan.*

After looking over the plan of the house Rose had supplied, he'd decided to approach from the river side. It was perhaps a trifle obvious as an opening move, but the front door of the house was on a well-lit, fashionable street which would have carriage traffic and patrols of watchmen all through the night. The di Ninevah docks boasted only a solitary watchman and his lantern, keeping an eye on the baronet's finely appointed pleasure galley.

Andreas had taken care of him with a single shot from a soot-blackened crossbow while their little boat was still fifty yards out. Not a bad shot, if he said so himself, from a rocking boat and against a target silhouetted only occasionally against his lamp. The guard had taken the bolt in the temple and pitched off the pier with a soft splash, inaudible amid the gentle creaking of the tied-up boats. No one raised the alarm when Andreas rowed their own boat in and settled it between the pleasure galley and a cargo barge, well-concealed from casual eyes.

Di Ninevah wasn't such a fool that he'd completely ignored the possibility of intruders getting in this way, of course. The stairway that led from the docks to the house was cut deeply into the rock, well-lit by oil lanterns, and blocked by a pair of wrought-iron gates with solid locks. It was also overlooked by a second-floor window, and any movement would be obvious to a watcher within.

To Andreas' trained eye, however, the twenty feet of cliff was not the obstacle that it might have appeared. The red stone was soft and crumbling—treacherous to be sure, but offering plenty of hand- and foot-holds. Beth was halfway up, moving slowly and carefully, a dark, spidery shadow in her soft gray working outfit. Andreas stood on the dock below, keeping watch, as she tested each new position with one hand before trusting it with her weight. A soft rain of pebbles below her testified to the necessity of these precautions.

In another twenty minutes, she'd reached the top. The baronet's enormous balcony, while no doubt ideal for dinner parties in the warm summer evenings, provided a perfect place to make the ascent shielded from any possible view from the house windows. Beth disappeared over the lip of the cliff in a final spray of pebbles, and a moment later Andreas could hear a metallic *clink* as she hammered a piton into the rock. A coil of rope fell toward him, unrolling as it went, and he caught it before it hit the dock.

With the knotted cord in his hand, the climb was quick and easy work, though his boots scraped more dirt and small rocks from the cliff. Beth was waiting for him at the top, crouched beside the anchored line, her face a pale oval in the light from the quarter-moon.

"Well done," Andreas said. Praise had to be given when it was due, that was a vital part of training. Beth smiled.

"Thank you, sir."

He nodded and moved deeper beneath the balcony, and she fell into step behind him. Around the sides of the house, there were gardens, but nothing would grow in the shadow of that overhang, so the space had been covered in flagstones and given over to the more mundane task of airing out old bedding and linens. Sheets hung from hooked stands, still as specters, and Andreas crept around them with utmost care. Stumbling into one and bringing the whole thing crashing down would lend the enterprise a comic-opera touch that he would *not* appreciate.

The door leading from the under-balcony space into the house was plain but strong, secured with a stout iron lock. Rose hadn't provided any information on its construction, so Andreas had decided not to rely on fiddling around with picks, which in any case had never been his strong suit. Instead, he took a small flask from his belt, uncorked the stopper, and tilted it gently into the keyhole.

The flask was full of gunpowder— not the ordinary coarse stuff one might use to propel a cannonball, but a much more finely ground variety sometimes called 'flash powder'. It burned faster and hotter than its common cousin, and it was so fine-grained that particles of it lingered in the air like an incendiary fog. A few pinches was enough. He restoppered the flask, motioned Beth to back off a step, and struck a match near the keyhole.

The powder went off with a soft *whumph*, producing a flash of light that would have ruined Andreas' night-vision if he hadn't already had his eyes tightly shut. As soon as he heard the noise, he grabbed the door-handle and turned it. Inside the lock, the tiny fireball would have blown all the tumblers outward; the handle resisted for a moment, then opened with a *click*, smoke still pouring out of the keyhole.

Andreas eased the door open. As Rose's plans had promised, it led into a servant's hall, just off the kitchens. It was late enough that the staff—except for the watchmen, of course—would have gone to bed for the evening. A back stair led up to the third floor, to the Secretary-Treasurer's room. *So far, so good.*

THE AMBUSH WAS waiting in the third-floor hall, where a concealed door led out from the servants' passage onto a well-appointed hallway. Andreas opened the door and glanced in both directions, satisfying himself that the hall was empty, and slipped through, with Beth close behind him. Just after the door closed, though, he caught the sound of running footsteps, and then a squeal as an iron bolt slammed into place.

Someone had been waiting until they went through to block their escape. Something at the back of Andreas' mind, the part of him that kept him alive when missions went wrong, had him reaching for his weapons before his conscious mind understood what had happened. He drew a short sword in his right hand and a curved fighting knife in his left, and when the nearest bedroom door burst open to disgorge armed men, he was already moving.

The men were ready for a fight, but they were not expecting their opponent to come at them so quickly. Andreas got only an instant to assess the grim-faced, mustached fellows in fighting leathers, slim swords in hand and small round shields belted to their opposite forearms.

The first one through the door way stopped in his tracks when he saw Andreas coming, forcing his fellows to pull up short behind him. Andreas feinted high with his sword, bringing the man's shield up. Metal scraped on metal as the butt of Andreas' hilt hammered the shield, but he was already pivoting to bring his knife around into the man's belly. His opponent doubled up around the wound, exposing the next guard, wedged awkwardly in the doorway. There wasn't time or room for a proper swing, so Andreas punched him in the face with the hilt of his sword, sending him stumbling backward with blood streaming from his nose. The third guard, who'd had a moment to get clear, stepped aside and raised his sword, only to find Andreas shoving the man he'd stabbed out of the way and slamming the bedroom door.

Behind him, the hallway echoed with the stupendous *bang* of a pistol shot. Andreas looked over his shoulder to find three more swordsmen closing from the opposite direction. Beth had shot one in the chest, and she tucked the smoking pistol into her waistband and drew another from the leather strap at the small of her back. The remaining two guards hesitated, not eager to charge a loaded pistol, and Andreas decided to use that opportunity to seek a better tactical position.

"Beth!" he said. "With me!"

Beth fired again, and he winced—the shot had probably been more useful as a threat. Andreas ran flat-out at a pair of double doors that gave way before his shoulder with a wooden splintering sound. He pulled up short in the room beyond—a hexagonal, nearly empty space, some kind of performance chamber—and Beth trotted past him, pistol still held in one hand. Andreas slammed the door behind her. He'd broken the lock, but there was an iron bolt, and he drew it closed just in time for the first of the guards to reach the doors and start pushing.

"That won't hold," he muttered, casting about. A glass-fronted drinks cabinet looked heavy enough for his purposes, and he gestured to Beth. "Help me with this."

She dropped the pistol, and together they managed to get the solid piece of furniture off the ground, glass bottles inside rattling and tinkling wildly. They parked it across the doors, and Andreas stepped to one side of the doorway, drawing Beth after him.

Men on the other side were shouting in a language he couldn't follow—not Hamveltai. *Daciai, presumably. Those fellows have an Old Coast look.* The Knights might be more commercial enterprise than marital organization these days, but evidently they could still rustle up a few soldiers when the occasion called for it.

"Holy *shit*," Beth breathed.

"Are you all right?" Andreas said. He watched the door, which was shaking as the guards pounded on it from the other side.

"Fine." She gulped air and swallowed hard. "I'm fine. I just...*shit*. I barely saw them coming."

"It was neatly done. Block the way behind us, trap us in a corridor between two converging teams."

"They were waiting for us."

"Indeed. Rose's information is apparently not as good as she believes."

"Any idea who those guys are?"

"Knights, perhaps. More likely Old Coast mercenaries." He listened for a moment. "There's at least six of them out there."

Beth crossed to the other side of the room, where three big windows looked out over the river.

"We're right over the balcony," she reported. "But they've got a man down there."

"Of course they do." Andreas unshipped the folding crossbow from its harness and snapped the ribs into place. "Find something to tie a rope to."

Beth drew another coil of rope from her small pack. "There may be more inside. Over the balcony rail once we get down?"

Andreas finished drawing the crossbow, hearing the catch click, then paused. "Over the rail?"

"And back down the cliff. To the boat." She looked back at him. "Or did you have an alternate route in mind?"

Escape. That was the correct option, obviously. The mission was blown, had been blown from the beginning; they'd been expecting a couple of sleepy watchmen, not a house full of hornet-mad mercenaries. The best decision was to withdraw and wait for another opportunity.

But the Gray Rose is watching. Would *she* withdraw, under the same circumstances? *Or would she get the job done, and be damned to the opposition?*

Beth was staring at him. Her eyes were wide, he saw, and her breath came quickly, but she wasn't panicked. *Good.* That guard in the hallway had been her first kill, and every trainee reacted differently to a first kill. *I've done a good job with this one.*

"We're not pulling out," Andreas said. "We'll drop to the balcony and go in through another window. They won't be expecting it."

Beth blinked, swallowed, and nodded. She hadn't been privy to the mission briefing; if he thought it was important enough to carry on, in spite of the risks, that was his call to make.

"Okay," she said, with only a slight tremor in her voice. With a few quick movements, she opened the window and tied the rope to the iron crossbar. "We're good to go."

"You may want to take this chance to reload," Andreas said, indicating the pistol she'd dropped.

"Right."

Beth fumbled through her pocket for a paper cartridge, and Andreas moved to the window. He leaned out, just for a moment, to spot the armed figure waiting on the balcony, then ducked back and fitted a blackened metal bolt to his crossbow. The man down there would be alert—the whole house had probably heard the pistol shots—but he didn't know where danger might come from.

"Ready?" Andreas said.

Beth nodded, and as though to reinforce the need to move, a pair of shots came from the doorway. The wood around the bolt cracked and exploded, and the doors shifted against the heavy cabinets.

Andreas raised the crossbow to his shoulder. "I'll shoot, you drop. Go."

Beth took a deep breath, put her pistols back in her waistband, and jumped through the open window, knotted line in one hand. Andreas leaned out after her, sighting on the guard, who had turned to face the house at the sound of more shooting. *Perfect.*

The crossbow *thrummed*, and the guard sprouted a quarrel just above the bridge of his nose. He toppled, shield clattering against the stones. Andreas snapped the ribs of the crossbow closed, secured it to its harness, and followed Beth down the line. It was only a fifteen foot drop, and she was already on the balcony, pressed up against the wall between a pair of windows. Andreas joined her, trying to recall the layout of the parts of the building he hadn't expected to enter.

"That hallway leads out to the main staircase," he said. "Most of them are still breaking down the door upstairs, so we've got a minute or so."

"They'll still have guards on the stairs," Beth said, her tone professionally detached. Andreas hid an admiring smile.

"Shoot one of them, I'll handle any others."

"Got it."

"Ready to run?"

She nodded.

Andreas drew his sword and slammed the hilt against the windowpane, shattering the expensive glass. No point in stealth now, with the house full of shouting men breaking down doors. He vaulted through, avoiding the dangerous shards still stuck in the frame, and Beth followed. A heartbeat was sufficient to assure himself that the floor plan matched what he remembered; then he broke into a dead run, with his apprentice close behind.

A well-appointed hallway rushed past, doors to sitting rooms and drawing rooms tightly shut. Andreas noted, absently, that whoever had planned this ambush must have made sure the domestic staff were given the night off, or there would have been a good deal more panic. Then they were turning a corner, out into the main hall, where a staircase with crimson carpets led in both directions.

As Beth had predicted, there were guards on the landing, three more men with sword and buckler. They were looking the wrong way, though, up towards the excitement on the third floor. Andreas ran straight at them, sword extended like a lancer, and took the first through the kidney from behind with a clean thrust. He slid off the blade, gurgling, and the next man to turn dropped with a startled expression as Beth's pistol-shot found him. The third man backpedaled, shouting, but Andreas didn't give him a chance to get his footing. He swung his sword at the mercenary's right side, forcing him to parry, then stepped in and snaked his other hand around the man's shield arm. The guard pulled away, opening himself up, and Andreas kicked him in the groin. He doubled over, and his momentum carried his throat across the blade of Andreas' sword, placed neatly in his path. Blood spurted, soaking the rich carpet a darker shade of red.

Beth jogged up. "Nicely done, sir."

"Thank you."

Andreas looked up the stairs. The hall led in both directions at the top. The left was toward where they'd gone out the window, the right led to Secretary-Treasurer Sepulveda's bedroom. Not great, tactically—

if they got bogged down, enemies could catch up from behind—but there was no way around it. He jogged up the stairs, peeked around the corner to the left, and swore.

Four men were heading back towards the stairs, weapons drawn. *They must have got the door down already, and figured out we got clear.* Or else they'd heard the shot from downstairs—he'd been hoping it was too noisy for that—and were coming to investigate.

"Go!" he hissed at Beth. "Third door on the right, get it open. Now!"

Beth nodded and threw herself forward, turning right at the junction. The guards saw her, and shouted in alarm, but she didn't hesitate. *Good girl.* Andreas sheathed his sword and grabbed the flask of flash powder from his belt. The container was stiffened leather, and it was the work of a moment to cut it in half with his knife. As the four guards came in front of the stairs, he hurled the mutilated flask into their midst, spraying powder as fine as milled flour in all directions. He followed it with a match, just as the men were turning to face this new assailant, and squeezed his eyes shut.

The powder went up all at once with a *whoomph* and a rush of heat that frizzled Andreas' eyebrow. The blast would blind and burn, but it wasn't enough to kill. Andreas would have liked to take a few moments to finish the guards off, but they still had their weapons drawn and flailing, and doing it safely would take longer than he could afford. Instead he slipped past them, following Beth. The door he'd indicated was open, and as he approached he heard a shot from inside. Wood exploded into splinters from the doorframe. Andreas spun through, exposing himself as little as possible, and dropped into a crouch.

The bedroom was a small guest suite, and he found himself in the receiving room, with a few armchairs and spindly tables. Another doorway in the opposite wall led to a dining room, and beyond that a closed door presumably concealed the bedroom itself. Beth was crouched behind a chair, one of her pistols lying on the floor beside her, trickling smoke. She had the other in her hand.

The guards would not be far behind him. Andreas pushed the door closed, paused a moment, then leapt across the line of fire from the inner door. A pistol shot rang out, the ball smacking into the plaster in a puff of dust. From his new position, he could reach the bolt, which he pushed home to buy at least a few minutes. That done, he squatted beside Beth, well out of sight of the dining room doorway.

"At least two of them in there," Beth said. "A pistol each."

"Two shots so far. We've got quite a few more behind us, too."

Beth grimaced. "We'll have to risk it."

Andreas nodded, picturing the two men inside frantically reloading. If they were fast—or if they had a second pair of loaded weapons—this was going to be extremely dangerous. Even a poor shot would have a hard time missing a target trapped in a doorway at this range.

"Okay," Andreas said. "Give me the pistol. You go first, move fast and stay low, try to draw a shot. I'll be right behind."

"Got it." Beth closed her eyes and took several deep breaths. Andreas could hear booted feet outside, and once again frantic pounding on the door. "Ready."

She reversed the pistol and handed it to him, then crouched by the edge of the doorframe. Andreas took a position behind her, ready to lean out as soon as she moved.

"Andreas…" Beth's voice was a bare whisper.

"What?"

"Nothing. Sorry, sir. Ready?"

"Go."

Beth pushed off, rolling through the doorway and throwing herself into a sideways dodge as soon as she was clear. Two pistols went off, almost simultaneously, roaring in the enclosed space. Andreas stepped into the doorway, drew a bead on a man crouching behind a long lacquered table, and fired. It wasn't a perfect shot, but the ball caught the guard in the shoulder and spun him to the floor. The second guard had discarded his pistol and drawn a sword, and Andreas did likewise. They stepped forward, the guard edging clear of the chairs tucked in around the table to get a clear space, Andreas giving ground slightly.

The mercenary snarled—he was an older man, with a badge sewn into his jacket, perhaps indicating his rank—and pressed forward. Then something went *thunk*; a throwing knife sprouted between his shoulder blades, as if by magic. It didn't sink deep enough to do real damage, but the guard turned to find the source of this new attack, and that was all the opening Andreas needed to drop into a neat lunge and put the point of his sword through the man's throat.

He hurried across the room to the other guard, in case he was still capable of offering any resistance, but the mercenary was only clutching his wound and moaning. Andreas finished him with a quick slash, sheathed his sword, and went back to check on Beth.

She was sitting up, with obvious difficulty, supporting herself with one hand and keeping the other pressed against her stomach. Blood, thick and red, welled between her fingers.

"Good throw," Andreas said. Recognizing good work was important for training.

"Thanks." Beth swallowed, the muscles in her throat working. "Not quite fast enough, though."

Andreas said nothing. Beth gave a weak smile and jerked her head toward the inner doorway.

"Go on," she said. "Finish the job. Then we'll see about getting out of here."

THE DOOR TO the Secretary-Treasurer's room opened with a creak, neither locked nor bolted. No lamps were burning, but by the light from the outer room Andreas could see dark shapes sprawled across the floor. He counted four of them—five, he corrected, seeing another curled up in one corner—all armed mercenaries, all dead. There was remarkably little blood. Each man had been killed by a single deep stab wound, to the head or to the heart. None of the five had managed to even draw a sword.

The bed, a big four-poster, was hung round with curtains. Andreas drew them back, already certain what he would find. Sepulveda was an old man, pale and liver-spotted, with wispy gray hair and long, quivering jowls. His mouth was open in a silent 'O' of surprise, and his cloudy eyes stared sightlessly at the ceiling. His hands were clutched over his heart, where a dark stain on his shirt marked the wound underneath.

"Rose?" Andreas said. "You're here, aren't you?"

A shadow extracted itself from the deeper darkness beside the bed. "I wasn't expecting you."

The guards in the outer room didn't know about this, Andreas thought. That meant that these men had died, not just without getting the chance to draw a weapon, but practically without a sound. *This wasn't a fight. It was a... dissection.*

"Did you know they'd be waiting for us?" he said.

Rose shrugged. "It was always a possibility. One of our local informants has been compromised by the Komerzint. Now that they've tipped their hand"—she gestured at the corpses—"we'll be able to find out who, and express His Grace's feelings on the matter."

"And you just decided to come in here and do the job yourself? You didn't think I'd make it?"

"I didn't think you'd try." She walked across the room to stand in front of him. "Retreat would have been the correct tactical option."

"But you waited here for me."

"As I said. I've read your file."

Rose slipped past him, out into the dining room. Andreas followed. The noise of the guards at the outer door had grown louder.

"If this is a test," Andreas said, as Rose knelt beside Beth, "did I pass?"

"That depends," Rose said. "Did you learn anything?"

Andreas looked down at the two women. Beth's eyes were closed, and her breathing was fast and shallow. Rose put two fingers to her throat, then gently pulled her hand away to examine the wound.

"I learned not to be the first one through the door," Andreas muttered.

"She may live," Rose said, straightening up. "If we can get her to a cutter soon."

"So what now? It sounds like there's at least a dozen of them out in the hallway. We won't have a chance if we have to carry her."

"Consider it another test. You're trapped in a room with a badly injured comrade and no escape route." Rose cocked her head. "What do you do?"

Andreas stared at her for a moment, then crouched beside Beth. He wasn't sure if she was conscious or not, but either way he moved so fast she had no time to make a sound. His knife went in to the soft spot under her jaw in a single, smooth motion. Her legs kicked, weakly, and the breath went out of her with a sigh. Andreas withdrew his blade, wiped it on her shirtsleeve, and sheathed it again.

He looked up at the Gray Rose, and she looked back at him, her expression unreadable. He wondered if, in that moment, he had finally surprised her. Then she was turning away, drawing a long, curved blade as the door broke open, and a moment later men were falling around her like wheat before the scythe.

THE BETYÁR AND THE MAGUS

S.R. Cambridge

betyár (n.): a highwayman in 19th century Hungary

Outside Győr

Kingdom of Hungary

1850

MY TEACHER JÓSKA Bajusz had died half a year earlier, and there was no fun in robbing the roads without him. You might imagine the life of a *betyár* to be all guns and riches and soft swooning women, but you wouldn't imagine the truth of it, the tedium, the long spans of night spent hiding and hoping for an unwary traveller to pass.

It was January, one of those days where the night steals in early, and unwary travellers had become a rare commodity. All I had to show for hours of waiting was a beard soaked through with snow, a sour mood, and half a *forint* from a shepherd who had been relieved, not afraid, when he realized it was a mere *betyár* who leapt in front of him.

Illustration by OKSANA DMITRIENKO ▸

People weren't frightened of *betyárok* then, not when there were worse dangers on the roads: Austrian soldiers, Habsburg men, who would name you a rebel and clap irons around your wrists before you could say *guten tag*. If you were lucky, you were held prisoner and conscripted. If not, you met your maker at the bad end of a firing squad.

I had been lazy with that shepherd, letting him go without even demanding one of his sheep, even though one of them would have fetched a good price. *But it wouldn't have been worth the trouble*, I told myself. *Sheep are stubborn.*

When Jóska was alive, before the war, I was never lazy, and never in poor spirits, even on the roughest of nights. With how much Jóska talked, I didn't have the chance. He was generous with advice, was Jóska, from the day he tried to steal a pig from me and instead decided to take me on as an apprentice *betyár*, although his habit was to begin with an insult before he got to anything helpful.

László, Jóska would say, *did your mother lay with a goat? It's the only explanation for that sad little beard of yours. Listen: if you apprehend a true Hungarian, then you take from him ten percent of what he has and let him go. That's what the churches do, after all. Frenchmen, Englishmen, take more. And if you rob an Austrian, take everything.*

Or, *László, you know there is a blind girl in Tata? There might be a wife for you, after all. Listen: you will rob many women. Treat them all with courtesy. The lady in her middle years, the one who was once a beauty, will respond best to romance. Speak kindly, look upon her as though you ache, and let your fingers linger on her throat. She'll be gladder to give you her coin if you give her a scandalous tale to tell other women about how she was nearly seduced on the road.*

The Russians killed Jóska during the battle at Segesvár. We'd come up with the brilliant idea to join up and fight for a free Hungary, Jóska and me. We ought to have stayed out of it. None of it had been fair.

We had been winning, honestly *winning*, and then the Habsburgs got scared and said, *oh, Russia, please help us crush the Hungarians*, and Russia agreed and that was that.

Jóska had been hit with a spell from a Russian magus, some burst of terrible white-hot light that had ripped him open better and faster than a bayonet ever could. They were organized, those companies of Russian magi in the service of the Habsburgs. Always they attacked in formation. We had magi, too, but none so talented, none so regimented.

I'd knelt before Jóska as he struggled to speak, gurgling out blood and incoherent sounds in equal measure. His insides had glowed unnaturally and spilled on the earth. Tragic, truly, that a man who talked as endlessly as Jóska Bajusz should be denied the right to spit out a last bit of wisdom.

My hiding place for the night was one of the best spots Jóska and I had found along the well-worn road from Pest-Buda to Vienna: a hidden cleft of rock obscured by trees, a few paces from a bend in the road. A fine site for an ambush. It was easy for a wagon or a carriage to get bogged down in the deep ruts of the road when it was muddy. Always a fortunate thing, when that happened. You could appear before the poor stranded travellers with a benevolent smile on your face and act the solicitous saviour before you started waving your weapons about.

That's what I did with the Countess Almásy, Jóska had told me once. *Pretended I planned to help her when one of her horses fell injured on the road.* If he wasn't doling out advice, Jóska was going on about the time he robbed the Countess Almásy. I was fourteen and stupid when I first set out with Jóska, so initially I had believed him, but he told his Countess Almásy story so often and so inconsistently that it did not take me long to privately conclude it was horseshit designed to make me believe that being a *betyár* was more glamorous than it was.

Sometimes the countess kissed Jóska, having fallen in love with the handsome *betyár*, and wept because she would never see him again. (*It was my moustache,* Jóska had explained, stroking the black bristly mass of it. *Women love my moustache.*) Depending on how drunk Jóska was when he told the story, sometimes the countess was more lusty than loving. Once Jóska claimed the countess had told him she'd murder her old unkind husband and make Jóska her count if only he would leave his nomad's life to wed her.

When Jóska got into his Countess Almásy story, he always began the same way. *Once I charged before a carriage*, he would say, *a beautiful one, all white, and who should be inside but the Countess Almásy…*

Jézus, I thought. *László Sovány, you've gone sentimental.* Foolish, but on the night, quiet and windless with the snow settling about me like ash on embers, I longed to hear Jóska tell lies about the Countess Almásy. A strange listlessness had taken hold of me since Jóska's death. All I wanted, then, was a bed and supper and enough pálinka to make me forget that I had to think about what I would do next. *Half a forint is enough for that.*

Before the war I had been rich, in secret. Jóska and I had hidden the spoils of our robberies in places all along the road, in the houses of friends in Győr and Bicske and Komárom, but the Austrians had seen to my newfound poverty. After the war, after the Hungarians surrendered at Világos, Austrian soldiers swept over the country, *taking*. In the weeks it took me to get home, I went to each spot. In every case the money and valuables Jóska and I had spent years collecting were gone, replaced with abandoned or burnt-out buildings, or upturned earth. The friends were gone, too: dead, fled or captured.

I climbed down from my hiding place. On the road, I patted my coat and pockets to ensure my few possessions were still on my person: two pistols, a dagger, a paltry excuse for a coin purse. It would be a slow trudge back to Győr, where there were places I could lodge for the night. I was unused to life on my feet. I had sold Lánya, my horse, a week earlier, demoting myself from a mounted *betyár* to a lowly footpad. (*Listen*, Jóska's voice echoed in my head, *a betyár must always have handsome clothes and a fine fearsome horse, or else he is nothing but a common rogue.*) I regretted selling Lánya, having brought her to war with me, but it was time for her to go when I began thinking of her less as my faithful steed and more as tasty horsemeat.

It was then, starting that dreaded trek back to Győr, when I saw it: far off, faint, but unmistakable. *The light from a coachman's lantern*, I thought. Then: *oh, oh, thank God.*

Grinning, I drew my pistols, unmindful of the cold on my bare hands. I loaded each with powder and ball. I felt as though I had been buried but had clawed my way to fresh air, so great and so sweet was my relief. I had not spotted a proper carriage with a coachman in *months*. Before it all, before the revolution and the Russians and that horrible spell killing Jóska, the road was lousy with the wealthy, all of them ripe for a robbing. Afterwards, though, the rich seemed to have collectively determined that fashionable jaunts outside the relative safety of Pest-Buda weren't *quite* the thing when some cockless wonder of an Austrian could ruin your fun by deciding to detain you.

I stepped to one side, concealing myself among the trees. The light from the lantern grew closer, a pale beacon bobbing like a fairy-light through the drifting snow. I could hear the hooves of a pair of horses beating in time, squelching on the mud. *Jézus*, I prayed, *let them have gold and jewels and no guns and fearful dispositions.*

The carriage drew nearer. White, it was. *Just like the Countess Almásy's*, I thought, smiling. The coachman was a fat lump in a long winter coat, with a pouf of a fur hat and a wound-up scarf concealing his face. The horses were a matched pair of handsome chestnut

Percherons, worth a fair bit more than poor battle-scarred Lányа.

It was time. I charged in front of the carriage, shouting, "Halt!"

The carriage stilled. (Part of me did notice, then, that the horses went utterly quiet, with nary a snort or a whinny from either to complain of such an unceremonious stop. However, this half-made observation did not pierce through the fog of my excitement.) "Good evening, sir," I called, feigning cheer.

The coachman lifted the lantern, casting a yellow glow on me.

"Don't move," I said. "I am armed, and I'm aiming at you, but I have no desire to harm you unless you give me cause." I raised one pistol into the light so the coachman would see the gleam of the barrel. "I shall not leave you stranded. I'll have one horse, not both, and I will speak to your master or mistress inside regarding what else you might have for me."

The coachman did not speak, but he (if *he* is the right word; I'm not sure it is) dropped the lantern. It shattered on the carriage perch, leaving the road dark again, with only the snow-beaten light of the moon. The coachman climbed to the ground, desultory, as though he were simply stopping to stretch his legs and not faced with a loaded pistol.

"Tread no further, sir," I warned.

The coachman did not listen, or perhaps he could not listen. I still couldn't see his face, just the hat and the scarf. Slowly, he went past the horses; his movements were more like *floating* than walking. By then a nervous knot had formed in my stomach, but I pressed on. "Stop now, or I *will* fire."

He stopped. His head tilted. Then he lunged at me, alarmingly fast, and I stumbled back and shot at him. The ball caught him in the thigh.

I could have shot him in the chest instead, if I had wanted. I was a good shot. Even Jóska couldn't make light of my skill with guns, so formidable it was. It even netted me something of a reputation during the war. Travellers weren't enemy soldiers, though, and I was no murderer. (*We are gentlemen*, Jóska would remind me, *not criminals.*) Rarely had Jóska and I encountered a target foolish enough to attempt to fight us, and on those occasions a careful shot to somewhere non-fatal would always quell the heroics.

The coachman's head fell back when he was hit, sharp and soundless, like a puppet with its strings cut. None of the usual: no screaming, no doubling over, no cursing at me, no drip of blood from a wound.

I've killed him, I thought wildly. "Ah—" I said, stepping forward, but before I could say more, the coachman's coat spun, as though he and he alone had been caught in a brutal wind. His fur hat fell. Where a head should have been there was a black cloud of nothing. The scarf unwound and cascaded, in a spiral around him, to the ground.

A second later, there was nothing left of the coachman but a pile of clothes. The horses watched, still as statues and uncaring, and I *knew*.

There was only one piece of advice Jóska Bajusz had never delivered with humour.

László. Listen. Never, ever, ever *try to rob a magus.*

"Oh, *shit*," I spat.

In the next moment, I was frozen, and bathed in a dark blue mist. I tried to turn, to run, but my legs were rooted in the road. My hands were heavy like anchors; my pistols fell from my clumsy fingers. My tongue was a hot leaden weight in my mouth. Before, I had only known magic from the periphery of it: the graze of a spell during a battle, the lightning-storm smell that permeated the air when magi fought. The pure violence of this magic stunned me. My innards felt like they had together decided to all at once age and fail and die. My throat constricted; I could breathe only in thin streams. I couldn't blink. *Was this what Jóska felt?*

The carriage doors creaked open. First, I glimpsed old scratched boots, and the bottom of a ratty rough-spun cloak. Then the magus himself. His hood was down. His hair was long, tangled, and not the colour you would expect on a magus: not white-blond, not blood-red, but an unremarkable peasant-brown.

He walked with a pronounced limp as he approached me, but he did not carry a staff like most of the magi I had seen in the war. When he stood before my trapped self, I could see that he was young. Eighteen or nineteen, at most. His face was ruddy. A few pimples dotted his chin. *My sort of luck lately*, I thought. *Dying at the hands of a crippled magus who's just out of short pants.*

But the magus did not kill me. He said, "You're no Austrian."

"Mmph," was my reply. It was impossible to speak.

He huffed impatiently, then pointed a bony finger at my throat and murmured a few indistinguishable words. *Horse's ass*, I thought. *You did this; don't get tetchy when I can't answer you.* Tendrils of smoke encircled my neck. I glared down at them, mistrustful, but my throat loosened and my tongue went back to normal. "Do I *look* Austrian?"

"No," the magus said. "You look poor."

"And I was hoping you and your carriage might be a step toward changing that," I said, adopting a jovial tone. "It appears I was wrong there, but, friend, no harm in an honest mistake. If you'll undo this spell and let me on my way—"

"You've ruined my coachman."

The magus gazed at the coachman's clothes, now speckled with fresh snow. He had bright blue eyes that belonged more on a guileless farm boy than someone who could kill you with a hand gesture. "That thing wasn't *alive*, was it?" I asked.

"Not like you and I are alive."

"So? You cannot wiggle your fingers and *magic* him back up?"

He sighed. "I see you have no understanding of how the Art works."

"I've had about five minutes of schooling," I snapped. It was true: I had no real family, not since I was small, and though I liked to read, every well-meaning attempt to put me in a schoolroom unfailingly ended once the Good Samaritan in question realized there was no keeping me from escaping formal education. "Somehow the nuances of magic weren't part of it."

The magus did not respond. He stared at me, calm and assessing, as though he were deciding what slimy creature he should snap his fingers to turn me into.

"Why would you even have a coachman? I've never seen a magus with a coachman. Or horses." You could tell a magus's carriage from the silent eerie way it travelled: unmanned, horseless, but lurching along with its wheels clacking and turning all the same.

The magus shrugged. "I've never seen a *betyár* with patches on his coat and holes in his trousers."

I ignored that. Jóska and I had once dressed in finery, since people had romantic notions of what *betyárok* should look like, but hunger had a way of making you not care about your threadbare clothes. "You can't fault me for attempting to rob you," I said. "It wouldn't be *fair*. I couldn't have known you were a magus."

"We live in unfair times," the magus said. His accent was from somewhere east of my own: the Carpathians, perhaps, or Transylvania. His voice dropped low. "You see, good *betyár*, I do not want *anyone* on the road to know what I am."

"I wouldn't—"

Before I could finish my sentence, the magus growled out more words I didn't know and held out both palms. Blue light, dark like the mist around me, arced from the magus's fingers and knocked me down. I howled, and tried to gain purchase on the ground, but the magic banded around my limbs and wrenched them back forcefully, as though an invisible strongman had pinned me. Trussed like a chicken, I craned my neck to look up. The magus loomed over me, the edge of his cloak tickling my cheek, his hands hidden in clouds of smoke, and the first thing I thought was *If I hadn't seen that damnable lantern, I'd be having beef and pálinka right now.*

The second thing was in Jóska's voice. *László, I should have made your pig my apprentice and made bacon of you. Listen: your pistols, your dagger, those are your weapons, but your words are your armour. Jóska Bajusz, you could sell a fur pelt to a fox: that's what the Countess Almásy told me of my charm. That's what you must do, if ever you cannot use your weapons. Use your armour. Sell a fur pelt to a fox.*

"Whatever you're doing, you're going about it wrong," I rasped.

If the magus heard, he did not show it. He lowered his hands, and an incredible pain shot through me, hot like fiery coals. From what I could see, my arms and legs appeared normal, but felt like they had been set afire. My chest burned, and I choked and sputtered before I managed to grind out, "I can tell you were in the war."

That did stop the magus. He balled his hands into fists. "And?"

Relieved, I took a gasping gulp of air, cold and sweet. "That leg of yours has to have been crippled by magic. Otherwise you could heal it, no? I would wager it was some Russian magus," I said, and again I remembered Jóska breathing his last. "Efficient, those Russian magi were, rows on rows of them casting God-knows-what at us in perfect time. It's a pity ours weren't so well-marshalled."

"*Betyár*, insulting me will not help you—"

"You thought I might be Austrian, and you were disappointed when I turned out not to be. You're travelling with the trappings of a wealthy man. You've a war wound. You're up to something – and I tell you, *magus*, you're going about it wrong."

The magus pursed his lips. He slashed one arm down. I flipped over, my limbs still bent and rigid beneath me. Snow seeped through my trousers and the skin of my ungloved hands, but, after the heat of the magus's spell, I welcomed it.

"My leg was hit at Segesvár," the magus said. "Scores of my brethren were killed, scores more wounded to the point where their magic was lost to them, and I was left with *this.*" He glared at his bad leg with disgust, as though he wanted nothing more than to hack the thing off.

"I fought at Segesvár, too."

He met my eyes and snorted. "Is this where we embrace like old friends and go find some ale and regale one another with stories of our battles and sing songs of mother Hungary?"

"...Yes?" I said hopefully.

He raised an eyebrow, a touch peevishly. "I thought *betyárok* were meant to be clever."

"You can think me an idiot if you like, magus, but if it's Austrians you want to fall for your phony rich man's carriage, it's not men like what you're pretending to be that the *Austrians* want. I suspect you're out here, hiding who you truly are, because you're scheming some revenge on them." The east, where the magus's accent marked him as from, had borne the worst of the revolution. "Did they turn your home into a battlefield?"

The magus was silent.

I nodded at his carriage. "A fine carriage like that, a coachman, a pair of horses – to me, that says *here's a good law-abiding fellow who'll accept any king who rules him so long as his taxes don't go up*. For the most part, the Habsburg men aren't out here bothering noblemen. They're not the men an Austrian soldier would want to apprehend."

The magus paused, his mouth still pressed into a thin frown. "And what man *would* he want to apprehend?"

Yes, I thought. I had him. *I may taste that pálinka yet.* "Men like me. Former soldiers, rebels, *betyárok.* All the vermin that has to be hunted after a war." The magus was listening. I could tell by the way his magic seemed to drain from me, slowly, as his concentration shifted to my words. "Why, not a month ago the *betyár* Józef Szarka was arrested for making a toast to the thirteen martyrs of Arad in a public house," I continued. "And Artúr Marek was found outside Tata with his throat slashed." (Both Józef and Artúr were men Jóska had always dismissed as puffed-up peacock fools, not true *betyárok*, but he would not have minded me invoking their names in the service of persuasion.) "I had a – a friend who died at Segesvár. He always had the same advice regarding Austrians."

"Oh?"

"If you rob an Austrian, take everything."

The magus smiled, faint but satisfied. "You are offering to show me how to play the *betyár*," he concluded.

"Better than letting you kill me." My arms and legs were coming back to me, but I remained still, not wanting him to notice. "But there would be no *play* about it. You learn to rob the roads, you learn to do it for real." The idea of it was beginning to appeal to me. *Imagine the robberies you could pull off with a magus.*

He looked at me thoughtfully. "What's your name?"

"László Sovány."

"I haven't heard of you."

Listen, Jóska's voice reminded me, *it is a fine thing to have legends told of you, but remember you cannot eat a legend, nor spend it, nor sleep beside it for warmth in winter.* "Nor should you have," I said testily. "I imagine you've only heard of *betyárok* who are fools. It's no time to go around proclaiming yourself to be a *betyár*, not unless you want a swift death."

The magus nodded. "It's a generous offer you make, László Sovány."

"I'm a generous man."

"But I would rather remain on my own."

The magus raised his hands again, and that horrible blue smoke rose, but this time I was ready for him. I rolled and kicked out wildly, aiming for his crippled leg. I knew I'd hit my mark when the magus screamed and collapsed beside me; it was as though I had knocked one leg from a rickety stool.

The magus's hands went to his injured leg. I got to my knees and scrambled for my dagger. As the magus tried to pick himself up, I lunged forward and sliced along the back of his right wrist. I had cut him only lightly, but a runnel of blood dripped beneath the blade and onto the magus's cloak. "I'll give you a severed hand to match that lame leg if you don't stop trying to kill me," I said, through gritted teeth.

He winced, but then he laughed. "Old man, you're not as useless as I thought."

"*Old man*," I repeated, incredulous. I was thirty-three, not *seventy*. "Just because you're not even old enough to grow a beard—" I pressed the dagger down a little more. "You try to cast something and I start *sawing*."

"Peace, László," the magus said, his eyes fixed on his pinned hand. His words were even, but the look in his eyes was that of a frightened animal. "Let me go. I'll not hurt you. I promise." He held up his free hand in a gesture of supplication: something you would do if you wanted to show you were unarmed, but no comfort from a magus whose hands *were* his weapons.

I held the dagger in place. "Swear it on your mother's sweet soul."

He blanched at that, though it might have been from blood loss. But, from his look, I would have bet my last coin (and I did only have one) that his mother was dead, and his father, too. He had a loneliness about him that I recognized: a hollow, worn, burnt-out look that you don't see in people who still have homes and families. "Swear it, magus," I said.

"Very well," he said, sounding almost petulant. "On my mother's soul, I swear that if you now remove your dagger from my hand, and if you do not try to attack me or rob me further, I will use no magic on you."

I had hoped he wouldn't remember to put that bit in about me not robbing him, but I couldn't be picky. "Swear, too, that you will not *harm* me. I don't want you taking a swing at me, magic or not."

"And I will not harm you."

"Good," I said. I withdrew the dagger and instead held out my hand. He looked at it suspiciously, then shook it. To my astonishment, a ribbon of orange light circled our handshake, first cauterizing his cut wrist, then streaming over our fingers. It didn't hurt. Unlike the other magic I had experienced, this magic was warm and cozy, like a good wool mitten. *Binding the magus's word*, I realized.

I could tell the magus was irritated from how he yanked his hand away as soon as the spell released him. I stood up, but he struggled with his bad leg. After a moment, I sighed and held out my hand to help him up.

Just what Jóska did, I remembered. I had been on the way to Pest-Buda with a sow from a hog farmer who had hired me to bring it to market. Jóska had burst out with a pistol and demanded the pig. Jóska had not expected a skinny fourteen-year-old boy to strike back, but I had grown up stupid and feral, without learning much in the way of common sense. To me, fighting a *betyár*, even an armed one, had been preferable to a whipping from the hog farmer. We had fought until we were both as filthy as the pig. I even bit Jóska on his big hairy forearm. And, in the end, he had laughingly helped me up from the mud and told me I had the heart of a *betyár*. (The sow, rest its fat delicious soul, became our supper.)

Grudgingly, the magus took my hand, and I hauled him up. "Why are you smiling?" he asked me, as he inspected his crippled leg.

"I'm not dead, and I'm smarter than you," I said. "Fine reasons to smile, both." At his surly expression, I grinned wider. "You haven't given me your name, magus."

He drew his cloak around himself and stood a bit taller. "Krisztián."

"Truly? *Christian*, that means," I said, as I retrieved my pistols. "Are not all magi godless heathens?"

"Indeed we are, but my mother liked the name."

"Well, far be it from me to speak ill of a woman who produced a specimen so fine as yourself."

Krisztián's face was easy to read: he very much regretted his vow not to harm me. He pulled his hood up to cover his hair and hobbled toward the carriage. I cannot say what made me do what I did next. Perhaps I felt sorry for Krisztián, with that pathetic limp of his. Perhaps I was enamoured with the idea of having a magus's powers with me, of having my targets stunned with magic as I went through their belongings. Perhaps, deep down, I shared Krisztián's apparent desire to take revenge for the war. Perhaps it was simple: it was cold and late and I was weary and I missed Jóska. "Krisztián?" I called.

He turned.

"My offer stands, if you still want me to teach you how to rob the roads."

I could not see his reaction, not with that hood, but he asked, "There would be Austrians?"

I thought of all the treasures Jóska and I had collected, and all the ransacked places I had found when I had returned from the war alone. "There would be," I confirmed. "And it would be a shame, with your spells and my skills, if we didn't relieve them of their possessions, not when most of them have stolen from good honest Hungarians."

Even through the snow, I could see the gleam of Krisztián's smile. When, at last, he spoke, there was a bright note in his voice. "All right," he said. "I shall try it. But if I do not like learning to be a *betyár*, I will leave."

"Oh, you'll love it," I said cheerfully. "Guns, riches, soft swooning women. Now, can we *please* use your carriage to reach Győr? My clothes are soaked, thanks to you, and I long for a drink."

"No," Krisztián said.

"No?"

He looked glumly at the coachman's clothes. "The spell in that coachman was what held everything together. That's why I was furious. You destroyed *weeks* of complicated work with a single pull of a pistol's trigger. I cannot merely wave my hands and enchant the carriage anew."

"The horses?" *Please*, I thought.

Krisztián snapped his fingers. The beautiful chestnut Percherons vanished.

"What in *the*—"

"Those horses were not real, old man," Krisztián explained. "The carriage is, but now we have no way to move it. We shall have to walk."

I must have looked rather chagrined at the word *walk* because Krisztián sighed, muttered more strange words, and made a broad looping motion with one arm. This spell was yellow, the rich golden yellow of honey. Once it left Krisztián's fingers it broke apart and fell all about us like hundreds of humming fireflies.

But I felt nothing. "What is this?" I asked.

Krisztián frowned. "It's protection against the cold," he said. "I can feel it. It should warm you, like you're sitting before a hearth." He raised his hand to try again, but before he cast the spell, he began to laugh.

"What?"

"*I will use no magic on you.*"

"Obviously, I don't mind when it is *good* magic."

"No, that's what you had me swear. I cannot use magic on you, for good or ill."

"Oh – oh, *shit*. You *fucking* ass."

"It's not my fault, László," Krisztián said innocently. "You made me swear on my mother's sweet soul."

"Let's go," I growled. I turned away from the carriage and stomped up the road, my saturated boots squelching on the ground.

"*I'm* quite warm," he added, still snickering.

"Please be quiet."

We walked in silence for a stretch. The night was still snowy, still dark, and I still had a long way to Győr with only half a forint in my coin purse, but, even with my body aching from residual magic and my clothes sodden and ruined, I felt lighter. I had known the road a long time, the road Jóska and I had lived on: the pine smell of the trees, the scattered stars, the curves of every well-worn rut. There was something restful in that road when it was not walked alone.

Then Krisztián said, "László." For the first time, he sounded as young as he looked. "The rumours of *betyárok*, it is often said…" He hesitated.

"Hm?" I prodded.

"Well, you mentioned *women*. It is often said that a *betyár* has great luck with women."

I had to stop and hold my sides and gasp for breath, so hard did I laugh. It felt good, after he had laughed at me. "Now I see! That's why you're coming with me. Vengeance, yes, patriotism for mother Hungary, certainly, but there's no compromise to those if you happen to tumble a few lovely ladies along the way—"

“Never mind,” he interrupted.

“Ah, Krisztián, not to worry,” I said, coughing to hide a chuckle. “About women – well, let me tell you a story. Once I charged before a carriage, a beautiful one, all white, and who should be inside but the Countess Almásy…”

THE WHITE ROSE THIEF

Shawn Speakman

THE FINAL NOTE of the *crwth* died in silence followed by raucous applause.

Rosenwyn Whyte lowered the stringed instrument and its bow, inclining her head in polite recognition. The audience cheered all the more. She sat upon a slightly elevated stage at the Raging Drunk, the largest inn and tavern in Annwn's northern city of Mur Castell, no other musicians accompanying her. Although larger than most, the Raging Drunk was like many such establishments she often played—smoky, loud, and the odor of crowded, unwashed humanity mingling with beer grown long sour. It attracted patrons from all castes, from the wealthy sitting in the upper balconies to the vagabonds who had managed to escape the notice of burly Byl Cornwyll, the owner. The Everwinter drove all of them inside, its snow and ice an indiscriminate hardship for all, while music and drunken fellowship offered the only solace.

The unnaturally long winter had been good to Rosenwyn though.

Illustration by ORION ZANGARA ▸

Music helped people forget the terrible season, and music was her trade. This night, the crowd had been large. Money emptied from pockets to fill flagons with beer.

Not that Rosenwyn saw much of either.

"Yeh were a might amazin' again, Rosie," Byl Cornwyll said, having pushed his way from behind the bar through the crowd to tower over her.

"A great room, Byl, as usual."

The owner of the Raging Drunk grinned, wringing his large hands on a damp bar towel that hung at his waist. A nervous habit that made her smile. "That was one helluva rendition of *The Ballad of Gor Dwallyn*. Never heard its like sung. Found damnable tears in me eyes, ah did. Had to turn away."

"You are too big a man to cry, Byl," Rosenwyn said, smiling, tucking the crwth safely away within a padded carrying pouch.

"And yeh are too beautiful to play in holes like this," the other said, winking. "Do yeh have plans for tomorrow night? Another go? If these people do not see me ask, they will burn the Drunk down, ah swear."

"I will let you know later tonight," she said, massaging the stress from her hands.

"Yeh know where ah'll be."

Rosenwyn nodded her thanks. Byl made his way back behind the bar. He would pay her when most had left the common room—and beg her to stay one more night. She might accept. The Raging Drunk was one of her favorite places to play in all of Annwn. And Byl paid her better than most innkeepers, which meant she received more than just food and lodging. But not much more.

"You play with magic, love."

Still gathering her things, Rosenwyn turned. A man stared at her with piercing blue eyes, as bold as any hunter's. He was younger than her but that would not matter in his mind. She cursed inwardly. These were the moments she hated.

"It is a gift," she said simply. "And I work hard to improve upon it. Thank you for coming to the Raging Drunk. It helps keep me playing here."

"I am Aron McManus. May I buy you a beer?" he asked. "Better yet, a meal?"

There it was. Men could be so transparent sometimes. He prized her more for her status and appearance than the woman behind the music.

"If there is one thing I already get paid in, it's the necessities of life," Rosenwyn said, smiling her best to defuse the forthcoming situation. "And besides that, I see you coming from a town away, sir. Better for you to find another woman to entertain."

His smile became uncertain. "If I gave you the wrong impression, I apologize. You play lovely music but it pales to your beauty. One drink. That is all."

"Flattery will get you nowhere this night."

McManus darkened. "I think you misunderst—"

"Lady Rosenwyn Whyte!"

Both Rosenwyn and her suitor cringed as a fairy flew into their midst, its rainbow-hued gossamer wings a blur. The fey creature was no more than a hand tall, his naked body the color of damp ash. Rosenwyn did not care much for the fey. But she was pleased this one had interrupted a conversation that was about to become ugly.

Rather than talk to her though, the fairy hovered before the man and gave him a knowing grin that held no humor.

"*Crotchlove*, leave before this becomes painful for you," the fairy said.

"Fairy, should I squish you right now?" he asked.

"I will only say it once."

McManus turned crimson. "Look here, you little snit, no one tells me wha—"

"I know why you stand here still," the fey creature said, his tiny black eyes now appraising Rosenwyn. "Her hair, red as flame, a powerful shade to possess. The alabaster skin, as if it has never seen the tarnishing effects of sunlight. The blue eyes, so deep one could drown in them. That tiny mole by her sensuous lips. The sharp cheekbones and lithe figure. A worthy prize to lust after." The fey creature magically called forth a tiny sword that flared briefly and returned his gaze back to the man. "But if you do not leave us to our business, *whelp*, I will start with your sight. Test me, and you will never view another beautiful woman again."

The words held impatience. And certainty. The suitor glared, assessing his small foe; with the sword, the lightning-fast creature could be quite dangerous.

The man knew this. Rosenwyn hid her smile as she watched McManus' bravado diminish. "I beg your forgiveness, Lady Whyte," he said finally and, giving the fairy an angry last look, vanished into the crowd.

"Not that red is your natural hair color, of course," the fairy continued, his sword suddenly evaporating into nothing. "White, isn't it? Not that I care how adept you are at disguise. I rather like the red. Fiery."

Rosenwyn frowned, chill prickling her skin. "Who are you?"

"One who was sent to find you."

The chill became ice in her veins, her anger rising. "Who do you serve? That sword of yours might scare randy buggers looking for a toss in the sheets but it does not frighten me."

"If it did, my benefactor would be greatly unimpressed by your fabled prowess."

"Play your game," Rosenwyn said, grabbing her instrument and deciding another night at the Raging Drunk was not in the cards. "I have my own. And they will not be dictated by the likes of the fey."

"A redhead's birthright. The game is about to get more interesting," the fairy said, blocking her path by flying in front of her to bow in midair. "I am Bazltrix. And I am here on the behalf of Lady Audeph Klestmark of Mur Castell, a woman in need of your help and great many talents."

"Never heard of her."

"She knows of you. *That* is what matters."

Rosenwyn hated being at a disadvantage. It was a part of her life though. Playing in taverns, surrounded by unknown people. Most of them simply enjoyed her music. Some had ulterior motives though. Bazltrix had scared off one such person but the man's motives had been easy to decipher. The motives of the fairy and his benefactor were not.

"What does she want of me?" Rosenwyn asked.

"That is for Lady Klestmark to share."

Rosenwyn appraised Bazltrix a moment. "Where is she then?"

"Outside," the fairy said, his charcoal face pinched with the gravity of his request. "Anonymity is a requirement. The Everwinter offers it best."

The tiny hairs along the back of her neck prickled warning. The area where the Raging Drunk conducted business was one of the safest districts in Mur Castell. Annwn had become more chaotic after the fall of Caer Llion though. Evil existed everywhere.

"To be alone on the streets of Mur Castell at night with an unknown woman and her fairy is not wise, I am afraid," Rosenwyn growled, already weaving her way past the flying creature. "I think your benefactor will have to find aid elsewhere."

"Lady Klestmark anticipated this," Bazltrix said, flying after. He removed something from a small cloth sack on his back. He then offered the item to her.

Curiosity trumping uneasiness, Rosenwyn accepted the item. She immediately wished she hadn't; a dark rage filled her as she held a small diamond spider, no larger than her thumbnail. It caught the candle and torchlight and glowed like the summer sun. It was a beautiful piece of art, symmetrical and flawless. There were only three in existence. And it was worth a fortune to the right people.

Its monetary worth did not matter to Rosenwyn, though. She gripped the spider, its legs cutting into her palm. The present world faded around her until all she could see was a past she had tried to escape, tried to forget.

This had once been her sigil. The Lleidr Corryn.

The calling token for a master thief.

"Unfortunately, someone else is not an option," Bazltrix sniffed with indignation. "I trust you are ready to go now?"

Rosenwyn cursed her luck.

THE EVERWINTER SWIRLED about her as she left the Raging Drunk.

After having donned her fur-lined sable cloak and boots, Rosenwyn followed the fairy as he flew through the streets of Mur Castell. She pulled her cloak and its cowl close for warmth, the crwth on her back comforting as well. She had spoken to Byl briefly, sharing she would be leaving the inn for a while, telling him only what he needed to know. He had nodded, worry darkening his thick features as he frowned at the fairy, but he did not ask questions. She knew Byl well. He would undoubtedly send one of his kitchen boys to follow and watch from the shadows—a modicum of security.

Despite his nakedness, Bazltrix flew through the Everwinter seemingly unbothered by the elements, a silent black form in a world become white. She did not know what to expect from the forthcoming meeting. Her past had found her, one way or another, and there was no escaping it. Not from someone who possessed the Lleidr Corryn. Right now, even as she walked through the chill, there could be a hundred crossbow bolts pointed at her. Or none. One never knew. That's how these kinds of transactions happened. The life she had left behind long before the Everwinter began had been one of high reward with high risk. On reflection, it should have led to her death many times. Back then, of course, that thought had never crossed her mind. She had been young and impulsive, fearless and naïve.

She was older and more cautious now. She had left that life for one of music. Old memories were kept where they belonged—in the past. She had changed.

Fingering a dagger in her cloak's inner pocket with one hand and wearing a knife-ring on the other, Rosenwyn felt a stab of irony twisting inside her.

Some things never changed, it seemed.

At least there was no moon or stars this night to worry about.

"Where are you taking me?" she asked darkly. "I thought you said she was just outside."

The fairy either did not hear or was ignoring her.

She kept her frustration in check; it would not serve her this night. They eventually entered the primary courtyard of the city, so large she could barely see the other side. In summer, a market blossomed here, filled with colorful tents bearing produce, clothing, weapons, sweets, games, and other bazaar items. It was now a gray void. Directly across from her rose the ruling castle of Mur Castell, its walls tall, thick, and coated in ice and snow, torchlight flickering from various places giving just enough light to see by. Rosenwyn kept a keen eye on the fairy as he flew directly toward a massive stake that had been driven into the courtyard's stone. There, a figure stood, waiting.

Rosenwyn considered the situation. She didn't like it. The courtyard of Mur Castell had become a place of death. Earlier in the year, Caderyn Llewellyn, the lord of the great city, had burned a witch to death at the stake, retribution for the murder of his wife. The city had watched. Rosenwyn had not seen it, but she knew the tales and they chilled her. The fire. The screaming for mercy. The stench.

Its length charred, the giant stake remained as a gruesome warning: *Do not attack the royal family of Mur Castell.*

While no one else appeared, it was an unsettling place for a meeting. And even as Bazltrix landed on the charred pole, a black stain amidst the Everwinter, the hooded figure by the stake did not move to meet her.

"Well met, Rosenwyn White," the woman said as the musician approached. "I am Lady Audeph Klestmark. I have to say, I am impressed. I could not hear you approach despite the snow and ice, your footfalls were so light."

"My craft often requires steady hands and steadier feet."

"And what craft is that exactly?" the lady asked with a hint of dark amusement. "A musician? Or a thief *unfettered?* No, do not answer. It matters not. I do, however, thank you for responding to my request."

"It felt like more a summons. One I could not deny," Rosenwyn said, fingering her hidden knife. "But you know that already."

"The diamond spider *does* possess that power."

Rosenwyn nodded, observing the other. There was not much to see. Like the musician, Lady Audeph Klestmark wore a cloak and hood, a tall, thin figure, cut like a dark blade. What light existed emphasized round eyes above sharp cheekbones, full lips, and a hint of black hair curled beneath her cowl.

"I am no longer a Lleidr Corryn," Rosenwyn asserted. "She was a master thief. And died long ago."

"You have many gifts, Lady Whyte, but playing coy in an attempt to deceive me is not one of them," the lady said coldly. "Do *not* be any more foolish than you have just been, *Spider Thief*."

Rosenwyn had once been a favorite tool and done the bidding of many wealthy patrons, from lords and kings to merchant princes and their wives. No matter her outward appearance, Lady Audeph Klestmark was not one of them. They possessed a languid, indifferent air. The woman standing before her emanated an icy righteousness and a willingness to risk everything. Lady Klestmark would do anything to possess the thief's talents—as evidenced by the Lleidr Corryn. If the thief denied her, the woman would have her killed. Outright. Likely this night. And if not tonight, there were two men who would love to know Rosenwyn's location and they would finish the deed. Chill not born of the Everwinter infiltrated her. Despite her youthful appearance, the woman's shadowy gaze possessed a hatred so potent it could never be refused, especially not by a mere thief, retired or no.

For the first time in many years, fear gripped Rosenwyn Whyte. Real fear, as bone deep as the Everwinter itself.

"The Spider Thief lives, yes. I hate that she does."

"A first for everything, I fear, my dear," Lady Klestmark said with a small laugh, the threat behind her gaze gone as quickly as it had come. "You are also the Unseen Hand. The White Shadow. The Caer Ghost. Several other colorful names you have undoubtedly heard. The rich and powerful in all cities have different names for you. You are a legend, albeit a dubious one cursed aloud in private chambers or uttered in dark whispers upon the wind. And I have need of your legendary talents. I will pay handsomely for them, regardless of the token I possess."

"That part of my life is *over*," Rosenwyn said.

"The past." Lady Klestmark scoffed. "The past is always a part of our present, Lady Whyte. Do not be so quick to dismiss that fact."

"What does this have to do with?" Rosenwyn, steeled by anger again, tried to maintain some kind of control over the situation, but she knew what would happen if she refused the offer.

"As I said, I need your talents."

"For?"

"Finally we are getting somewhere useful," Lady Klestmark said. "A bit of background first though. The story of Saith yn Col. Once, the ruins were not ruined, rather a castle and keep called Caer Dathal where the first Druid Order built their home upon arriving in Annwn from those long-lost Misty Isles. The Druids worked hard at acquiring knowledge of all kinds. And people benefited from that. But when a dark faction overtook the order and tried to enslave Annwn, the most powerful fey of the Tuatha de Dannan gathered and destroyed that menace. The rebel Druids were killed. Caer Dathal of Old was destroyed in those battles, renamed Saith yn Col. It has remained that way since, a reminder of the danger excess power creates.

"The Druids who did not join the rebels were free to begin their order again, this time at Caer Dathal the New, where they live to this day."

"Then you want me to break into Caer Dathal and steal something that has been kept there from the days since it moved?"

"No." Lady Klestmark smirked. "I want something from Saith yn Col."

"I am a thief, not a ruins digger." Rosenwyn hated to admit still being a thief.

"Do you think for one moment I would need to acquire your services if I could just visit the ruins of Saith yn Col myself and take what I desire?" Lady Klestmark said, laughing without humor. "Maybe you are not as bright as I have been led to believe."

Rosenwyn hated being mocked even more.

"Have you played your music at Caer Dathal?" Lady Klestmark asked.

"Several times." Rosenwyn's breath plumed on the air. "It is a beautiful keep. Arch Druid Aengus Doughal is always warm and welcoming. So too his Druids and students."

"You know of the grotesques that ward that keep then?"

"The gargoyles? Yes," Rosenwyn said. "They sit about the keep. I have never seen one move though. Probably just mummery, to scare visitors."

"Oh, they are more than alive, my dear. Caer Dathal of Old had similar magical creatures protecting its walls. They could not withstand the might of the Erlking and Tal Ebolyon's dragon might. The grotesques were destroyed like their rebel Druid masters, reduced to broken statuary and dust. All but one." The lady paused. "One grotesque survived, the strongest among them, and this stone creature has been there ever since, within the ruins of a keep he could not protect."

"I am to steal something from this gargoyle then?"

"He is named the Nix, a terrible creature, powerful and ancient." Lady Klestmark's gaze intensified. "It should have perished as the rest of his brethren. Caer Dathal of Old is destroyed; there is no need to protect Saith yn Col. Yet the Nix remains. He does not possess the power to leave his ruins, magic binding him to the former Druid keep. But I believe he is gathering more than just secrets from that age."

"If the Nix cannot roam free, how does he gather anything?" Rosenwyn disliked the fact she was already intrigued.

"No one knows. Perhaps a thief in his employ. Or a magic unfamiliar to me. Regardless, this task I ask of you will be dangerous for numerous reasons."

"I have heard those words before. All too often."

"Little is known about the ruins beneath Saith yn Col," Lady Klestmark said. "It will be fraught with peril. Less is known about where the Nix holds his treasures. It will be dangerous, even for one of the Lleidr Corryn."

"My price is steep then, perhaps too steep for one such as yourself." Rosenwyn stood straighter, showing her resolve. "You possess the Lleidr Corryn and you have a certain amount of power over me because of it, but no power over my price, which I and I alone set."

"Hear that, Bazltrix? She knows her worth." An icy smile crossed Lady Klestmark's pale features. The fairy nodded, barely interested, even as the woman removed a glove to reveal rings adorning every finger. "You are right, Lady Whyte. Jewels. Precious metals. Like these. These would be poor attempts at acquiring your talents. I wonder though, looking at you, knowing something of your past, if you would rather gain the ability to walk in the light—sunlight, moonlight, starlight—without others staring at you, hating you, or questioning you? Would that be an adequate payment for your services?" She paused. "What is the *price* for being human?"

Rosenwyn barely breathed. Lady Klestmark knew of her bane, the very thing that shackled her to the shadows. If she completed the charge, the reward would be a chance at something she had wanted since childhood.

A normal life.

"That is impossible," she whispered.

"Is it?" Lady Klestmark asked, just as serious. "Even Bazltrix does not know the full extent of my standing. With wealth comes power and with power comes opportunity. I know people. More importantly, I know the *right* people. There are those in my employ who possess magic. A great deal of magic." She smiled. "How ironic. The music you have replaced your former life with might be the very talent that undoes that past."

"Why would you say that?"

"Because grotesques are fond of music."

Rosenwyn now knew why she had been chosen. She had once been a master thief, true, but she was also a musician. The other two Lleidr Corryn were not.

It made sense.

Long moments passed.

"Not that I am accepting—because there *will* come a time when my death is more desirable than a job I am to take—but what am I to steal?"

Lady Audeph Klestmark smiled. Both women knew she had won her thief.

"The Grimoires of the rebel Druids, Lady Lleidr Corryn."

LOST IN THOUGHT, Rosenwyn ignored the Everwinter chill.

She rode Wennyl eastward out of Mur Castell, cloaked in a black as dark as the Rhedewyr she sat upon. Wennyl had been the price of one of her first heists, a miraculous animal that had become her best friend, strong in ways normal horses were not, aware of her every mood and circumstance. Rhedewyr were difficult for humans to come by; if one lost its first rider to death, the horse usually died from sorrow. Some did not though. Rosenwyn and Wennyl had bonded upon meeting and they had been together ever since. The fey mount had carried her over much of Annwn, seen her through the most difficult thefts, and now the stallion moved through the snows toward the ruins of Saith yn Col, the elements barely a hindrance.

As Mur Castell faded behind her, she embraced the solitude of the peaceful road, senses always attuned to possible danger.

And thought about Lady Klestmark's offer.

From her earliest memories, Rosenwyn had been a thief. She did not understand the moral implications of such a life. Few four year olds needed to. She had learned them from the hardest of lives, to survive the river city streets of Velen Rhyd, to eat when others would starve. She rarely thought about her painful childhood—one spent stealing while evading the Red Crosses even as she outwitted older bullies and those who would try to exploit her abilities. But being summoned by the Lleidr Corryn token brought those memories to the fore, like angry slivers buried deep beneath her skin. Velen Rhyd was a threadbare city, barely able to sustain even its poor and, having lost her parents and older siblings to fire, she alone had survived. She hid the secret of her magic even then despite the fearful whispers on the streets. Halfbreed. Fey.

More witch than little girl.

No one back then knew her an actual secret. But children can sense truth without actually witnessing it. There was a reason she only ventured out at night. There was a reason she kept her skin covered. Her family had known. The night had replaced the family she had lost, become her first friend, camouflaging her unpredictable magic.

As she grew so did her thieving abilities, not because of the blood that flowed through her veins but because stealing ensured survival.

It did not take long for her to come to the attention of Vrace Erryn. Young but already accomplished, he had trained Rosenwyn, shaping her like a master artist does a sculpture. Together, they had stolen from the capital of Caer Llion. Together, they had cheated Magwyn Mog within his spell-protected wizard warren. Together, they had taken a rare dragon egg from Tal Ebolyon just to watch it hatch.

And together they had become Lleidr Corryn.

Until the day Vrace broke her heart. Had tried to kill her. And she vanished from the game, beginning a new life as a wandering musician.

As far as she knew, Vrace and the older Rol Macleod remained in their trade. She had thought herself safe, far enough removed from that former life to escape notice from everyone, including the death the two men owed her for breaking the Lleidr Corryn vow.

Lady Audeph Klestmark had proven that thought wrong.

If she could find her, who else could?

Wennyl snorted, a ghost plume dying on the air.

"I know, boy." Rosenwyn patted the stallion's great neck, her annoyance matching his. "We will disappear again soon. I promise."

The path continued, the Everwinter a constant companion. The snow had stopped. No stars appeared, leaving Rosenwyn thankful. They possessed a light, no matter how faint, that brought the magic in her blood to life. Even though all parts of her skin were covered—including her eyes by darkglass goggles and a veil over her mouth—she had to be vigilant. It was a danger she lived with every day.

To be free of that curse would be worth one more theft.

If she survived.

As midnight came and went, the two companions came to a stone marker set along the road where another, smaller path intersected it, the marker's worn face covered in ice and snow.

Rosenwyn dismounted. She struck a match into life.

She could just make out the age-worn words chiseled on the stone sign.

ROSENWYN GRUNTED. THAT castle keep no longer existed. At least not in this part of the world. It had become Saith yn Col, home to one lone stubborn piece of rock.

"Easy part over," she said sarcastically.

Wennyl snorted and she remounted. They left the road for the smaller path, the forest closing in on them as if to strangle their passage. Rosenwyn ignored the feeling; unlike many thieves, she was not superstitious. The great oaks that suffocated the trail grew wilder the deeper they traveled, until frozen limbs threatened to unseat her. She dismounted then, sending her senses into the Everwinter around her, abilities honed to feel danger no matter its quarter. Nothing presented itself; no sound betrayed otherwise. With Wennyl quietly behind, Rosenwyn crossed over icy streams, the trail shrinking as it winded over small hills, until the ground flattened and the great oaks began to thin, the musician become thief-once-again finally viewing beyond her immediate vicinity.

She almost could not comprehend what she saw. Saith yn Col laid before her, the remnants of Caer Dathal of Old spreading into the distance. She gauged the situation from the forest. It did not look promising. The ruins were a black mess, the height of dead stone heaving out of the world making it difficult to measure the breadth of it all. She could imagine Caer Dathal then, the grand towers and buildings that had once filled the sky, the bustling, lively community, and pennants flying in the wind—all brought low by a battle waged centuries earlier. It spoke to the might of the Unseelie Court and the dragons of Tal Ebolyon. Many people had died, their remains crushed beneath. Caer Dathal of Old was no longer a place of learning; it had become a graveyard of stone and buried bone, a place where death had taken up ancient residence.

Only one tower remained, once probably the shortest. It had outlived its brethren, tall compared to the thief, its merlons ripped free but otherwise intact.

Rosenwyn took a deep breath, cursing Audeph Klestmark all the more. She moved Wennyl back into the forest, out of sight for anyone—or any gargoyle—that did not know of the fey horse's presence.

"Wish me speed and silence, old friend."

Wennyl stared back at her, his awareness mixed with fire.

She rubbed his nose, already looking back toward Saith yn Col. With footfalls light upon the frozen snow, she moved with soundless purpose. The last hours of night were upon her world, a clock ticking against her magical ailment, and while she shielded herself from the light it would not do well to linger, being exposed to the very thing that could alarm the gargoyle if her clothing and goggles failed. She strode the perimeter, not venturing into the ruins. Yet. If Audeph Klestmark was to be believed, gargoyles were perceptive creatures and the thief's continued anonymity would serve her best.

She crept into Saith yn Col as a ghost, ferreting its secrets. It had been many years since her last theft, but she found her skills right where she had left them, all too eager to be used.

It left her even more annoyed

The past remained, no matter her attempts to discard it.

Finishing her initial appraisal of Saith yn Col and not finding anything, Rosenwyn entered the short tower, grappling to its exposed top and dropping inside on cat's feet. But the structure had long been a dead shell, possessing nothing of interest. No treasure trove. And thankfully no grotesque. She then silently scaled the mounds of broken walls and buildings, searching outward from the center of Caer Dathal of Old in concentric circles, looking for any entrances into the rubble. That too yielded no results. She cursed silently. Saith yn Col was as unlike any situation she had entered. In that past, having accepted a job, she had always prepared, learning all she could. Surprises could get one killed all too easily and knowledge could be the key to living another day. But the destruction here wrought centuries earlier had left Caer Dathal of Old a formidable riddle, with none of the entrances and exits of her previous thieving forays had possessed.

Hating to admit defeat and her chance at a normal life, she leaned against a broken wall of the inner keep, considering her lack of options.

That's when her instincts tingled.

A lesser thief might have ignored them. Rosenwyn cocked her head, listening to an odd deadness on the air. Trusting those instincts, she shrunk down and moved over the ruins, quietly searching. It did not take her long to find an intact wall where the rubble had been moved aside.

Another wall—once part of the keep—met it. And where they intersected, a hidden maw of blackness waited where steps vanished into the bowels of Saith yn Col.

Massive footprints. Pressed into the snow around the opening. Unlike any Rosenwyn had ever seen.

Sign of the Nix.

And this was most likely the only entrance—and therefore the only exit.

Thieves abhorred such things.

Heart quickened, Rosenwyn retreated to crouch behind stones atop the ruins a short distance away, her eyes never leaving the wide hole leading to some unknown subterranean depth. Long moments passed. They became longer. Rosenwyn still did not move, thinking. The sky to the east began to lighten as a new snow fell. The day would soon be upon her. She fought the cold that threatened without as her thoughts turned icy within. Saith yn Col was an impossible task, she realized with real regret. She knew many a foolhardy thief, but few who would risk such a passage as that yawning gap. She simply did not possess enough information to overcome the terrible odds. Undoubtedly, the Nix waited for her below. A creature created to protect, it would have installed any number of physical or magical traps to protect Caer Dathal of Old.

Worse, the gargoyle could be waiting, right where true darkness first blinds.

Able to end her life easily.

No matter how much it galled the Lleidr Corryn, the situation was beyond her.

"Enough of this," she whispered, not happy having to convince herself of the truth. She was no coward but it had to be more equal than this.

She would return to Audeph Klestmark. This job was no job.

It was suicide.

That is when she saw the glowing eyes.

Rosenwyn almost thought it a trick of her imagination. In the feeble illumination of the night, even her eyes—eyes that had become as strong as any cat's—could not decipher what stared at her. The orbs looked like tiny lamps that floated in the dark, unblinking and unwavering.

"I see you are aware of me, Woman of Many Talents," the darkness rumbled from within the entrance, the voice deep like stone grinding against stone.

Rosenwyn froze, torn between flight and intrigue.

"Standing still will not help you disappear," the darkness mocked.

"I did not think it would."

"Good. Now go. These ruins are no longer for the living."

Rosenwyn took a deep breath, bolstering her resolve. "Who do

I have the pleasure of conversing?" she asked, fighting to keep her voice free of fear.

"I was wrong, in part. A *well-spoken* Woman of Many Talents," the voice digressed. It carried authority and something else. Curiosity? "An oddity in these broken wilds, that much I know." The Nix paused. "Tell me, Woman of Many Talents, should you not leave? This is where our conversation parts."

"Why do you keep calling me that?"

The eyes shifted in their tunnel. "Beauty is truth, truth beauty – that is all ye know on earth and all ye need to know."

"I was not prepared to meet a poet."

"It is not my own. Yet I hold it close." The eyes wavered as if leaving. "Go. There are warmer climes for your frail form than these stones." She did not move, willing the other to notice. "Do you woo death?" the Nix grated finally.

There it was. The threat.

At least the gargoyle had not left.

"I will not leave," Rosenwyn said. "Not until you step free of your home and truly reveal yourself. I have come a long way for that very thing."

The Nix grunted. "Unlike you, *I* was created with patience."

The eyes vanished. Rosenwyn waited but they did not return. She wagered the Nix would not be gone long. He would reappear. Eventually. Curiosity ruled the creature. She had sensed it with every lingering sentence the gargoyle had spoken. And something else. Loneliness?

Rosenwyn slowed her adrenaline from the meeting and navigated back toward the forest. She needed to think. She had not expected to meet the Nix so quickly—especially a creature of such intelligence. It changed her approach in acquiring the grimoires she sought. Carefully exiting the ruins, she found Wennyl first, gathering a pack containing her supplies and a heavy blanket that would help ward off the chill while she built a fire. As the sky lightened in the east toward dawn, she did a quick visual of herself, ensuring no skin had become exposed during the night, and then sparked a small fire to life, its warmth chasing the cold that had followed her from Mur Castell.

The Nix did not appear throughout the day. It did not bother Rosenwyn. Thieves also possessed great patience. The gargoyle would emerge again during the day.

If he did not, she would be ready.

When night began to fall on Saith yn Col and the Nix still had not revealed himself once more, she pulled free her crwth and its bow from their case.

And closing her eyes, she began to play.

Rosenwyn chose *The Fall of Tember Tu*, the ballad describing the destruction of a mythical castle, beautiful quartz spires banded in silver brought low by the forces of dark midnight spawn. She poured all of her emotion into the epic song, building the tragedy of the city as well as the sorrow of two young lovers separated when the battle began. The Lleidr Corryn left her past behind then, a musician once more, letting her crwth and voice weave together in ways that had reduced the hardest men to tears. She bled her craft, the music infiltrating Saith yn Col. Rosenwyn felt the ghosts who now inhabited the ruins, and it made her sad that such grandeur could die in the world.

When the last note faded altogether, Rosenwyn took a deep breath and opened her eyes to the dying day.

"You are a mistress possessed of beautifully haunting music."

Suspecting her actions would bring the gargoyle, Rosenwyn feigned surprise and located him. The Nix sat regally tall on massive haunches where the forest met Saith yn Col, a stone dragon three times her height made from dark gray stone laced with tiny veins of silver. But unlike the dragons that flew over Annwn, the Nix appeared crippled, his long tail, wings, and left arm shattered, broken stone. His eyes burned bright though; no weakness stared at her. Power radiated from the ancient guardian. It remained a force to be reckoned.

A silver shield containing a single oak acorn winked from his left breast, reflecting the orange and yellow light of the fire.

"Thank you," she said simply.

The Nix looked into the branches of the frozen oaks, eyes lost to the past. "*The Fall of Tember Tu* had long been one my favorite songs. Poignant. Sorrowful. The cost of human loving in a world fractured by hatred." The gargoyle frowned. "The song took a new meaning when the stones of my home began killing those I was formed to protect. I have not heard it sung for centuries—and not as well sung. It is beautiful still but tainted with memory."

"I am sorry," Rosenwyn said. "I did not mean to cause you pain."

"The instrument you hold is also beautiful," the Nix rumbled, eyeing the crwth with interest. "I have seen its kind and yet have not."

"I have made modifications," she said. "Yes."

"You have added frets."

"Frets?" she asked, confused.

"Yes. Poet John Keats speaks of fret, I believe," the Nix said. "Fret is a word that came into existence in the Misty Isles, the world beyond this one. There are many such newly wrought words, apparently." The Nix thought on it. "The Heliwr of a century past brought me a book from his world, a book filled with poetry and song. The word 'fret' has two meanings though." The Nix gazed over the modified crwth. "I believe those raised areas along the neck of your instrument are of what he spoke."

Rosenwyn had made some changes to the design, true. As far as she knew, her crwth was one of a kind.

She found that she liked the Nix.

"I would like to hear you play again," the grotesque said. "It has been many centuries since I have heard music, longer from one so talented."

"Thank you."

"But first to serious matters," the Nix said. "Why are you here?"

The stone creature's sharp gaze daggered into her. Rosenwyn found it difficult to look away. "I am merely traveling. My grandfather would tell stories of Caer Dathal of Old's grandeur. The beauty. The prestige. The stories he told had been passed down from his fathers before him. I was hoping to view you as well as see... something... of that famous castle, to know those stories were real. You are more than I could ever have imagined."

"Stories have power." The Nix ignored her platitudes. "And shared stories grow in the telling, especially when those stories are told over centuries. Caer Dathal was beautiful, once. No longer. That beauty has vanished with time," the Nix said with a hint of anger. "And I am not a mindless beast as some of those stories make me out to be. I do not take kindly to strangers. Men and women and Seelie and Unseelie are all alike—they trespass to dig for imagined treasure or magical artifacts. I trust no one."

Rosenwyn returned her crwth and bow to their case. Pulling her cloak close, she stood much as she had against Audeph Klestmark—tall and strong. "I am not here to dig for artifacts," she said.

"My question remains unanswered with true honesty."

"There is beauty here," she said, looking toward Saith yn Col. "Even one such as you would seek it out."

The Nix squinted. "Go on."

"You are right about one thing: you are more than the stories suggest, a powerful presence amongst the bones of sorrow. And you are lonely," she said, hoping beyond hope she was correct. If she wasn't, she'd be soon dead. "Music brought you from your home, returned you to the light, my life's blood calling you from the shadows. I only wish to see your home and what remains of the beauty of Caer Dathal. If you wish to hear me play again, you will grant me this small request."

Rosenwyn had a hard time not holding her breath. If she lived. If she died. If the curse that had been upon her since she was a child could be lifted. Everything hinged on the next few moments. She had never been so reckless.

She had never so much to gain.

Eyes thoughtful, the Nix mulled it over. Rosenwyn prepared for the guardian to turn her away or, worse, kill her.

"It is a small price to pay for a song," the Nix mused.

She nodded. "True."

"I require your oath, your word, your promise, that your intent is not ill."

Rosenwyn had expected as much. "You have my oath as a musician," she promised, hating the sour taste of thief falsity on her tongue.

"What is your name, Woman of Many Talents?"

"Rosenwyn Whyte," she said. "And yours?"

The Nix bowed his head and then turned, ignoring the question. "Follow me."

He moved toward the entrance to the bowels of Saith yn Col, as silent upon the Everwinter as Rosenwyn had been. Giving Wennyl a last look, she followed. Rosenwyn marveled at the massive stone dragon, the fluidity of the rock that composed his body, the power in every silent stride. She had a hard time imagining how Caer Dathal of Old could fall with several dozen similar entities warding it. She suddenly wished she had met the Nix before the fall of the great Druid castle, unbroken by war and failure.

The grotesque did not look back to see if she followed. He simply vanished down his large staircase into darkness. Worried she would be unable to see where even the faintest light could not penetrate, she was surprised to find that every sixth stone comprising both walls and floors began to glow with a faint bluish-white light. The Nix strode in front of her, the illumination coming to life as he passed. Magic, most likely, of a kind she had only seen in the wealthiest houses. The hallway quickly opened into a grand hall, where massive pillars supported a ceiling lost to gloom. The Nix had brought her to his home, once a long banquet hall. She shivered. The ancient part of the keep had likely not been seen with human eyes for centuries.

A scent of parchment and ink mingled with the must of ages. With thief eyes, she began searching for the Grimoires of the rebel Druids. It would not be easy. Shelves as high as the ceiling stretched the length of the great room, filled with books, baubles, and items Rosenwyn had never seen before.

The grimoires were here. Somewhere.

"You need not wear the glass over your eyes, Rosenwyn Whyte," the Nix said, observing her. "You are safe from day and night's light here."

She hid her surprise. "How did you know?"

"It merely takes eyes to see."

She removed her goggles, thinking. The Nix could tell she possessed magic. He had deduced that and its trigger.

All of a sudden, she felt very transparent.

"I am Nicodemys Rothyn, First Warden of Caer Dathal," the Nix said, appraising her anew as if he could read her mind. "And I know there is more to you, Rosenwyn Whyte, than you have thus shared. Dragons covet their treasure. Trolls, the trinkets they gather from wayward travellers crossing bridges. Me? I was designed to cherish beauty in all of its forms, to keep it safe, no matter the cost. What do you treasure?" He paused, looking about him. "Despite these ruined halls, I still see beauty here. I protect it. I possess terrible secrets that should never leave these ruins, secrets so intrinsically powerful they could destroy Annwn and beyond. I protect as I was created—able to sense magic when it is close." He paused, looking down on her with sad eyes. "But I truly do miss from those former days of Caer Dathal's glory the music that filled these halls. The revelry. The joy. The laughter that kept the darkness at bay. And you, my dear, possess beautiful music."

"You know my secret," she said. "You know of the magic I carry in my blood."

"It weighs on you heavy, an anvil."

"I want nothing more than to be normal, to be whole," she said, unable to believe that she was opening up to one such as the Nix. "I suspect you know a thing or two about that. Wanting to be normal. Returning to what was once known."

The Nix glanced down where his arm should have been and then around the hall.

"Perhaps."

All of a sudden, she questioned the oath she had given to gain entrance to this ancient room of Caer Dathal of Old.

Could a person become more damned?

"This is your home now?" she asked, changing the subject.

"It is. Mine and mine alone, sadly. Once I lorded upon rooftops. Now?" the Nix dropped his head and looked away. "Long has guilt been my only companion. But guilt is not a true companion, is it? I am cursed with memory and it is filled with dragonfire and terrible shadows." He sat upon his haunches. "I suspect you know of this past of which I speak. Not everyone who walked these halls were evil. My kin and I were unable to keep safe those innocents who lived here. Now only I remain, evidence of past defeat."

"That must have been truly painful," she said, the other's pain tearing at her heart.

The Nix said nothing. Long moments passed.

The silence stretched and Rosenwyn became very aware of the other's scrutiny. She gazed about the room, letting her thief senses learn all aspects of it. She had a sudden thought—and a plan formed that she knew would damn her.

"You mentioned a book by a poet. A poet named John Keats, I believe?"

"Yes, yes I did," the Nix rumbled. He strode deeper into the hall. Rosenwyn followed. "The library under my care is a pittance compared to the grandeur of the Druid collection housed here eons ago. But I have managed to save a number of those volumes from their graveyard and acquire more by… outside means. I am fond of reading. When one lives eternally, reading can be the only solace."

With bluish-white light from the ceiling illuminating their way, the gargoyle and thief entered a part of the hall where one large shelf contained volume after volume. Rosenwyn was impressed. Books were not easily come by throughout Annwn, a privilege of wealth and, while she had seen larger libraries, this one held at least several thousand tomes. They came in various sizes and colors, all of them kept neat and orderly.

The First Warden of Caer Dathal of Old grabbed a book unlike any of the others, well made and bound in crimson leather, its cover filigreed with silver.

The Nix opened the book to a ribbon-marked page.

And read:

"Darkling, I listen; and, for many a time
I have been half in love with easeful Death,

Call'd him soft names in many a mused rhyme,
To take into the air my quiet breath;"

As the Nix recited from the poem, Rosenwyn sought the grimoires, books that would be like none of the others. She hoped they were here and she could end her search before he finished. It did not take long. High upon the shelf sat the objects of her hunt as described by Lady Audeph Klestmark—five books bound in black leather, their spines thick and left unadorned by text or title, the blank exteriors hiding powerful knowledge inside. They could be none other than what she sought.

The Grimoires of the rebel Druids.

"Beautiful," she whispered as the Nix finished reading.

"I continually return to this passage," the gargoyle said. "It seems John Keats knows me quite well. Although I am incapable of breath."

"And death, it seems," she offered.

The massive stone dragon said nothing.

"You have an impressive library here, Nicodemys Rothyn," she added.

"Thank you, Rosenwyn Whyte."

"You mentioned that you required 'outside means' to get some of these," she said hoping to keep her interest in the grimoires secret as her mind raced with how to steal them. "What did you mean by that? Can you not venture from Saith yn Col?"

The Nix grunted. "I am tied to the stone. I cannot venture abroad without leave from the Arch Druid of Caer Dathal. I will remain as long as this stone remains."

"We have a great deal in common," Rosenwyn found herself admitting.

"A great sorrow hangs upon you, a past where pain mingles with guilt," the Nix said. "It is easy to recognize because I know its source all too well. Did a lover do this to you? Or is this something else entirely, Rosenwyn Whyte?"

She shook her head, remembering her childhood.

"A man did hurt me. But he is nothing to me now."

"Something before this man then. When you were a child."

The Nix said it as though he already knew. Rosenwyn thought back to the day her family died. The lightning. The fire. The smoke. The screams. She alone had survived. The destruction of her home and her inability to stop it had created a guilt so deep it would always be there, right beneath the surface. Some memories could be carved into stone and hearts equally, for eternity.

"I will never be free of it," she said. "Like your own pain."

"But music helps."

It was not a question. Rosenwyn nodded.

"Then I hope you play music until your heart is healed," the Nix said.

Rosenwyn didn't have the heart to tell the Nix there was no amount of music in the world to do that.

"A song now, perhaps?" the gargoyle asked, all too eager.

Rosenwyn smiled, putting the past where it belonged. She needed time to devise her next few moves and the Nix offered her time to do so. She grabbed the padded case from her back and pulled forth the crwth and its bow, moved to a block of stone that had fallen from the ceiling, sat, and began to play. She let the music flow through her and into her instrument, a continuous recycling of notes and emotion, each feeding on the other in a wave of creativity. Usually playing for dozens if not hundreds of people, Rosenwyn now played for only one and let the music take her elsewhere even as she tried to discover a way to be free of her greatest and worst curse.

The Nix closed his eyes, listening, his strong presence at peace.

In the middle of playing a third song, a light-hearted tune called *Fly, Fairy, Fly*, the Nix rose up suddenly on his hind legs, towering over Rosenwyn who stopped playing immediately, the peace he had found while she played replaced by a fire of anger so potent she could feel it vibrating the air.

"*Thief!*" the Nix roared.

And the very ruins shook with his fury.

ROSENWYN CRINGED, WAITING for a massive clawed fist to deliver death.

It took her a moment to realize she yet lived, that the gargoyle had not killed her outright, that he hadn't finally discovered her secret in coming to Saith yn Col. Instead, the Nix frantically probed his subterranean home, every shadow and nook, ignoring her entirely and incensed beyond any rage she could believe the stone dragon to possess.

Thrusting her crwth and bow into their case, she madly scanned the area.

She saw nothing of what threatened the Nix or his home.

"What's going on?!" she screamed.

"Thief, I know you are here," the Nix snarled, not looking at her. "I sense your magic. You *dare* enter my home, to steal. Show yourself and end this now, before Death becomes your assured reward."

Nothing. No one answered.

Not that Rosenwyn would think anyone that stupid.

The ruined gargoyle swiveled toward her then, suddenly dwarfing her, a stone cliff ready to collapse and kill.

"Accomplice! You know of what transpires!"

Rosenwyn shrunk to the floor, hands up and placating. "No! I am not! I have no idea what is going on right now!"

"Conspirator!" the Nix hissed. "*Liar!*"

Rosenwyn cringed and furiously tried to discover what was going on. The stone dragon cocked his head as if trying to discover a sound that was just beyond hearing. He gazed back at the library then toward the exit of the hall that led to the world above. His eyes sweeping the shadows, the gargoyle finally settled on Rosenwyn for a moment—a moment that frightened her more than any moment in her life before it—and he bunched like a cat about to pounce, the stone of his muscles filled with sheer power.

Then the Nix leapt at her.

No, not at her.

Over her.

In a single bound, the Nix tore toward the opening that led back to the surface. Rosenwyn inspected the shelves where the grimoires had been.

The books were gone.

And she had been used like a pawn in a chess game.

Cursing, she chased after the Nix, already replacing her goggles, the thief part of her become icy certainty seeking a reckoning. She now knew stealing the grimoires had never been her role. The books were gone, taken by someone else. She had been a mere diversion, put in direct conflict with the Nix to draw attention away from the real thief. She had been used. And she hated that more than even Vrace Erryn. Anger bolstered her resolve as she ran through the hall, up the steps, and returned to the Everwinter.

The snow of the previous day had given way to dark clouds wandering in an azure sky, allowing patches of early morning sunlight to reach Annwn. Rosenwyn found tracks almost immediately. They led hastily away from Saith yn Col, to the south where the forest thinned over a series of slowly rising hills. Rosenwyn could not see the Nix but she could hear him; it sounded like the gargoyle was tearing every icy limb free in the forest in his hunt. She wanted the stone dragon to find the thief. She knew what would happen.

She knelt. It was easy to follow the other thief; the fresh snow that had fallen more than aided her. The tracks were distinctive.

A small foot. Pointed boot.

Another woman had entered Saith yn Col and fled into the surrounding forest.

"*Beautiful, did you miss me?*"

She spun aside, turning to find the voice's owner. It took Rosenwyn a moment to place the young man from the Raging Drunk. Aron McManus. He had dressed more warmly during his travels from Mur Castell but the sly, arrogant smile remained.

He held a sword and, based upon his stance, knew how to use it.

"What the hellfire are you doing here?" she spat.

"You'll find out," he snarled and attacked.

Rosenwyn bounded backwards, her knives filling her hands as if by magic. McManus circled her calmly after his initial swipe, never taking his eyes off her, his footwork precise and practiced. He feinted. She ignored it. He thrust. She stepped lightly to the side. He was testing her, but she knew it. She held the knives with skillful purpose, the blades deadly extensions of her will. In her line of work, carrying a sword hindered her movements. She had been in many fights, most of them while Lleidr Corryn, and she knew she would have to be fast and precise to best the younger foe.

Already annoyed, his arrogance driving him forward, he attacked then, the sword a blur of efficiency. She backpedaled, waiting for the opportunity to strike back. It didn't take long. In his fury, he overextended his reach, if by a moment. She filled the void and slashed back, aiming for his neck.

But the blade caught his cheek instead, opening it wide.

She tried to escape his reach but he backhanded her to the ground, causing black spots to dance before her eyes.

He stood over her, his tongue able to stick through the bloody cut in his face.

"Bitch!" McManus roared.

Thunder drowned out the killer's anger then, filling the forest.

He barely had time to look up before Wennyl struck him with the galloping full force of his barrel chest, the fey horse maddened in his protection of Rosenwyn. The attacker flew through the air, bones broken. McManus' pain did not last long. He screamed once, then died bloodily beneath the fall of the Rhedewyr's flashing hooves.

Rosenwyn didn't spare the fool a second thought. She leapt onto the stallion's back and together they tore through the forest, seeking the Nix. He was not hard to follow. The path of destruction the stone dragon had left in his wake—the forest floor torn and shattered trees as big around as her waste—made it easy. She kept her wits about her though. She did not want to fall prey to another attack if Lady Audeph Klestmark had hired more than a killer and a thief.

Wennyl cleared the forest, following the havoc, until both woman and horse burst from the trees into a long meadow that rolled over hills into the distance.

Nearby, the Nix tore huge frozen swaths from the ground

The body of Audeph Klestmark lay just beyond him, untouched by violence.

It wasn't until Rosenwyn realized the gargoyle lay fixated on some-one else that she saw the old crone. The woman fled upon her own mount, trying to gain the safety of the forest through the meadow. A black speck flew at her side.

The fairy Bazltrix.

"Go after her!" Rosenwyn screamed at the stone monolith.

"I cannot go beyond the *boundaries* of Caer Dathal," the grotesque roared, voice thick with rage. "I am *chained* and cannot go after the witch."

"A witch?"

"Yes, Rosenwyn Whyte," the Nix grated. "A witch."

Rosenwyn watched as sunlight punctuated the hills, the snow-cover blinding as it reflected the sun. She then looked to the body. If Audeph Klestmark laid dead and not the thief, who did Bazltrix accompany in flight?

Her own rage replied to her question.

"If I help you, will that be proof this was not my intention?"

The Nix nodded with bearish ferocity. Rosenwyn dismounted. She sent Wennyl back into the forest and then walked in front of the gargoyle, throwing off her fur-lined cloak. The icy air bit her but she did not feel it, her thoughts elsewhere.

Instead, she removed her gloves and pushed up her sleeves.

Exposing her skin.

The moment she did that, the day darkened, the countryside become draped in pervasive shadow even as she began to brighten, her fair skin flaring with light. Closing her eyes, Rosenwyn focused. The magic in her blood illuminated the countryside and all within it, the power that she kept hidden as a secret now fully exposed to the world and its elements. The light built until her skin writhed with it, power that filled her with dread and euphoria. Dark memories flooded her, of a time, as a child, when she stood at her window in a cloudless night—and moonlight bringing to terrible life the magic that would change her life forever.

Older now and having learned more about her curse, Rosenwyn still barely controlled it. It grew inside, a caged beast, and before it consumed her, she unleashed lightning upon the air, a swollen flood thundering through an obstinate dam. It blasted from her, into the earth, into the sky, into the morning. She sensed the Nix thrown away like a rag doll. The air sizzled and Rosenwyn concentrated on what her body had become, a gathering rod of sorts, capturing the sunlight and changing it into violence. The lightning arced and she sent it as best she could toward the fleeing woman and her fairy companion. As the lightning met the witch, a bright burst of wicked green flared, one not of Rosenwyn's making.

The crone vanished in an eruption of Everwinter elements.

When using her magic began to overwhelm her, Rosenwyn covered her skin anew, darkness swimming in her vision.

And collapsed, drained.

Silence more hollow than a graveyard followed, stillness so intense it rang in her ears. She breathed hard, fighting faintness. When she had recovered enough, she pushed up off the ground and focused on what she had done.

In the distance, the horse the witch had been riding lay unmoving.

Of the witch and the fairy, there was no sign.

The Nix untangled his stone body from crushed trees where the lightning had thrown him. "Woman of Many Talents," the stone behemoth growled a laugh, striding up to her. "I sensed your magic but I was not prepared for it."

"Are you hurt?" she asked.

"No," the Nix rumbled. "I have been struck by lightning more times than I can recount. It is nothing to me." He looked deeper into the meadow where the horse smoked. "You will have to approach with utmost caution. I cannot go with you. Be wary. The witch has guile and all too surely hates you for what just transpired."

Exhausted but determined, Rosenwyn nodded and mounted Wennyl. Both made their way to the horse's remains. The lightning had torn a hole in the mount's side, killing the mare instantly.

Having searched the area, Rosenwyn returned to the Nix.

"What did you find?" the gargoyle asked. "The grimoires?"

"No," she said, frustrated. She dismounted and went to the side of Audeph Klestmark. "The fairy is dead, reduced to black ash on the snow. The witch vanished though. The lightning threw her free of her mount but she regained her feet. The tracks led about twenty paces before they disappeared, like she never existed."

"Magic protected her and then concealed her passage. She will not be easily found," the Nix said, gently picking up the body of Audeph Klestmark with his remaining massive fist. "Come."

Rosenwyn nodded, the defeat like poison in her mouth and followed the great stone behemoth back toward his home. She first made certain the man from the Raging Drunk was dead. Aron McManus couldn't be more so. One eye stared up through the trees, the rest of his skull crushed beyond identification. Rosenwyn then went to the body of Audeph Klestmark where the Nix had laid her just outside the entrance to his lair. The wealthy woman stared to the side, her mouth agape. The thief checked over the body. She could not find a cause for the woman's death.

"You were attacked by this man here?" the Nix said, observing the remains.

"Wennyl finished him," she said.

"A fine Rhedewyr, a finer friend." The grotesque examined Audeph Klestmark then. "She was a vessel. And this was a plot," he growled.

"What do you mean by that?"

"Look upon her. Note what can be seen."

Rosenwyn did so. It did not take long to compare the difference from their previous meeting in Mur Castell—discarded gloves revealing fingers devoid of rings.

"Her rings are gone yet necklace and earrings remain," Rosenwyn observed.

"It means the rings held more worth," the Nix said. "And when it comes to magic and power, gems are priceless in the province of the witch."

"And the vessel?"

"This woman did not die, not by another's hand. No wounds. No bruising," the Nix said, inspecting the body. "An innocent. Housing a very rare evil. That evil overtook the body of this woman, similar to how a shadow infiltrates another shadow. Unseen. A witch, ancient, one whose body has long since decayed to dust yet the spirit lives on in a different body. One such witch even courted one of the rebel Druids of Caer Dathal. It is said she fled while my home—and her Druid partner—fell." The Nix looked into the forest as if the witch would be there. "And she would want the grimoires back. For their power... or something far more grave for Annwn."

"The grimoires of her fallen brethren," Rosenwyn said. "What have I done?"

"A terrible omen. No good can come of this."

Rosenwyn hated that she had aided the witch. More than she hated even herself.

"Tell me your role in this," the Nix rumbled. "With detail."

Rosenwyn did. She had no reason not to. She started with her childhood and the magic that she possessed—the same magic that had killed her family and plagued her life since that dark day. Talking briefly about becoming a Lleidr Corryn, she instead related her time as a musician—until the night when the man at the Raging Drunk had offered his company and the fairy intervened, leading to a clandestine meeting with Lady Audeph Klestmark and her promise to help rid Rosenwyn of her debilitating curse in exchange for the Grimoires of the rebel Druids.

"The man who tried to kill you," the gargoyle said. "He aided the witch. He was hired, under the supervision of the witch, to help deliver another vessel body. In killing this Lady Audeph Klestmark, you now have no lead to follow. This witch is devious. And she has her freedom." The Nix punched the ground, making Rosenwyn jump. He ignored her discomfort. "She stole dangerous knowledge," he said. "Quite possibly, the most dangerous books under my care."

"What makes them so dangerous?" she asked. "How can a set of books be that worrisome? They are only bound paper and ink."

"Books are quite possibly the most powerful items in the world, Rosenwyn Whyte," Nicodemys Rothyn argued. "These particular grimoires especially. They possess dark magic. That knowledge, in evil hands, could be a terrible bane on Annwn." The gargoyle turned to her, his dark eyes penetrating. "You were a part of this. I wish it were otherwise. I rather like you."

Rosenwyn thought the gargoyle about to attack. There would be no surviving.

"I did not sense the witch's magic," the Nix growled. "Because of you."

"My magic masked her magic."

The Nix nodded, still angry. "Do you wish to make amends?"

She realized she did. Nobody made a fool of her and lived to tell it. "I do," she admitted honestly. "Very much."

"Very well," the Nix said. "You start now."

"Start what?"

"You have power, Woman of Many Talents," the behemoth rumbled, his voice reverberating through the chill air. "It is powerful. You can also go where I cannot. You will become an extension of my will, for a time, until you have paid back the debt of your involvement. A Lleidr Corryn will become the White Rose." Rosenwyn was about to protest when the Nix raised his fist for silence. "Once, after the fall of Caer Llion, I had one such as you retrieve those lost grimoires from the private collection of the High King. In time, you will discover this witch. And regain what she stole."

"Where is that thief who stole the books from Caer Llion?" she questioned.

"Death comes all too soon in my presence, it seems."

Rosenwyn did not know what that meant. But if anyone could steal the grimoires back, it would be her.

"Do you accept this proposal?" the Nix asked finally.

"There may be a time when I am discovered. By those who would see me dead for abdicating my role as Lleidr Corryn," Rosenwyn said, hating the thought of confronting that part of her life. "In the past, I avoided Vrace Erryn and Rol Macleod by playing in a different town almost every night."

"Like the wind," the Nix said. "Constantly moving."

"Very much so," she said. "I can not guarantee others will not search for me here—and find you in the process. And all you possess. My life is tied to the master thief's token. They *will* come for me."

"The two other master thieves," the Nix grunted. "We will worry about them when the day of their reckoning comes."

The gargoyle said it so nonchalant she actually believed him.

The Nix gazed at the dark clouds roaming their blue sky:

"Was I deceived, or did a sable cloud
Turn forth her silver lining on the night?

I did not err; there does a sable cloud
Turn forth her silver lining on the night,
And casts a gleam over this tufted grove."

"What does that mean?" Rosenwyn asked.

"That is a verse from a John Milton poem, my White Rose thief," the Nix said. "Another poet from the world beyond Annwn. The passage means not every evil turn is for ill if one is capable of perceiving it."

"That is quite appropriate, I guess," she admitted. "The sable cloud has entered our lives. But that same cloud has brought us together." She patted Wennyl who nuzzled her back. "Time to find the witch and end her *own* silver lining."

"I could not agree more," Nicodemys Rothyn growled.

Life had a way of changing course, like a swollen river escaping its original banks. It could not be fought, only accepted. Rosenwyn went to gather her things. If the Nix could endure the change in his role from gargoyle atop Caer Dathal of Old to living in its ruins, she could adapt and become something more.

She breathed in the chill and returned to the ruins.

And her new home of Saith yn Col.

THE MUTTWHELP

Edward M. Erdelac

DARK DAYS IN Wayphar.

The Fey Folk of Oldwood had been left pinned to their trees like butterflies by the spears of the goblin hordes. Spars of the White Armada lay shattered at the bottom of the Billow Ocean, and Rentellevaire, the shining city-state of the August King, was threatened by the Witch Queen herself.

Behind the Black Army of Odius Khan, the Plains of Daroosh were furnished in fire. Thick curtains of smoke marked the pyres of the famous Thunder Riders, every man and horse slaughtered, their bones gnawed clean by crag trolls and other fell folk with a penchant for such meat. Below the Black Army's grimy encampment, down in the Valley of The Golden Lap, the plump little village of Glean huddled amid its waving wheat fields. To the east, its elder sister town, Crossbow Hollow, was ablaze. The orks scurried among the burning buildings like angry ants, and the tall shapes of trolls pulled down the tower keep with a resounding crash. The last true bastion of mankind between the orks and the Heartbreak Sea had fallen. The tall, red sailed warships of Admiral Athkabode waited at the coast to carry their forces north, to join the Witch Queen's dread host on the field of Bantilloy. Only Glean remained.

Mogarth Muttwhelp considered the stone bowl of mushy field gruel with a flare of his porcine nostrils, and decided to tip the sour smelling slop into the spluttering fire. He would almost rather eat raw man flesh than the stuff the ork cooks concocted.

The black little crow-nosed goblin squatting across from him, chewing at a raw dog's leg, looked at him aghast with his beady agate eyes.

"Boss, the next time you ain't going to eat your stew, give it to poor hungry Redshat," he squeaked, shaking the flopping, sandy-furred joint at him.

Redshat was the last of the old Bellygasher Gang. Picknose had been killed on forage detail by a farmer with a pitchfork while coming out of some henhouse with a chicken in his arms and a mouthful full of eggs. A clutch of peeping chicks had hatched in his dead, grinning maw moments after they'd pried him from the wall of the coop. Hangnail had tripped over his flapping feet on the march across Daroosh and been mashed flat by one of their own lumbering trolls, and Cockblood and Footwart had been spitted on the same blue lance in the last charge of the Silver Lancers at Corbin Keep.

Their brigand days in and around Crossbow Hollow had never been so deadly. They had made a decent living, the five of them, cutting throats in the alleys at night and unhorsing lonely riders on the back roads with a length of cord strung across the lane. As their boss, the lion's share of the gold had gone to Mogarth. The gobbos had been content to work for fresh meat.

Mogarth had fallen into the leadership of the Bellygashers by happenstance.

As a muttwhelp, the son of some nameless ork raider who had ravaged his human mother and left her hanging half-dead and bleeding from an oak tree on his grandfather's farm outside Glean, he had never quite fit in anywhere. Most muttwhelps never made it to the birthing, or were hacked to death in their cradles or drowned. His tenderhearted mother had suckled him, even though his tusk nubs had scarred her nipples. She had raised him, even though it had isolated her from her own family and neighbors, and educated him by the hearth light when the scowling master at the Glean schoolhouse had turned him away, an ugly, green skinned babe snuffling snot and bitter tears into her apron.

He had worked down in those golden fields till one winter when his mother had caught a deep chill in her chest and sickened past caring, wasting to death when the robins returned. He had tried to keep the old farm going after that, but none of the merchants in Glean would buy his yield or sell him seed, and he couldn't afford any intermediary agent.

He had burned the farm to the ground and salted the fields to ensure none of the hateful pinkskins could use it in his wake.

He rubbed his rough hand over his stubbled head. He could still see the bare patch of land down in the valley where his home had once stood.

Mogarth had departed for Crossbow Hollow, the eastern gateway to the Golden Lap Valley and its most populous city, taking only the old blue shirt his mother had woven for him and the silver handled whip his father had left tied around her scarred throat.

The whip. His only heirloom. A cruel black thing with a barbed popper and a gnashing jackal's head wrought in tarnished silver encasing the knotted handle.

"Home again, eh, boss?" Redshat said, having noticed Mogarth's eyes, staring down at the valley waiting to be crushed flat and burned by the Black Army.

"No home of mine," Mogarth grumbled.

In truth, the closest thing he had to home after his mother's death had been with the Bellygashers, though he'd never admit it to Redshat.

The people in Crossbow Hollow hadn't treated him any better than the humans of Glean. No one would hire him, not even the stableyard master. Unable to secure work he'd taken to making money any way he could. Naturally large, he had earned a meager living fighting in the sawdust pits for a time, when a scheming promoter had convinced him it was possible to retire on a brawler's winnings. But the crowds, most of them missing limbs or loved ones from the frequent ork raids, had hated him, and when it had been suggested he begin losing to please them, he turned to cutpursing and bashing the skulls of drunks late at night.

When the Hartslayers had brought in the Bellygasher Gang one night and left them locked in the jail wagon out in front of Bintu's Tavern while they threw themselves a congratulatory celebration, he had gathered with the rest of the drunken crowd and watched them jeer and pitch dog shit and beer at the five little sable-skinned goblins gripping the bars and gnashing their black needle teeth within.

The Bellygashers already had a reputation for waylaying travelers. Their leader, Picknose's brother Pickscab, had thought it a great joke to tie travelers alive to trees, cut their stomachs open, then fasten their intestines to the saddle horns of their own horses and lash them down the road to town.

The Hartslayers, unappreciative of his humor but savoring irony, had done the same for Pickscab. They'd slit him open and tied his guts to the back of the prison wagon. They'd made him march behind until he'd died and then dragged his carcass the rest of the way to town.

Picknose had tried to cut his brother loose, but his claws couldn't reach through the bars. He had borne the gray scars of his effort on his skinny arms till his own death.

Something in the cruelty of the Hartslayers had rankled Mogarth, even though he'd known well it was deserved punishment. The sight of the town dogs tearing Pickscab's corpse apart as the squealing little pink children fetched up the goblin's cast off genitals and flung them back and forth at each other had boiled his blood.

Maybe it was because somewhere back in his own cursed heritage, gobbos were kin to orks. Maybe it was just the ugliness on display that night. He didn't know.

He'd set fire to the Hartslayers' constabulary and, while everybody had gone off with buckets to fight the blaze, he'd picked the lock of the cage and gone running off into the dark with the tumbling, chittering goblins.

It hadn't been easy leading that bunch at first. Gobbos weren't bright, and they were disgusting. A few times that first night he'd woken to find one of them gnawing at his toes, or two of them trying to tie his hands and feet, but after giving them a respectable thrashing, they'd relented to his company. Once he'd made them understand there was more to be gained from robbing travelers of their gold than in simply torturing them, they'd even accepted him as their boss.

He had maintained his innocuous presence in town, but he used the money from their subsequent robberies to build a cabin in the foothills on the outskirts where he pretended to raise sheep. In actuality, he bred them for the Bellygashers, who exchanged live mutton for gold and jewelry. Picknose still insisted on honoring his late brother's memory with the occasional disembowelment, but Mogarth was able to keep them informed as to the Hartslayer's movements. They charted the forest and even the sewer tunnels beneath the town so they always had a place to hide.

It could not be called happiness. It was never quite a family, but it was contentment.

Then one night the scouts of the Black Army had come to Mogarth's cabin, three muttwhelps, like him. He had never seen so many all together, and one, Bashka, was a female.

Odius Khan had emerged at the head of the united ork tribes from somewhere past the Broken Tooth Mountains, and allied his people with the Witch Queen and her numerous retainers among the dark folk of Wayphar. The animosity with which the five tribes regarded each other was legendary, and so this alliance under the great Odius was unprecedented. Combined with the might of the Witch Queen, it meant the end for the humans and the dwarves and even the elves and the fairies. It meant a new world for folk like him.

So Bashka and the other muttwhelps had told him.

He didn't know now quite why he had bought into it so readily. Maybe it was the sight of Bashka. She had been no prize, certainly, with her too-broad hips and pendulous chest, her dripping snout and ornamented tusks, but nevertheless, she'd been female and willing. Maybe it was the thought of not having to live in isolation, or to pay well above the market price for the touch of some pinkskin woman.

So he and the Bellygashers had joined the Black Army. Orks, goblins, ogres, and trolls, all under the command of Odius Khan and the Ork Lords. They had skulked and scouted, fought and died, and he and Bashka had rolled and bucked to his content for a time.

But for what?

The orks treated them no better than the humans had. The muttwhelps were worse than servants in camp, bullied and ordered about like slaves, as hated for their human blood as he had been by the valley dwellers for his father's. Bashka was expected to present herself to any rank and file ork or ogre in the host, and did so readily, submissively, until the perennially drunken orks raucously encouraged her coupling with an overeager crag troll and she was killed, torn nearly asunder.

The gobbos fared no better. They were kicked around by the larger soldiers when they were noticed at all, and driven in the forefront of the fighting always, to die by the scores. The trolls dipped them in barrels of pitch and hurtled them over the walls of castles on fire. They were instructed to roll across the thatch roofs or run through the enemy stables for as long as they could, if they landed alive.

Mogarth and his Bellygashers avoided such treatment after Mogarth himself had set a precedent.

One day, not long after the death of Bashka, a burly Broken Tooth Clan sergeant had tried to bend him over a cask of bilemead. The Bellygashers had scurried out from nowhere and swarmed the offender, biting, clawing, stabbing, and digging in with their hooked iron ankle and elbow spurs all at once. The sergeant's shrieking had brought his orks, and Mogarth had taken up his big iron cleaver and stood over the gobbos while they did their bloody work.

Of the score ork soldiers he faced down, four had tried to come through him to the aid of their superior. One he cut from the top of his head to the middle of his neck. The second he sheared off below the knees. The third he swept both eyes from, and the fourth died in a tug of war over his own innards with one of the ravenous camp wolves.

After that day the word spread through the orks that the muttwhelp called Mogarth and his goblins were not to be touched.

As a reminder, he stuck the sergeant's gaping head on a pole outside their mule hide tents.

The gobbos had swatted the flies away every morning and picked the meat from the face by increments to chew on the march. It was just a grinning black skull now. Mogarth had carved designs into the tusks in his off time, and he wore them from a necklace, along with the claws of a werebear champion he had slain at the Battle of Kantrivone Grove.

The Black Army was relentless. They had scoured the eastern half of the continent in a bloody, four month campaign before returning west where Mogarth's own journey had begun, here at the edge of the Valley of The Golden Lap.

Though he hated to admit it, Redshat was right. It *was* like coming home.

Except now, it was just the two of them.

Mogarth could see the highways leading north and west from the burning buildings of Crossbow Hollow. They were blocked with inching caravans of refugees. The ones to the north were being ridden down by wolfriders, the orks and goblins no doubt raping, slaying, and masticating their way through them. They were being slaughtered on their desperate flight north, to the dwarf stronghold of Stonehewn, a sanctuary that no longer even existed. It had been conquered by Odius Khan himself three days ago.

The last of the defenders and commoners, perhaps Duke Pastorlak himself, were racing toward Glean, an indefensible little scattering of cottages, silos, and farmhouses that would shortly be their killing ground.

The only thing that spared them thus far was Odius Khan himself. The great ork leader had sent word to halt the advance after the fall of Crossbow Hollow, so he could ride down from Stonehewn and oversee the fall of the valley personally.

Dark clouds were the only aid rolling in from the north to help the people of Crossbow Hollow. Maybe soon their homes would burn a little less in the rain.

Mogarth spat in the dirt.

Crossbow Hollow had fallen all the quicker because he and Redshat had known the secret ways under the city, and led the orks into the middle of town via the sewers. The orks had bypassed the city defenses and surprised the garrison from within, decimating them almost without resistance.

He and Redshat returned to camp once they played their part, not engaging in the slaughter. The deaths of the Bellygashers had soured him on army life. He didn't know if Redshat could be sated in blood, but Mogarth had his fill. He had seen and caused enough bloodshed and mayhem to last him a lifetime. They had waded in dead men, and though the orks and gobbos and even Redshat had used the women harshly in every county and kingdom they had crushed, Mogarth had refrained, thinking always of his own childhood and the scars around his mother's neck and down her back from his father's hard attentions. What place would his own bastards have in the world to come? If the treatment of the muttwhelps in camp was any indication, they would fare no better than him. So he fathered none.

Now he wondered what would become of him and Redshat once they reached the sea. Would they be loaded onto the red-sailed ships with the rest of the army to go and fight the August King and the Sabrelords, or would they be left behind on the coast with nothing but the burning valley behind them?

This business of burning and razing; while he found enjoyment in the utter destruction of those who had mistreated him in his past, when he thought hard on it, it made little practical sense. The Khan had promised the Black Army's soldiers a land free for orks once all was said and done. But what kind of land would that be?

He thought of how he had salted and burned his own home prior to leaving Glean. The Black Army had done the same on a larger scale. It seemed sort of foolish now. What would they have conquered?

Nothing but a wasteland of ash and cinder.

A war horn sounded at the north end of camp, and a wild shout went up.

Redshat jammed his dog joint in his teeth and shimmied up a nearby fir tree.

Moments later he jumped down.

"Looks like Big Khan here," he announced excitedly.

"Well," said Mogarth, getting to his feet. "Let's go see him."

A light rain began falling, cool and steady. The dirt at their feet began to shine.

They joined an excited rush of loping goblins and clanking, gorilla-like orks striding toward the center of the excitement, which proved to be a group of heavily mailed riders atop immense horned and barded warbulls, the mount of choice for the Five Ork Lords. These were escorted by tall, deadly looking orks in red stained armor. The janissaries; personal guards of the Khan.

There were four riders in all, and two empty, but saddled, warbulls guided by janissaries, representing the lords of the Boogaht and Kill-Kill tribes who had fallen in battle with the elves.

The orks nearest the retinue began to clash their weapons to their breastplates and chant;

"O-di-us! O-di-us! O-di-us!"

The largest of the four riders was an impressive looking ork masked in the dwarf-forged helm of the Iron King of Stonehewn. He was garbed in piecemeal costume attesting to the peoples he had conquered. His greenweave cape had belonged to an elvish noble, and his filigree breastplate and pauldrons had come from the Master of the Knights of Cendreeve, whom he had personally slain. A necklace of desiccated pixie queens adorned his neck, each one pierced neatly through the temple by a silver chain.

He stood in his stirrups and wrenched off the helm, revealing a scarred, white haired ork with moss green skin. One tusk was chipped off, the other was gold. He roared deeply, and the orks bellowed their approval.

Redshat tugged Mogarth's hand, unable to see, and he let the gobbo clamber up his leg and mount his shoulders like a child.

Odius Khan opened his mailed fists and the orks ceased their shouting immediately. His command over them was astounding. Even the captains of Mogarth's regiment had put the scourge to the backs of the unruly soldiers when the fighting was thick to keep them at it. In the presence of the Khan, every savage brute reacted with military discipline.

Even Mogarth felt an indescribable sense of pride in his commander. Previously, he had only seen the Khan from afar, and never without a helm. Odius had gained a reputation for personally leading attacks and the orks loved him for it. He was the sole reason they had put aside their ceaseless feuds. Never mind the far away Witch Queen to whom the Black Army ostensibly owed its allegiance. The orks fought for Odius Khan and none other.

He shrugged closer through the crowd.

"Look at you!" Odius bellowed. "Five tribes, five fingers on the hands of the ork people. Together," he said, throwing one fist forward. "The fist of the Black Army!"

The orks roared again, and struck each other in their enthusiasm.

"How you have fought! What glory you have achieved! You have torn down castles and dragged forth kings weeping! You have picked your teeth with the bones of heroes! Now, of those so-called bright folk, who in the past have driven you to drink bitter waters in black lands and to hide in cold, dark places, only old men and women remain to quiver and clutch mewling children to their wrinkled breasts, for their champions and their kings even now are lapped by the thirsty fires of hell!"

He thrust his finger down at the valley.

"Smell the smoke of ruin! The delectable aroma of man-flesh slow-roasting in the stone rubble of their homes! This is the holy incense of our struggle, the sweet fragrance of our victory feast! May the Witch Queen bless us as we prepare this table in her name! All that remains is to smear the spineless pinkskins that remain beneath our heels!"

Redshat clapped his hands excitedly, giggling.

Mogarth watched the splendid figure of Odius as he gesticulated. He was a leader born, as far above the undisciplined savages that made up his army as was a lord from the beasts that tilled his fields. Perhaps there was a hope for this new world. Surely the great Odius would not deliver his people to blight and starvation. Maybe the bountiful lands around Rentellevaire would be their promised country.

"Tonight, the Golden Lap will be the Black Lap! And in the morning, we will sail north, to pluck the August King's head from his shoulders!"

The orks erupted in furious cheers and chest thumping.

Redshat yelped as the ork behind Mogarth plucked him from his neck and began to excitedly whirl him around overhead by the ankle.

Mogarth turned and drove his elbow into the ork's face, feeling a tusk snap off. The ork fell flat and did not move, and Redshat scurried back up his arm like a monkey and resumed his place.

"Look! Look!" Redshat cackled, as if nothing had happened. He swatted the top of Mogarth's close shaved pate repeatedly and pointed to the Khan. "See? See? It's like yours, Boss!"

Mogarth ignored the goblin's ravings.

He saw a few unfortunate goblins tossed into the air, laughing stupidly as they were passed over the crowded ork soldiers, then squealing as they were flung to the muddy ground and vigorously stomped without warning.

He gripped Redshat's ankle.

"Like yours! Like yours!" the goblin was still yelling.

"All right! All right! Enough!" Mogarth hissed, reaching up and cuffing him upside the head.

"And now!" Odius said, raising his hands again to the gray sky for silence. "Let us kneel and give thanks to our mistress, the Witch Queen, from whom all dark blessings flow!"

"And to Odius!" one of the captains shouted.

Odius grinned as the soldiers nearest him prostrated themselves.

Mogarth was caught up in the feeling. His earlier doubts were almost gone. He pulled Redshat from his shoulders and let him drop to the ground.

The goblin tugged at the whip hanging from his belt.

Mogarth pushed him away and dropped to one knee in the mud, bowing his head.

Redshat came back, pulling insistently on the coiled leather.

Mogarth glared at him. All around them was the clatter of steel and iron and the creak of leather as the orks genuflected in ecstatic worship.

He did not know this Witch Queen, but now that he had laid eyes on Odius Khan, now that he had heard his voice, his ork blood sang in his veins as it never had before. He was of a people. And the future now belonged to them. There *would* be a place for him.

Redshat, peering up at him, held up the silver handle of his whip and pointed again.

"It's like yours!"

Mogarth followed the goblin's black finger, uncomprehending.

And then the spell was broken.

For a spell it had been, surely, a spell to cloak his mind, to ignite him, like good wine before a battle.

Some glamour, a boon of this Witch Queen.

It took no arcane counterhex, no mystic pass or ancient ward or light of the autumn moon to break it.

It took only a glance at the silver handled whip on Odius Khan's belt.

As Redshat had said, very like his own.

WHEN THE BENEDICTION was complete, Odius Khan lowered himself to the saddle of his warbull and led the ork lords in a line down the center of the Black Army, which opened to receive them. The orks rose and hastened out of his way, clearing his path, yet straining to reach across the entourage of marching janissaries and touch his knee as he rode past, like pilgrims venerating. He cradled the helm of the Iron King in his elbow and reached down from his mount to touch the heads and squeeze the hands of his soldiers.

Then his bull stopped short, and snorted.

A single ork obstructed his path. No, not quite an ork. It was one of these half-caste, fatherless muttwhelps, with the unnatural eyes of a human, so unnerving in the otherwise handsome, olive green face of an ork. The tusks were not so prominent either. Another way to tell a pureblood from one of these pitiful, corrupted bastards. He was dressed in a dirty woven blue shirt of human make, and a boiled leather hauberk and greaves. There was a heavy black iron cleaver in his fist, the hand and a half handle of plain oak.

A little black goblin clutched his knee with one arm and dug deep in his nose with the tip of his finger.

Odius gave his spurs to his bull and urged the lumbering animal forward.

The muttwhelp put up his open hand and stopped the warbull with an insistent shove that made the animal snort.

Several orks stepped forward, cursing, to pull him out of the Khan's way.

The muttwhelp mashed one's nose with the butt end of his weapon and kicked another in the balls. When the offended ork dropped to his knees, groaning, the muttwhelp put his foot to his face and kicked him away.

A third ork tried to intervene unseen from behind, but the little goblin spun with a snarl and drew an elbow spur across the back of his leg, leaving him howling and rolling in the mud.

The muttwhelp stared up at Odius, saying nothing.

"Stand aside, muttwhelp!" he commanded.

The half-ork said nothing, but unhooked something from his belt and let it uncoil to the ground like a long black snake.

"Father Khan," said the ork. "This is yours. I return it to you."

With that, he pulled back his arm, and the whip cut the air. It lashed around his throat, the cruel popper winding around and splitting his upper lip.

In the next moment he was pulled from his saddle, and landed with a crash and a huff of surprise in the mud.

MOGARTH HELD THE Khan at the end of the whip like a dog on a leash. He waited till the stunned Odius, his mouth awash in blood, got slowly to his feet.

The janissaries moved in, growling unintelligibly, brandishing their weapons, and behind them the ork soldiers leapt and bellowed, but the Khan held up his hand and they all halted.

Odius drew the single-edged yatagan at his side and cut the offending whip away with one swipe.

Mogarth circled the Khan, warily checking to see that none of the janissaries swept in to intervene. The mud sucked at his boots.

"Do you think to challenge me, you miserable castoff nothing?" The Khan laughed.

"Here, *great father*," said Mogarth, holding up the handle of the whip. "You forgot the rest."

He tossed it lightly across the distance, and the Khan snatched it out of the silver slashed air. He was about to fling it down when he glanced at the silver handle. Then he stopped short, and turned it over in his hand. He snorted and looked at Mogarth appraisingly.

"I left this trifle knotted around a pinkskin whore's throat a long time ago." He grinned and patted the whip at his side. "I've replaced them both since," he said.

Mogarth's fingers flexed about the cleaver handle, trembling at the slight to his mother.

The Khan opened his hand and let the handle roll from his palm into the mud. "Bastards are due no birthright," he said.

Mogarth shook his head, his lip curling, baring his tusks. His fingers flexed on his cleaver.

"It's not your birthright I want."

The Khan nodded. He turned to the janissaries, and for a moment, Mogarth expected him to give the order to kill him.

"This rape-spawn is mine," he said.

The Khan whirled and rushed in, eager to end the fight with a swift downward stroke.

Mogarth slipped the attack and landed a blow on the Khan's back that rang against his armor.

Odius growled his frustration and spun. The Khan's sword whistled just over Mogarth's head as he came in chopping with his heavy blade.

He dented the golden armor and broke the chain mail between the Khan's neck and shoulder, sending blood trickling over the bright cuirass.

Odius kicked Mogarth's leg out from under him, and he stumbled back. The Khan slashed his arm and caught him again on the backswing, his sharp sword cutting into his hauberk and ploughing a shallow furrow in the belly beneath.

Mogarth groaned and batted away the Khan's stabbing sword. He gave ground, defending. The Khan hammered furiously away at him.

A few swipes landed glancing strikes, and Mogarth answered with quick, clanging blows against that impenetrable armor, the two of them fighting back and forth, slipping in the mud, sending it spraying all around them.

No one cheered, no one shouted. The Black Army stood stark still. Even the Ork Lords and the janissaries made no move.

Mogarth didn't know why those sworn to protect the Khan were not attacking, or why the droves of fanatic and undisciplined hero worshippers behind were allowing him to cross swords with their deity. He supposed the Khan's word really was absolute. If a blow came from some unexpected quarter or an arrow flew out of the crowd and struck him down, so be it. Mogarth had enough to worry about.

Their weapons clashed and locked together, exerting all effort each against the other, but there was no yielding in either of them. The face of the older ork was close, his skin beaded with sweat, his blood red eyes slits alight in his face, snout huffing excitedly.

The face of his father, straining to kill him.

Mogarth threw his head forward and swiped his tusks across Odius' face, ripping the Khan's left cheek wide open to the eye.

The Khan stumbled back, shaking the blood from his face.

Mogarth leapt at him, driving him down for all he was worth, frantic, landing a shuddering blow for every scar on his mother's back.

Odius Khan fell to one knee, jamming his own sword into the dirt to keep from pitching over.

Mogarth started in low and swung upward. His heavy blade broke through the Khan's lower jaw and struck it off. It turned high into the air, trailing his tusks and broken teeth with a splash of blood.

Odius fell forward on his hands and knees, blood pouring from the grievous wound, his tongue hanging and twitching down where once it had nestled in the bottom of his mouth.

Mogarth kicked him on his side.

Odius rolled on his back in the mud. The rainwater had flattened his hair to his skull.

Mogarth bled from a half dozen cuts, but the bright crimson washed away as fast as it streamed out of him.

Odius gagged and shook his head, blood pooling and bubbling in his throat. His eyes rolled and darted wildly, and in them Mogarth read his befuddlement at this strange defeat from so unexpected a quarter at the pinnacle of his greatest triumph.

The Khan looked up at the gray sky, blinked, tried to breathe, gargling and choking.

Mogarth thought again of his mother and their myriad sufferings. He thought of the gobbos he had led to death. He lifted his blade and split his father's face and the skull beneath it.

He straightened then, fully expecting the horde to close in upon him like a ravenous mouth, too tired to fight them anymore.

But the orks all shuffled in place, looking at him expectantly.

The janissaries were impassive in their armor.

The ork lords looked at each other. One turned his mount, and slowly plodded off to the north.

A slew of orks broke rank and followed him. Members of his tribe.

Another headed east, back toward the now smoldering plains, the inferno that had been Daroosh diminished beneath the increasing patter of the rain. The previously raging fire of Crossbow Hollow, too, was withering.

Another followed the first. Another went south, both with their respective hordes. The ogres and the crag trolls wandered off toward the hills, jostling each other as they went, spreading out, preferring solitude to each other's company. Each of the janissaries went his own way.

None went down into the Golden Lap.

Like a wheel without its hub, the spokes scattered to the eight directions.

Mogarth stood over the dead Khan and watched them all go.

Something tugged the bottom of his hauberk.

It was Redshat.

"We go now, Boss?"

Mogarth lifted the goblin onto his shoulders.

TO THE WEST, Admiral Athkabode paced the rolling deck of his red sailed flagship and watched the rain washed coast impatiently.

In her black pavilion on the blood-glutted fields of Bantilloy, the Witch Queen smashed her scrying mirror into a thousand shards and collapsed onto her pale, unicorn hide setee in an exasperated rage.

Her generals in the command tent listened nervously to the reports of their scouts and her soldiers watched the rising dust in the far north with dread and wondered about their reinforcements.

They glanced at their mistress' silent pavilion and waited anxiously for word.

Any word.

MOGARTH AND REDSHAT rode down into the Valley of the Golden Lap, hunched under the drizzling rain on a dead ork lord's warbull.

Its tail swished idly.

THE LONG KISS

Clay Sanger

SIX SHIPS, SIX months, and two thousand miles. That's how far Raddox Edorian, former Captain and sole survivor of the Blackfish, had to run until he finally felt safe. When he reached the City of Kos, nestled along a stretch of exotic eastern shore he couldn't pronounce, he thought that just maybe it was far enough.

Less than one in ten people here spoke his mother tongue. These people were a mix of Sundish and Pahji and other folk he was largely ignorant about. He couldn't tell them apart anyway. As far as Raddox was concerned, all the strange people that filled this howling city looked alike, and that meant they looked nothing like him. That suited him perfectly.

The aging mercenary stood head and shoulders taller than the average local. Men like him, burly pale-faced Westermen, were rare here which made them easy enough to spot in a crowd. It was those sort of people that held the price on Raddox's head. The people of Kos and all these other folk along the Sundish shores couldn't have cared less about him.

Illustration by OKSANA DMITRIENKO ▸

Haj'adann. That was the word he'd heard the locals use to describe men like him, westerners and northerners from Galadyr and beyond. He didn't suppose they meant it politely. It made him laugh.

The City of Kos was good. Loud, busy, full to bursting. Fragrant and exotic. There was music here he'd never heard before. Food he'd never tasted. Women he'd never had. He even saw a great gray beast with a wizened little man on its back and a coiling serpent for a nose. *Yphant,* the locals called it. It dropped great piles of shit in the streets and boys with wicker baskets would come along to collect the droppings. Raddox found that comical. Little sun-darkened men pulled on the yphant's great flapping ears with hooked sticks to steer the hulking beasts like mules.

Raddox even saw a great fat man in purple robes and a silly hat accompanied by a tiny and hairy man dressed in a set of clothes that were identical in every stitch. The little hairy man climbed all over the huge fat man and sat on his shoulder squawking and clapping like a court jester. The speechless little fool even had a tail like a beast.

The fat man and the little hairy man danced and twirled for coins, singing loud brassy songs as they tottered up and down the streets. Folk here seemed to appreciate their talents. Raddox was not so impressed. The fat man's language sounded like two goats humping.

Kos was perfect. It was the other side of the world in Raddox's estimation.

If he went any further east, he'd be circling the world back home, he thought.

And there, he was a dead man.

RADDOX MADE HIMSELF at home in Kos and the days turned into weeks. Back home, the world was full of problems. Big problems.

War. Namely a war that he himself had been paid to start. Those things were no longer Raddox's concern though. He had small problems. Like a keeping a belly full of wine that outclassed his tastes and getting a regular bathing by beautiful women. That included finding a whorehouse that suited his liking, which he did. Though they didn't call them whore houses here. They called them *sunkiri damash*, which he understood meant pleasure house, or near enough.

He learned quickly that Kosian pleasure houses weren't like whore houses back home. They weren't dens for drunks and lechers. Here in Kos, visiting the pleasure houses was a classy, respectable pastime. Men of wealth and standing did that, and women too. Business was conducted. Deals were sealed. It was all very civilized. There was etiquette to be observed, or you'd find yourself in the street.

Raddox liked his wine and he liked his women, so he adapted.

On a jasmine-scented evening nine weeks after arriving in Kos, Raddox visited his favorite pleasure house, the Crimson Circle. He was still working on how to say the name in the local tongue, damnable and finicky as it was.

The madam, a smiling and polite hostess, always made him feel at home. She was aging, too old for his tastes if he was paying for it. She no longer worked the baths or the pillow rooms anyway, but she spoke his language. And she had a sense of humor. Raddox liked her.

She greeted Raddox with a kiss on each scruffy cheek and smiled.

"It is my Western Sun," she declared happily, taking him by the hand and leading him beyond the plush curtains into the parlor. "How do you fare this fine evening?"

"Well enough," Raddox replied. "I think I'm seeking Milaeka tonight."

The madam tisked. "Milaeka is not in the house tonight. But… there is a new girl."

Raddox frowned. He liked Milaeka best. She had talents he truly appreciated and was more round and voluptuous than many of these slender eastern girls.

"What's her name?" the expatriated mercenary asked.

The madam smiled. "Whatever you wish it to be."

"And what are her… talents?"

"Whatever you desire."

Raddox considered it, pondering the playful light dancing in the madam's eyes.

"I'll take her," he said at last.

"Shall we discuss the terms?"

Raddox laughed. "If she's worth it, she's worth it. And I can pay it." He was proud of that, of his wealth. Gold enough to last five lifetimes, bought by blood and betrayal. Pockets full of gold was the only thing he had left to be proud of, after all. Everything else about him was a disgrace.

"As you will," the madam said with a respectful bow.

Raddox caught something then. A shift in her eyes. A sense of tension, perhaps. Something not entirely warm and welcoming.

"What is it?" he asked plainly.

The madam realized then that he'd spotted her flicker of misgiving. She cleared her throat and composed herself.

"She is… very expensive."

Raddox laughed. "Then she damn well better be worth it!" he declared happily.

If there was a lie in her eyes, the raucous mercenary missed it. The madam took him upstairs to the bath and the woman he desired.

THE ROOM WAS hot and steamy from the bath, rich with the

scents of incense burning in nearby braziers and oils wafting up from the marble tub. Raddox promptly disrobed, hanging his clothes and sword belt over the back of a carved wooden bench. He would keep them close. Raddox was at ease, but not foolish.

The door on the opposite side of the chamber opened and the lithe, cat-like silhouette of a young woman came into view. Gliding weightlessly on tiny feet, she breezed into the room and bowed low before him.

She was young, very young. Bronze skinned, raven-haired, with dark, almond shaped eyes. Silk veils draped her shapely form, leaving little to the imagination. The girl was, as the madam had represented, stunning.

"What is your name?" Raddox asked her and hearing his voice, she rose from her low bow. There was non-comprehension in her dark smoldering eyes. "Your name, girl. What is it?"

She offered a small smile and another bow.

Raddox chuckled. "You don't speak a word of the Galatti, do ya?" Doe-eyed silence was her answer. That was good. It meant he could dispense with much of the etiquette and pleasantries. As elegant as Kosian pleasure houses were, they could learn a thing or two from the gritty sex stores that were the brothels back home.

She gave him a brilliant smile and motioned toward the large steaming bath. He nodded and stepped that way, sliding into the hot water with a relaxing sigh. With a few graceful movements, she disrobed and slid into the water beside him.

There she took up a scented sea sponge and rubbed it with a rind of pale pink soap. Once the sponge was rich with lather she began to meticulously bathe him.

Raddox almost liked this part best. It was soothing in a way that even the sex wasn't. She scrubbed and massaged his scarred, muscle-knotted arms and he closed his eyes, basking in the warmth.

"You're a damn sight better at this part than Milaeka," he commented after a bit.

The girl only looked back at him with sheepish, non-comprehending eyes. She said something in her own tongue, as if in apology, and continued to bathe him.

Raddox pondered that for a bit. Then he said, "I suppose... I suppose you can say things to a whore what don't speak your language you can't even say to a father-confessor, can't ya?"

The girl had no reply.

Raddox was quiet for a long while as she finished scrubbing and massaging him down. While he continued to soak his cares away, she left the bath and brought back a silver goblet and round-bellied flagon of wine. He drank without fear. The circle of runes tattooed around his neck had cost him a bloody fortune, but they protected him from poison, just as the little bald-headed Pahji mystic had promised. Raddox had even made him prove it, and sure enough, it was so.

He was a man with a price on his head after all. If he died from some assassin's poison with all that gold in his pockets, the bit he *hadn't* spent would do him no good. He'd paid it, just for the peace of mind of being able to eat and drink without wondering if every meal or cup was his last. As he filled his belly fearlessly with the little whore's wine, he deemed it, as he usually did, a price well paid.

Yes, if a man wanted Raddox Edorian dead, he'd have to earn it. With steel. And in that, Raddox was no easy kill. No easy kill at all.

He drank and he was in no hurry. He'd seen in the bath that all her parts were where they were supposed to be and he owned her for the night. She wasn't going anywhere and the rest of what he was after would be waiting for him when he was ready for it. So Raddox drank, drank until the wine made his face numb.

As he drank, his mood darkened.

"I'm a murderer," he said to her and a humorless smile twisted his mouth. "A murderer, and a killer, and a raper." Raddox laughed, a joyless sound. "I done worse than that, too."

She refilled his goblet, dutifully pretending to listen even though he knew she didn't understand the words.

"I remember this lad, Turro was his name. When we'd first hired him on, he comes to me back from some brothel one night. And he's covered in blood and he's crying like a babe. He says to me 'I done murder!' Like it was something... special. So I says to him 'Welcome, brother. Ain't we all.'"

At that, Raddox was quiet for a while. When he spoke next, his voice was grave and his eyes stared off into the distance well beyond the walls of the bath chamber.

"Back home, there's killin' and dyin' a plenty going on," he said. "I started a war. And boys is lining up to die in it now." He nodded. "Just like I was paid to do."

The girl refilled his goblet once more.

Raddox drank. He told her about it and she listened.

ON THE DISTANT western edges of Outer Galadyr, there was always tension. Tension between the persistent growth of Imperial Galadyr and the native savages who dwelt there. Chief among them were a fierce and territorial people called the Tarqs. But between two kings reluctant to go to war with each other, there was peace, fragile as it might have been.

There were those, however, who felt the peace an unnatural, and unprofitable, condition. And such men set out to change the course of things in Outer Galadyr. Captain Raddox Edorian and the Blackfish were one such cat's paw thrown secretly into the gears by powerful and ambitious men.

Their mission was clandestine, as was their employer secret, known only to Captain Raddox himself and he kept that knowledge close and quiet.

Raddox and the Blackfish were to start a war with the Tarqs.

Making enemies was the sort of job the Blackfish excelled at. Raddox and his boys took to the wilds of Outer Galadyr to see it done and to bathe in the gold that would come with their success.

Not long after arriving in the frontier, with autumn in full flame, Raddox's scouts picked up the trail of one of the Tarq's savage princes. The Captain smelled the opportunity they'd been waiting for. He gathered eighty of his men and set out after the barbarian prince and his dozen riders.

Raddox and his vanguard caught up to the savages at Bitter Ford along the River Toreg.

The Tarqish Prince and his riders were watering their horses and stretching their saddle weary legs when Raddox and his van rode into view across the way. The Tarqs were skittish, seeing so many riders beneath a banner of Galadyr riding up on them in the wild. The savages held their ground and went about the business of watering their mounts and preparing to cross the river. They would yield the ford when they were done, but they would not be run off by outlanders.

"What do you think?" young Turro asked nervously. His horse, smelling the Tarqs across the ford, stamped and whickered.

Raddox smiled. "I think... we're about to get paid." He nodded to the rear of the van to Old Oliver, who took a dozen men and cantered off south down the flank, disappearing through the blazing yellow birches and alders. The remainder of Raddox's van held their ground at the top of the ford.

The Tarqs watched the company across the river with suspicious eyes. A member of their party ran back to his Prince, who was a tall lanky fellow with red hair and beard in long banded braids. He was stripped to the waist and knelt washing beside the stream.

Steering his horse down the bank, Raddox rode out to midstream, slowly and deliberately toward the Tarqs. The Prince and his men withdrew from the water's edge reaching for weapons, the Prince himself throwing a flowing shirt of iron mail back over his head as he moved beside his horse.

"Oy!" Raddox called out across the way. "Do any of you sorry cunts speak my language?" The scroungy mercenary smiled when the Prince himself bristled. "Are you son of the Graymantle King? Prince Vyan?"

The Prince cinched a belt with sword and axe about the waist of his chain shirt and spat in the river.

"I am, and I speak your tongue, outlander," he declared in clear and well-spoken Galatti. "What business would you have?"

Raddox's eyes twinkled. "A pleasure to finally meet you, Prince of the Tarqs."

Then the golden autumn air filled with the whistle of streaking arrows.

Three of Prince Vyan's men went down straight away under Old Oliver's hail from the south. The Prince himself took an arrow through the calf and two more of his men limped away wounded as well.

Men scurried for cover. Horses screamed and reared in panic. The chaos of battle set in.

"Boys!" Raddox bellowed. He ripped the spear from his stirrup and hefted his shield. "Have at 'em! Spare the Red-Haired Prince!"

With a laughing roar Raddox charged and the sixty men remaining in his vanguard came on with him. Horses snorted and dashed through the bubbling river, pounding across the ford in a thunderous wave.

Scrambling, desperate, out-manned, the Tarqs tried to reach their mounts to escape. Well-placed arrows cut more of them down, dumping them into the rocky river brush in choking bloodied heaps.

Raddox's howling horde was upon them as fast as they could gain their mounts.

A hulking yellow-bearded Tarq shivered Raddox's shield with a two-handed blow from a great iron axe. Twisting in the saddle, Raddox plunged his spear down through the Tarq's throat in a bloody tear.

To his right, a bald-headed Tarq wearing a black wolf-pelt on his shoulder unhorsed poor Turro and stoved his head in with a scarred old mace. Knobber from Gilder Bay put a spear through the brute's back and ended him.

As his men poured onto the Tarqs like an avalanche, Raddox swung down from his stirrups and stalked through the melee in search of the Prince.

Shin deep in the river, hobbled by the arrow through his calf, and bleeding from handful of cruel cuts, Raddox found the Prince hedged in by four of his boys.

A Tarq with a tattooed face and gory gash in the side of his head charged from the chaos to come at Raddox swinging a long handled axe. Raddox got his broken shield between the tattooed Tarq and the axe for two swings, recovered his footing, and shoved back with a brutal shield bash. The Tarq was unbalanced and Raddox rushed in low, bringing his spear up with a twist, knifing it through his enemy's leathers deep into his ribs. Grinding his blade in the savage's chest, Raddox drove him to the ground and finished him.

It was over as quick as it had begun.

Of the prince's twelve men, all but two were dead and the Prince himself was surrounded in a growing ring of Raddox's fighters.

"Enough!" Raddox roared. "Throw down or die!" Old Oliver's boys closed in from the south and bent their bows. Raddox's vanguard tightened the circle, bristling with cruel steel. The only sounds were the last moans of the dying, the screams of horses, the sigh of the wind, and the babble of the river over the rocks.

Prince Vyan spat a mouthful of hot blood and pitched his sword and axe into the stream in disgust. His last two men followed his example.

"Good," Raddox grumbled. "Get him up here." Once ashore, Bolbo cracked the Tarqish Prince in the small of the back with the butt of his spear and drove him to his knees. Wounded and stunned, the Prince of the Tarqs knelt and complied.

"You belong to me," Raddox told the Prince as he cast aside his ruined shield and stripped off his gauntlets. "I intend to keep you and ransom you back to your little cunt of a father, that is if he's king enough and has cock enough to come get you." Raddox made sure the furious Prince met his eyes. "Do you understand?"

The Tarqish Prince nodded.

"Tell them," Raddox ordered, nodding toward Prince Vyan's remaining men.

Eyes burning with hate, face streaked with blood and sweat, the Tarqish Prince did as his captor commanded. He spoke to his men in the tongue of the Tarqs and as he spoke they looked sickened and stunned. Raddox figured that meant they got the point.

"Send them back to your father-king," the mercenary captain ordered. "You tell them I'll trade your sorry hide back to him for ten thousand crown or its equal. Not a penny less. And you tell 'em, if he don't pay, then I'm gonna drag ya behind my horse all the way to Westergate, tar ya, string ya up in a tree, and set ya on fire. Divine help me so."

The Prince relayed this to his battered kinsmen.

"You're a good fighter," Raddox offered. "Some of your men was even fair fighters. But I'm gonna have a piss in your face anyway, just so your boys here know I'm serious."

Prince Vyan scowled and Raddox's men clamped down on him and held him firm as their Captain unlaced and proceeded to piss in the captive Prince's face. The Prince's surviving men howled in outrage, just as Raddox intended.

They seemed to get the message.

"Cut 'em loose," Raddox ordered when it was done. The two surviving Tarqs scrounged up a single healthy mount between them and rode off frantically back toward the northwest.

The wind shivered the forest again, bringing down another shower of golden leaves as the boys of the Blackfish finished off the enemy wounded and tended their own.

The gambit was only just begun, but whichever way it turned out, this would be the last big score for the Captain of the Blackfish. Soldiering was a young and lucky man's game, and Raddox Edorian knew he was fast running out of both.

BY THE TIME Raddox was done with his story, bath time was over and he was drunk and hard and ready to make the little bronze-skinned doe weep. He groped and grabbed and she laughed and played, but rather than take him to the bed, she led him back to the wooden bench. Drunk and chuckling, he flopped down beside his gear and pawed at her.

She grinned and babbled at him in that meaningless language of hers and carefully, she pulled away, showing him gestures that seemed to indicate she was willing, but that she wanted him to wait a moment.

Raddox was drunk and happy and miserable, so he complied.

When she came back to him she brought a black silken satchel with her. It was decorated in a beautiful constellation of silver thread. She set the satchel beside him on the bench and began to meticulously move through its contents. The girl produced several little vials of ink and a quill adorned with a red and black feather.

Raddox laughed. "What's this about?"

The girl smiled. Reaching into the satchel, she produced a polished bronze mask. Giggling she placed it over her face, but it had no slits for eyes, mouth, or nostrils. Its surface was solid, and Raddox saw it was the face of a man, not a woman. There was something familiar in the shape of the face, but without eyes, beard, hair, and the tone of polished bronze rather than flesh, it eluded him.

The girl peeked out from behind the mask, grinned lustily, and set it aside.

She was half Raddox's size, if that, and he wanted to manhandle her like a doll. But she laid a gentle hand in the middle of his chest, gave his manhood a playful squeeze, and he played along, drunk and laughing.

She opened her three inkwells and dipped the quill in each. Then, with fluid and practiced movements, a mischievous smile on her face the entire time, she began to inscribe flowing calligraphy across his bare chest. The ink, so dark as to be almost black, but not quite, did not run in the damp heat of the room.

Raddox wondered what ridiculous Kosian love ritual this was and how long he'd be tattooed by the little girl's handiwork. Surely she was invoking the blessing of some little goatish love goddess before bouncing away merrily on his cock like she was paid to do. He chuckled and prattled on while she tickled his skin with her little quill.

"Oh, hell, did the boys love to torment that damn Prince," he muttered. "And they did. They fed him live rats and made him piss in his own face." Raddox laughed without humor. "Guess I inspired 'em, huh? And his father-king was gonna pay up too, if you can believe that. He was riding to treat with us at Grippa when that little cunt of a son of his tries to escape. Well... we couldn't have that, could we? So Old Oliver puts two arrows in the Prince's back and there wasn't nothing for it then but to take the hammer to his head and be done with it."

Raddox's face darkened, and his eyes grew once more distant, the little girl scribbling her funny sigils across his body all but forgotten. His grim smile was all teeth and no joy.

"The King of the Tarqs was mighty unhappy when he rode up to pay his ransom and found his son and kinsmen all dead. You shoulda seen his face when I says to him 'Your son was worth ten thousand... how much is *you* worth?'" The grizzled mercenary laughed, both sickened and amused by his own story.

"Ah, we set on the big gray-bearded bastard then. Set on him good. Killed half his men and kicked the gooseshit outta the other half." Raddox nodded, self-satisfied. "Then they got away... the King and his men we'd offended... Just like they was supposed to."

The girl offered no reply. She continued to scribble away with dexterous little flickers of her quill.

"Then the Prince's brothers, they just kept comin' south. Smashed right into Outer Galadyr, burning farms and sacking at Valnya. And that... was that. There was war then, whether anybody wanted it or not."

Raddox nodded. "A job done perfectly, I estimate. And so we was heading home to get paid." He was suddenly very quiet. His distant eyes teared up and his voice got husky. "I got a funny feelin' about it, ya know? Like maybe what we done wasn't something the men who'd hired us could afford to let get out. And they're the sort o' men who can move mountains if it suits 'em."

A tear fell then. Just one. It rolled down his scruffy cheek and dripped from his chin to land on his rune-inscribed chest. The ink did not run, even under the salty tear.

"So I did a very uncaptainly thing to my boys," Raddox said. "I robbed 'em blind and I ran. Took everything I could carry and made for a port and a boat as fast as I could fly." He blinked the tears away and tried to laugh. "And I wasn't wrong. Misfortune done caught up to all my boys, one by one, and fast. Tall men got their war. I got my boys' gold. My boys got their deaths."

Raddox wanted to reach out for his goblet of wine. He didn't like feeling these things, and wine was a cure for that.

Only then did he realize he couldn't move.

There was no humor left on the girl's face as she finished the last rune with a flare of her quill. She stood up, naked and beautiful, skin glistening in the steamy bath chamber heat.

But Raddox felt suddenly cold.

Weight pushed in on his chest, making it hard to breathe. With each breath he let out, the pressure tightened, making the next one he took in smaller and smaller.

"Wha...." he wheezed, frozen as a statue as the girl produced a small, keen, curved knife from the black satchel, wicked as a barber's razor.

The runes inked on his flesh seeped into his skin, like glowing iron melting into ice, but cold rather than hot, dark rather than vibrant. No poison could take him, not with the runes of protection about his throat. There were few men he feared to face with steel in hand.

But this witchcraft, this was something he was wholly unprepared for.

Helpless, he watched as ghostly faces of his dead and betrayed comrades began to appear in the mist and the incense smoke. First one. Old Oliver. Then poor Turro. Knobber. Five Fingered Jack. They were there. They were coming.

His breath was gone. His lungs would not expand.

"What do you see?" the girl whispered to him flawlessly in his mother tongue, even though clearly he could not answer.

The ghosts in the mist pressed in around them as she took up the glittering, evil razor. They whispered to him in the flickering nightmarish gloom. "Welcome, brother."

Voice by ghostly voice, the chorus grew. Raddox would have screamed if he'd had the breath to do so. He looked desperately to the girl but found no more comfort there.

Taking up the little silver blade, she angled it along his jaw.

With a long, sweet final kiss, she began to cut.

HALF A WORLD away and many weeks later, Giori Dondain glided along the docks of Westergate like an alley cat. The hour was late and legitimate business was sparse. The groan of old planks, the creaking of ropes, the lap of the sea, the occasional bursts of distant laughter from the sailors' taverns. These were the only sounds.

Giori was accustomed to this environment and the lateness of the hour. Such was his trade, from his days as a humble knife-boy for the Harbor Rats to his more lucrative and recent days currying favor with the wealthy and powerful. There was no rough dock or darkened alley that intimidated Giori Dondain.

Meeting face to face with one of the Gray Sisters, however, was another matter. Dwelling on it too much slowed his pace and made his feet heavy, so he did his best to put it out of his mind.

The ship he sought flew beneath a Sundish flag and he could read the rolling foreign script on the fantail marking it as the *Silver Voyager*.

He walked up the gangplank like he owned the ship and the

hidden shadows guarding the deck did nothing to bar his passage.

He found her waiting for him below in a chamber lit by a single lantern.

She was a tiny woman, a raven-haired beauty with rich bronze skin and dark almond shaped eyes. Her attire was simple, functional. She was the embodiment of stillness, seated at a small round table beside the pale glowing lantern. There were no guards with her in the chamber and no weapon in sight. That did nothing to ease Giori's sense of apprehension.

"It is done," she said softly, her voice touched with the accent of Valar.

"Are you certain?" Giori asked.

The woman smiled. "With the certainty of my own hand." Reaching down beside the table, she produced a box and slid it across to Giori.

With a nervous swallow, Giori removed the lid from the box and did his best to hide his revulsion. He'd seen his far share of violence, done his share of killing. Brutality and death were never pretty.

However, he'd never seen a man's surgically skinned face so meticulously tanned and mounted to a bronze mask before. That was a first, even for a scoundrel as worldly as Giori. The likeness of Raddox Edorian was unmistakable. Alien and lifeless, with bronze teeth showing between thin lips and empty bronze eyes showing through sleepy, half-closed lids, but it was the man, nonetheless. Pale as fallen snow and dead as a doll, the fate of Raddox Edorian was certain as far as Giori was concerned.

"We are... most pleased," Giori offered, putting the lid back on the ghoulish box. "All arrangements will be seen to, in good faith, as promised."

"Good," the tiny woman offered with a gracious nod.

"If we were... to need your services again, how would I find you?"

"You and I will never see each other again," the woman assured him plainly. "But if you have need of us, my Sisters will find *you.* As we did before."

"Understood," Giori offered with a forced, but charming smile. He swallowed and asked the hardest question of the night. "As... arranged... there are no means known to... compel Raddox Edorian to divulge secrets... even in death?" Most men would scoff at such a notion, but Giori knew it to be possible. He'd seen it, with his own horrified eyes. His employer knew it to be possible too.

The little woman smiled, radiant and beautiful, even in the pale lamplight.

"He who holds *this*, holds all the man's secrets," she offered, touching the tips of her fingers lightly to the gruesome box. "I assure you, no man's soul escapes the Long Kiss."

The price of such assurances was nothing short of monstrous. But there were men in this world who could pay such prices. Giori's employer was among them.

With that the little woman rose from behind the table, handed Giori his box, took him by the hand and led him back above decks to the gangplank.

"It has been a pleasure," the Gray Sister told him. Then, stretching up on tiny tiptoes, she kissed him on the cheek in parting.

For a moment, Giori's breath froze in fear, then he let it trickle slowly out.

The woman smiled, her eyes twinkling in the moonlight.

"Fear not," she said. "That is only a small kiss."

Giori, wanting no part of her kisses, Long or small, counted his blessings and shuffled quickly down the gangplank with his gruesome box. Before he was out of sight down the docks, the *Silver Voyager*'s rowers were underway and she was moving into the harbor, sails unfurling in the moonlight.

Neither she, nor the Gray Sister, would ever visit Westergate again.

Of course, neither would Raddox Edorian. Or his secrets.